MANNING WOLFE

HUNTED
BY
PROXY

PROXY LEGAL THRILLER SERIES | BOOK 2

STARPATH BOOKS, LLC

Starpath Books, LLC
Austin, TX
www.starpathbooks.com

Paperback: ISBN: 978-1-944225-54-4
Ebook: ISBN: 978-1-944225-55-1

Manufactured in the United States of America
10 9 8 7 6 5 4 3 2 1

1

Tommy Joe (TJ) Hobbs did his usual walk around his big rig, not knowing that this night run would be far from usual. He adjusted his Freightliner cap and attached his tractor to the trailer of a large cargo van bearing the logo of Speedy Transportation Services. With a lightning bolt making up the top of the T, the brand was easily recognized as one of the largest trucking services in the world. Hobbs had been hauling freight for STS for a few months on a contract basis. He owned the semitruck, but STS owned the trailers, which were already loaded and ready for him to pick up for the haul. He never knew exactly what he might be carrying on each trip, only the total weight. Sometimes it would be dry goods, sometimes groceries. Often, he didn't know exactly what was in the haul until he arrived at the delivery destination, if at all.

The setup was like any other job, so far. He hitched the coupling system, including the fifth wheel and the trailer kingpin, completing the connection of the power to the payload. He did a final safety check, walked all the way around the rig in his oil-stained boots, and spit out a plug of tobacco. Hobbs climbed in, adjusted the radio to country music on KILT - FM Houston - The Bull, and poured coffee from a dented silver thermos into an insulated cup. He waited his turn and sipped caffeine in anticipation of the drive.

Hobbs usually had about an hour to spare on this particular run so he fantasized about getting on the CB radio on the other side of Houston and calling up his favorite hooker, Trick or Treat. She often ran the roads around that part of the state, blasting out her call sign, in hopes of a quick buck with a horny truck driver on a run through her territory. Hobbs had hooked up with her several times over the last year, and she was dynamite. He began to feel a slight tingle at the thought of her climbing into his cab.

When he got the thumbs-up from the yard supervisor, he released the air brakes, pulled out of the truck yard, drove over crackling caliche to the frontage road, then headed into the setting sun on Interstate Highway 10 leading west out of Houston. Hobbs cranked up the radio as it played Johnny Cash's *I've Been Everywhere,* and settled in for the short drive to San Antonio. He sang along loudly, missing only a few of the cities in the lyrics.

Charlotte Collins thought it was going to be a good trip. She picked up her seven-year-old daughter, Lily, from school and buckled her into the seatbelt in the back of their white Toyota Camry. Lily, wearing her favorite pink dress with matching socks, played with the necklace hanging around her mother's neck as she was secured for the one hundred sixty-five-mile drive from Houston to Austin for a mother-daughter weekend. Charlotte smiled at the child and handed her a pink stuffed teddy bear and a favorite book, *Oh the Places You'll Go.* "There you are, all safe and sound."

Charlotte got into the front seat, buckled herself in, looked back, and pulled away from the curb. "We're off."

Lily mimicked her mother as she opened the book. "We're off."

Occasionally, the single mother smiled into the rearview mirror at her daughter who read quietly and happily. Charlotte wove through their small neighborhood and drove up and onto the entrance ramp of Interstate 10 in Houston, west toward Katy.

A crew of Texas Department of Transportation highway construction workers set up an overnight work zone, complete with signage, night lighting, cones, temporary guardrails, and flashing lights on the portion of Highway 10 that started in Katy.

The crew chief, Victor Rodriguez, checked to make sure all twelve workers were wearing orange reflective vests, hard hats, and steel-toed boots. He'd had three hundred sixty-four days without a work incident, and he planned to keep it that way. The project involved completing the addition of a new ramp to help lessen the burden of traffic on the frontage road and feeder onto the massive freeway.

The crew was organized, well trained, and most had done this type of work for some time. It was a beautiful clear night to be outside and Rodriguez was happy in his work. He was a new father to a three-month-old bouncing baby boy and lived his life in gratitude. He was blessed and he knew it. When he'd kissed his wife goodbye, she offered her daily admonition, "Be careful. Love you."

Allison Parker, young, pretty, and blonde, traveled on Interstate 10, on her way to the diner where she worked the night shift, past the TxDOT construction crew in Katy. As she accelerated after the slow zone, she felt the lurch of her junky, clunky car as she crested the overpass just before the Katy exit. The 'piece of crap' car, as she liked to call it, had been on its last leg for months and she and her brother, Luke, had been coaxing it along with duct tape and bailing wire, trying to get another week out of it until her next paycheck. Obviously, the 'piece of crap' had another idea and finally died just as she got to the top of the crest of the overpass.

She pulled over as far as she could onto the shoulder, pressed the flasher button, which, of course, didn't come on, and called her brother, Luke, on her phone to come and get her. While she waited, she rolled down the window with the hand crank, lit a cigarette, opened the app for Angry Birds, and took the aggravation out on her phone with her thumbs.

Jesse Peters powered up his Harley Davidson Pan America 1250 Adventure Bike and buzzed down his driveway and onto the neighborhood street of the home where he lived with his new bride, Viola. He wore a helmet, a leather jacket, and jeans and obeyed all the usual traffic laws.

He loved riding the motorcycle and the sense of freedom it gave him. He especially enjoyed swerving in and out of traffic, making his drive into Sugarland on the Katy Freeway shorter than most and a lot more fun. Sometimes he would pop the clutch and give himself an extra thrill, but not today. There was a lot of traffic, and he was sensitive to the fact that often drivers did not register a motorcycle as easily as a car or truck. He was extra careful.

Hobbs, driving the eighteen-wheeler, progressed on I-10, carefully passed into the TxDOT construction zone, decelerated to the speed limit, and watched for a gap to open so he could move into the middle lane. He wanted to get out of town before heavy traffic, so he crept ten miles over the speed limit for trucks on I-10, waiting for his chance to change lanes.

When the semi crested the overpass, Hobbs spotted Allison Parker's car on the right shoulder and slowed a bit to pass it. As Hobbs was about to reach Parker's car, an opening appeared in the middle lane. He put on his blinker, accelerated again, and began to pull the big rig to the left.

As he entered the lane, Jesse Peters appeared on his Harley. It wasn't clear to Hobbs if Peters had pulled around the big rig or been in the lane initially unseen. When the truck driver did register his presence, he began to slow the eighteen-wheeler and return to the first lane next to the curb. He overcorrected and seeing that his trajectory was directly into Allison Parker's car, pulled back toward Peters on the Harley. Peters was caught between the eighteen-wheeler and an SUV in the middle lane.

Peters accelerated the Harley, shot out ahead of the big rig, and zoomed on down the highway, flipping the bird over his shoulder, not realizing that the big rig was out of control. He continued his journey, unaware of the gravity of the situation he had just narrowly escaped.

Hobbs felt the payload shift to one side of the truck, becoming aware that it was over the quoted load weight and unsecured in the trailer. The shift in weight and load motivated Hobbs to overcorrect again, causing the big rig to begin swinging back and forth. Hobbs hit the brakes as the sway grew further out of his control. When the trailer swung outward, he was unable to stop and it began to grind against the coupling holding it to the truck.

The twist and groan of the metal was the last thing that Allison Parker heard in her 'piece of crap' car. She dropped her phone, looked into the silver metal grill of the truck, and went over the side of the overpass to her death below.

On impact, Hobbs lost all control. The big rig jackknifed causing it to flip on its side with the truck on the guardrail and the trailer on the highway. The truck ground down the overpass rail like a skateboard, dragging the trailer, and scraping down the abutment. It rested in a precarious position, rocking back and forth like a teeter-totter on the overpass wall.

Charlotte Collins slowed the Camry when the TxDOT construction site came into view, moved into the middle lane to give the workers a wide berth, and continued along at a moderate speed. She noticed that the traffic was getting heavier but attributed the slowed pace to the construction. She hit the brakes to slow down, but too late, and was caught in a wall of cars on each side and behind with the jackknifed trailer across four lanes of traffic in front. She hit the brakes again and harder, causing Lily to catch in her seatbelt and cry out in fear. "Mommy."

Charlotte swerved, hit the car next to her with the passenger-side fender, which threw her into the jackknifed trailer, where her car came to a stop. She looked in the rearview mirror and saw the cars and trucks behind her approaching at a rapid pace. Brake lights lit up before her all across the highway and the contraflow lane. There was no place to go and nothing she could do as one car after another crashed into her and the cars around her. She felt the jolt of the pickup truck behind her just as she was hit on the driver's door by a large SUV. Lily's cry was the last thing she would ever remember.

Every car behind Charlotte's Camry began to swerve and plow into the car in front of it, stacking the vehicles in turn, with the eighteen-wheeler at the epicenter. As the crashing cars mashed into the ones before them, the pileup grew longer until the vehicles were crashing and swerving into all four lanes and over the shoulder into the TxDOT construction site. The traffic canyon caused the vehicles to smush together like an accordion.

Rodriguez yelled at his highway workers who also reacted to the sounds of the crashing metal and moved far into the shoulder behind the guardrail. An orange self-moving van skidded into the workers' temporary guardrail and pushed it toward the side of the highway wall. Rodriguez and several workers jumped over the wall and onto the grassy shoulder of the feeder road below. Rodriguez went down on a bad knee from his former football days and shattered the joint. He gasped in pain, unable to get up.

Back on the freeway, dozens of vehicles crashed for miles, in the corridor leading up to the construction zone, until finally the pileup petered out and drivers were able to stop in time to prevent being rear-ended by the next wave of traffic behind them.

Since the crash happened around 6:00 p.m., many hospital and emergency technicians were heading from work to home, so some of those involved in the crash were health care workers and emergency responders, including police officers. Those who were able began to tend to the needs of those in the crash by directing traffic, or triaging wounds as best they could, while waiting for highway officers and EMS to arrive.

Police cars, EMS, and tow trucks could not get down the shoulder to the wreck because of the pileup and jackknifed truck. Multiple tow trucks began to work their way to the epicenter of the accident, from both ends of the wreckage, by disentangling and hauling away the cars and trucks one by one. The sheriff's office landed a helicopter in the middle of the highway at the head of the pileup, on the west side of the big rig, and began to sort out the priorities of both helping and investigating.

Multiple commuters were trapped within the confines of their vehicles requiring the use of hydraulic rescue equipment by EMS in order to extricate them, including Charlotte Collins. Charlotte lay across the front seat, with the airbag deflated around her, covered in glass from the shattered windshield. The engine of the car was crushed into the passenger compartment and had her lower extremities pinned. As she bled out, she moaned and cried out in pain. Lily, who had awakened from her own experience with a side airbag and multiple crush injuries, called out for her mother through tears and anguish. "Mommy, mommy, mommy."

MedRun, the ambulance service for the area, finally reached the epicenter of the accident by following the tow trucks in. As the day wore on, sixty-five people were taken by ambulance from the crash site, including twenty with critical injuries. Numerous others were treated at the scene and released. Police cars transported those who could walk in and out of the epicenter to waiting vehicles to take them home.

It took all night, but by early morning each car had been searched and police were confident that anyone who may have been trapped was extricated and taken to the hospital or morgue.

By the time the press fought their way through traffic and arrived on the scene of the accident, Charlotte Collins was dead. Crews were working to clean up the area, following a fuel leak and lettuce and cabbages spilling out of the trailer of Hobbs's eighteen-wheeler. News helicopters flew overhead showing traffic backed up for miles, as only one lane was now open.

A well-known local reporter with HNN, Terri Emery, blonde and wearing a recent facelift, stood before the wreckage. She moved as close as she could get without crossing the police barrier, motioned to the cameraman to roll, and spoke into a handheld microphone.

"Officials tell us that eight people are dead and multiple commuters were trapped in vehicles after a pileup on west Interstate 10, involving about one hundred fifty cars."

Emery paused to allow the magnitude of the incident to sink in as the Houston police chief passed by her. "Chief. Chief. Just a moment, please."

The police chief stopped and appeared to be in shock.

Emery pressed him for information. "What can you tell us, Chief?"

"The scene here today is unlike any other we've ever seen in Houston, and we pray to God we will never see again." He rushed on toward the epicenter of the incident where police lights were flashing red and blue.

The camera followed the chief out of sight, then returned to a closeup of Emery.

"It is not known if the driver fell asleep at the wheel or

suffered a medical emergency. What is alleged is that the 80,000-pound rig veered out of the lane due to driver's error. The eighteen-wheeler crashed into the overpass concrete wall and slid on the overpass like a skateboard, scraping down the wall in a grind."

The cameraman panned over to the trailer laying sideways on the concrete then up to the truck hanging precariously over the side of the overpass wall. It tilted back and forth like a rocking chair.

"At this point, the finger of blame is being pointed at the person behind the wheel. What is not yet known is if outside factors or other drivers contributed to the accident. Officials have asked for any witnesses with video of the scene that might help in the investigation to reach out to the Houston non-emergency number. More at ten on HNN."

Emery made a slicing motion across her neck as she lowered the microphone and moved to another location for the next shot.

At midnight, municipal agencies were still on the scene, which officials described as an expansive geographic area. In the final tally, there were eight fatalities and hundreds of injuries.

It was reported that a large number of people who were victims were in scrubs with hospital IDs. Three police officers were injured who were en route from work, and one while working on the scene after the crash. All medical workers and police officers were released from the hospital with mild to serious injuries except for one policeman who remained in critical condition.

It was determined that only three children were involved in the pileup due to the time of day that the accident took place.

One of the three was Lily Collins who remained in the hospital for necessary surgeries. The other two were released to their parents after treatment.

On all the local news networks, and some national outlets, the phone number to report information ran under footage of the accident scene for three days. The pileup held the spotlight until a news story involving a crooked politician, allegedly bribing a witness, took the attention of viewers who were ready to say goodbye to pictures of the gruesome crash.

2

Quinton heaved a box of thick books onto the conference room table in the new Law Office of Quinton Lamar Bell in Houston, Texas. He'd recently moved to The Galleria area around Westheimer and Post Oak and opened a solo practice. Quinton was now what they called a loop lawyer, one who offices around and outside the 610 Loop. It circled the city from Interstate 10 to Highway 45 to Highway 59 surrounding the downtown high-rises poking out of the ground in the middle of the ring. He had been working downtown for the last year but, seeking distance and maybe a little safety from the legal community, found his perfect new office and began to make it his own.

Clients were not hard to come by as Quinton had created a reputation on his last big case, a murder involving the defense of his friend and lover, Joanne Wyatt. That seemed a lifetime ago, and he had become a loop lawyer in part to get a fresh start, but also to protect his former firm, Jamail, Powers & Kent, from his past life in New York City. That's another story, for another day, but it involved Quinton's pseudocide off the Staten Island Ferry.

Quinton Lamar Bell was not his real name, it was Byron Douglas, but only he knew that and one other person. A potentially dangerous person. When Quinton had opened his new office, he thought he was the only one on earth who knew he had faked his own death in New York and come to Houston to hide in plain sight. He looked different with a little plastic surgery, and had assumed not only the face, name, and demeanor, but the entire life of a childhood friend. He did so, not because he hated his prior life but because it was too dangerous to live it anymore. Besides, Q, as he'd dubbed his friend and benefactor, no longer needed his name or his face as he had been cremated and sprinkled in the Gulf of Mexico. So, in essence, Quinton had been killed twice, and he wasn't even dead.

The new Quinton had worked for a downtown Houston firm at the insistence of his faux father, Judge Sirus Bell, who was also now deceased, in order to establish himself as Quinton. When he'd left the downtown firm, on good terms, he'd agreed to split any profits fifty-fifty on the files that were open prior to his departure. Any new cases were all his, even if they were referred by the old firm. It was generous to Quinton. He'd been supported a great deal by the three women partners in his prior office and would not forget their kindness. It was one of the reasons for the separation and move, to protect them, and to get out of their hair.

The women's firm didn't really want criminal cases running through their office and Quinton didn't want the firm to get caught in the crossfire, in the event that his past came back to haunt him. And his past did haunt him. He could never go back. He'd broken the law, lied, cheated, stole, and taken Quinton's legacy as his own. Now, he went through each day hiding in plain sight and living the life of a dead man.

After Judge Bell's death, he'd found that he, as Quinton, was the sole heir of the Bell estate. He'd put most of the inheritance into a charitable trust, but had kept one asset, and only one asset. He loved the Bell house in Galveston, a beautiful Victorian home near the beach, that he could not bear to part with. It was the source of many childhood memories with both his friend, Q, and mentor, Judge Bell.

Giving the bulk of the estate to charity was the right thing to do, but if the authorities found out about his true identity, his altruism would not stop them from charging him with crimes from fraud to murder. Yes, murder. That's the aforementioned part of the long story for another day.

With the help of Judge Bell, Byron had stolen Quinton Bell's persona, deliberately adapted to his new life in Houston, and felt that he had truly escaped the danger he'd left behind. After a while, it felt to the new Quinton like he'd learned another language and was now immersed in it. He actually became the new Quinton Bell, a fusion of his former self and new persona speaking the acquired language as if he'd been born to it. Still, he'd walked on proverbial eggshells every day for months, finally settling in, to what he thought was a fairly safe place.

That is, until a strange card arrived in the mail at his new office. It revealed his former name, Byron Douglas, shook him to the core, and left him wondering who knew about his past and what they wanted from him. It had been several weeks since the card had been delivered. One side was adorned with a photo of the New York skyline and the Staten Island Ferry. The other side had a cryptic note: "Hello, Byron. I know who you are, and I know what you've done. Be seeing you."

No demands, no further contact, and no requests of any nature. It was like waiting for the proverbial 'other shoe' to drop. Was he going to be blackmailed? If so, why send the card? The sender wanted something, but what? Would Quinton one day be arrested without further notice? Law enforcement wouldn't send a warning. Who was the sender, and what did they have planned for him?

"Be seeing you." It gave him a chill. Waiting to find out was worse than the many scenarios he imagined would flow from his discovery.

———

After setting up his new law firm, Quinton hired an investigator, Dart Owens, to assist with the firm's cases. Dart had been a client over a year ago, a court-appointed case in which he'd been accused of murdering a narcotics dealer in a drug purchase gone bad. Quinton was able, in court, to assert and prove self-defense and get the big not guilty verdict that was hard to come by in a town like Houston. Dart had been forever grateful and started doing a few research projects for Quinton from time to time.

Eventually, Dart had gotten his private investigator's license, with Quinton's support and at his request. Dart was the only person in the office Quinton really knew or intended to know. Quinton would never share the truth of his secret prior life, and current deceit, not even with Dart. But, in the event that something dangerous did happen, Dart could take care of himself.

Quinton intended to hire an office manager as soon as he could. He'd placed an ad in the back of the Texas Bar Journal and hoped to find a suitable candidate when the Journal went out in a week or two. For now, he had a temp, Lacey Brooks, covering the receptionist's desk, making copies, and answering the phone. She didn't have the skill set to function as a paralegal or to keep the books and run a law firm, but she made great coffee, was cordial, and seemed happy for the job, however long it lasted.

Dart and Lacey had already developed a flirtation, which Quinton would have preferred they kept out of the office. However, Quinton couldn't really blame them, as they seemed meant for each other. Dart looked like a big black refrigerator with a neck. He had muscles bulging out of every opening of his shirt. Lacey looked like a stripper with long red hair, obviously fake, and breasts bulging out of the top of her blouse, obviously not fake. Her platform heels clacked on the floor when she moved around the office, giving Quinton plenty of warning that she was about to burst through his door, as she often did.

If she had been more than a temp, Quinton might have gotten rid of her, or told Dart to cool it, but business preoccupied Quinton, as the office had just opened. He had better things to worry about, like setting up shop and the blackmail note, if it was to be blackmail.

3

"Judge Robert Blaylock calling," Lacey yelled from the outer office.

Quinton laughed and yelled, "Use the intercom, please. This is a dignified office."

Quinton saw the name of the judge, Bob Blaylock, spelled out on the caller ID. The judge had saved Quinton's bacon and that of several others when he'd taken out an active shooter with his self-protection piece, a .357 Magnum, that he kept hidden behind the riser in his courtroom. Unfortunately, Judge Blaylock wasn't able to protect Joanne that day, no matter how large the weapon, and neither was Quinton.

Quinton's love for Joanne had not died with her, and he still mourned her every day. Some days, he could feel her dying in his arms again. Some nights, he could feel her alive in his bed. Neither helped the emptiness nor regret he suffered when he thought of her.

He hit the lit button on the desk phone, putting Judge Blaylock on speaker. "Hello, Judge. How are you doing?"

"Great, Quinton. Just great. Busy down here in court. Haven't seen you in a while."

"I took some time off to settle Dad's estate and clean out the Galveston house. I've just set up my new office digs at the Galleria. Planned to visit you soon."

"I heard. Loop Lawyer. Sounds good. Sorry about your father. I missed telling you that at his memorial. It was so crowded."

"Thanks, Judge." Not wanting to go too far into that conversation, Quinton changed the subject. "Have you been swimming?"

"Yes. I've gotten in a few laps lately. You?" Quinton and the judge shared a love of lap swimming, the judge to stay in shape and Quinton to do the same and more importantly to manage stress.

"I've been downtown to the club a few times, but I plan to find a pool closer to the office and home—when I get moved." Quinton didn't tell the judge he'd been to the Coushatta Indian Reservation to gamble for stress relief, as well. "I'm looking for a house closer to the office. Need to stop renting."

"Good luck with that. Don't overlook the zoning laws, or rather the lack of zoning laws in Houston. Make sure you get a place in a planned community with deed restrictions. Anyone can throw up a business on any old street corner here and drop your property value right into Buffalo Bayou."

"So I've been told. Thanks for the warning."

"Sure."

Quinton got down to business. "What can I do for you?"

"I have a case I'd like for you to consider. It won't be pro bono, you'll get paid, but it may require an investment of time upfront before the money comes in. Can you get down to the courthouse this week and drop by?"

"Sure."

"Thanks. I'm in court from ten to four on Tuesday; otherwise, I should be available."

"Great, I'll be by tomorrow morning, and I'll bring breakfast."

"I'll have the coffee on."

———

Quinton entered Judge Blaylock's dimly lit and empty courtroom, walked down the aisle, through the swinging gate and circle to the right of the riser toward a door marked *Judge's Chambers*. Before he could reach the door, he stopped dead in his tracks. He was sweating and felt woozy.

Quinton dropped his briefcase and the bag of food he carried, grabbed the wooden rail around the jury box, and slowly slid to the floor. He gasped for air, loosened the knot of his tie, and released the top button on his shirt. The room went milky white, and he could not see.

Quinton's heart pounded in his chest as he struggled to regain control of his breathing. His vision slowly returned, but was still blurred, and his head throbbed with an overwhelming sense of dread. He looked over at the defense table and it appeared to be on its side on the floor. As he slumped against the jury box, he could not stop the replay of memories in his mind. He could see Joanne lying in a pool of blood next to Mo. He heard the deafening roar of the gunshots from Judge Blaylock's .357 Magnum. He could smell the gunpowder and blood and hear the screams of the reporters trying to exit the side door.

The scene had been haunting his dreams for months, but he had not had an episode like this before. He clenched his trembling fists, his knuckles white as he fought to bring himself back to the present. He struggled to rise, as he dreaded anyone walking in to see him in this vulnerable state. Summoning his strength, he pulled himself up using the wooden rail and staggered toward the side exit, his steps unsteady, his mind a whirlwind of fear and confusion.

When he reached the hallway outside the courtroom, he leaned his back against the cool marble wall that offered some relief from the suffocating memories. He took slow, deliberate breaths to quell the emotions he was experiencing as he looked around to see if anyone was watching him. Thankfully, no one seemed to notice.

Slowly the milky haze began to lift and his vision cleared. Quinton had heard clients talk about the effects of PTSD in his New York practice, but he had no idea how out of control those men and women had felt in the grips of a flashback. He felt a newfound empathy, and was ashamed that he had not been more sympathetic to their plight.

He often recalled one particularly gruesome case involving a New York Yellow Cab and a pedestrian. He had represented the woman who'd been struck by the cab while crossing the street at the light. She was a young mother of two babies who was relegated to a wheelchair for life. She had endured unimaginable pain and suffering, her remaining days forever altered by the fateful collision. During the trial, the courtroom had buzzed with hushed whispers as Quinton, then Byron, meticulously presented the evidence. It was a classic case of he said, she said, a battle of narratives.

Byron had painted a vivid picture of the young mother's once-vibrant persona. He spoke of her dreams and aspirations and the promising future that was now cruelly yanked away. As the trial progressed, Byron had skillfully dismantled the defense's arguments, exposing inconsistencies and highlighting the cab driver's culpability. His client had been awarded a record-setting sum of money, but her PTSD had stolen away her ability to move forward. She eventually took her own life.

Today, Quinton was the one suffering. As he tried to steady himself in the hallway, he grasped for reality with his mind's eye, but felt as if the floor was shifting beneath him. He continued to breathe deeply and tried to look normal. After a few minutes, a large, uniformed man with a militant posture, fit, clean-shaven, a buzz cut, came down the hallway and approached Quinton. When the man came into view, Quinton recognized George Grant, Judge Blaylock's bailiff of many years.

As Quinton settled his breath, Bailiff Grant supported Quinton by his elbow and took some of the weight off his legs. "You having a flashback?"

Quinton nodded. "How did you know?"

"I still get them every time I go to the garage. I get sweaty, can't stop looking over my shoulder, almost run to my car some days."

One day after court, Bailiff Grant had escorted Judge Blaylock to his Cadillac in the municipal garage and headed to his own vehicle. A hooded man, wearing jeans and boots, ran toward the bailiff and clobbered him from behind with a tire iron. Thankfully, Judge Blaylock saw the attack and drove his Cadillac toward the mugger, forcing him away from Grant. The judge used the Caddy as a weapon and saved Bailiff Grant's life. George had been mugged during the murder trial, to allow his temporary replacement to smuggle in the handgun that ultimately caused Joanne's death.

Quinton looked at the bailiff with sympathy. "George, I had no idea."

"Just take it easy for another minute or two and it will pass, Quinton. Your color's looking better already."

Bailiff Grant helped Quinton over to a bench that looked like a church pew. So far, the two had not drawn the attention of others navigating the hall. Quinton felt his body start to cool off and the sweating stopped. After a few more breaths, Quinton said, "Thank you. I dropped my things by the jury box. Could you get them for me?"

"Sure. You okay for me to leave you for a minute?"

"Yes."

"Don't try to get up yet."

"I won't."

Bailiff Grant returned shortly with Quinton's briefcase and the bag of food. He sat beside Quinton on the bench. "Is that the first time you've been back in there?"

"No, but it's the first time the courtroom was empty."

"It can be dark and eerie in there with the lights down and nobody bustling about."

"No shit." Quinton laughed.

Bailiff Grant laughed too. The two men just sat for a while.

Quinton began to stir. "I have a meeting with Judge Blaylock."

"Right. Why don't you stop by the men's room and splash a little water on your face? I'll let the judge know you're here and come back and escort you in the back way. No need to go back into the courtroom today."

"Do you have to tell him?"

"Of course not."

"You're a saint, George."

"No, just a fellow survivor."

Quinton sat before Judge Blaylock's desk and took four fat breakfast tacos out of the brown paper bag that had a little grease residue on the bottom. He showed no signs of the turmoil he'd just experienced and made an extra effort to be upbeat.

Judge Blaylock sniffed the air. "Taco Fuego?"

"Where else? You have a choice. Chorizo and egg or bacon and egg? Both have cheese and jalapeño."

Judge Blaylock placed a cup of steaming hot coffee in front of Quinton and sat down. "I'll take one of each."

"Excellent decision. I'll do the same," Quinton said, as if he had a choice given what was left. "Salsa?"

"Yep. Tell me what you've been up to."

"It's been good to have a break, get my own office away from the old firm, and sleep a little." Quinton didn't mention the days and weeks of sleepless nights he'd endured after the Joanne Wyatt murder trial, and Judge Bell's suicide, much less the recent incident in the courtroom.

Judge Blaylock took a big bite of breakfast taco and washed it down with a swig of coffee. "I understand. You should do well in the new office. I think you'll fit right in as a loop lawyer."

Quinton laughed. Some thought the term loop lawyer to be derogatory, but Quinton thought it very descriptive. When he took a drink of the coffee, it was so hot it made him grimace and shake his head.

Judge Blaylock picked up a file from his desk. "Let me tell you about this case I'd like for you to consider."

Quinton put down his taco, wiped the grease from his hands, and pulled up the Notes app on his phone. "Shoot."

"You heard about the eighteen-wheeler accident on Interstate 10, near Katy?"

"Sure."

"I'd like for you to get involved in the case."

"You want me to represent the driver of an eighteen-wheeler? I thought those companies had attorneys on retainer for that type of thing. Is he being charged with murder?"

MANNING WOLFE

"No. I want you to cross over to the civil side and represent the child and estate of a woman who was killed in the accident."

"A tort case? I don't know, Judge. I plan to take a few civil cases, but mostly stick to criminal law. Someone else might be better suited to the task."

Judge Blaylock nodded. "I understand, but this is going to be very complex. The truck driver is being charged with vehicular manslaughter. He has an attorney for that, and his insurance company has hired counsel for the civil case, but the criminal case will bleed over into the tort suit."

"I assume the trucking company will have civil attorneys as well."

"Right. And there might be several more defendants and plaintiffs involved in the accident. Matt Johnson has been rounding up some of the victims from the pileup. He has six of the seven death cases signed up."

Quinton laughed. "The Houston Hammer? Attorneys left and right in this one."

Judge Bell nodded. "Since this is an unusual case, we need someone who understands both civil and criminal litigation. It appears the eighteen-wheeler company, Speedy Transportation Services, is likely going to settle. I just want you to make sure they give the girl what's due. The driver will likely go to jail, but I want you to monitor that side of it and make sure they don't let him off too easily."

Quinton scratched his chin. "I don't know how much control I'd have over that. What's the client's name?"

"The girl's name is Lily Collins. Her mother was Charlotte Collins. Just look out for the girl."

Quinton softened, and he knew he'd take the case because the judge had asked him to. "Okay. I'll look into it. Is this all the file you have?"

"Contact Judge Antonio Garzon. He's a colleague of mine and is expecting your call. He's asked me for a referral for the child's attorney and will also be appointing a guardian for her health. It will be up to you and Judge Garzon to finalize a representation deal and set the fee."

Quinton got up to go. "Got it. Thanks for the coffee."

Judge Blaylock held up the remainder of his taco, a gesture of thanks.

On Quinton's way out the door, Bailiff Grant held a card that he discreetly tucked into Quinton's breast pocket. "This guy helped me. Maybe he can do something for you."

"Shrink?"

"Sort of. Works with lots of veterans. Office is in North Houston. Just in case. No pressure."

"Thank you."

4

Quinton returned to his firm and Lacey pounced on him the minute he walked in the door. She scurried behind him, clacking her heels all the way, as he headed to his office. She handed him a stack of messages. "A Judge Garzon has been trying to reach you. I left a message on your mobile."

Quinton looked down at his phone. "Sorry. I forgot to unmute it after my meeting with Judge Blaylock. What did he say?"

"Just wants you to call asap." She pointed to a stack of documents and envelopes as she clacked away. "Mail's on your desk."

Quinton carefully checked the mail, as he did every afternoon. The ominous note he had received in the post about his prior life had left him reeling, but nothing new in today's delivery. He was sure everyone who knew his true identity was dead. Almost. He assumed that blackmail would be requested, and in his mind began to form an image of an ominous shadow figure, as he watched the mail day after day, but no one showed and no new cards arrived.

Just in case, Quinton had added five thousand dollars more to his offshore account, what he called 'Plan B' money. He could flee at any moment if the New York Dannon mob or Houston law enforcement appeared to be closing in. He hoped and prayed he would never have to use the money, but he didn't feel completely safe and stayed ready to leave town at a moment's notice.

Quinton kept a bag in the car with an extra laptop, cash, and fake credentials, just in case he had to bolt. He recently had added a second suitcase that he called a go bag and had selected the luggage with both handles and concealable back-pack straps, to make it easy if he had to run quickly. In the bag was a dop kit with toiletries, extra cash, a jogging suit with running shoes, and two disguises that he'd put together from Goodwill purchases.

He'd also included a Spyderco Dragonfly 2 Salt Lockback Knife in a bright neon yellow. It was just like the one he carried in his pocket, but that one was dark blue. Since these were dive knives, he hoped that he could talk his way out of it being seen as a weapon, if ever searched by law enforcement.

Keep telling yourself that.

He'd learned how to hide in Reno after he'd first left New York, and employed some of those evasion skills to assemble a nerd outfit with khakis and glasses, and a construction worker disguise with flannel shirt and Home Depot ballcap. He debated whether to make a duplicate go bag and keep it in his office, but that seemed overkill. *I hope.*

He knew that someone was tracking his movements to have found his new office. He also knew that they had discovered him some way through his past and followed him into his new life. After days of worry without further contact, he started thinking of the note writer as a shadow. He imagined a real person with an agenda that threatened his livelihood and maybe even his life. He imagined him or her always watching and following his every move.

Today, after he checked the mail, he tried not to think about it and went about his business as if the threat weren't hanging over him, but it was always in the back of his mind like a whisper that he couldn't quite hear, nor could he ignore.

5

Q uinton entered the inner chamber of Judge Antonio Garzon. It was a dark room because of the heavy wood on the walls and hunter green drapes on the windows. What kept it from being a cave was a long band of florescent lighting on the ceiling. Of course, there were books and files on every available shelf and table. The judge sat at his desk, unrobed, with his shirtsleeves rolled up and a cigar smoldering in an ashtray the size of a hubcap. Judging from the ash and butts, it wasn't the first cigar he'd smoked there.

"Bienvenido, Mr. Bell. Take a seat."

"Gracias, Your Honor." Quinton sat erect in one of the two guest chairs and waited.

The judge tamped out the cigar. "Don't rat me out about smoking in a government building. I only take a toke or two and put them out. It's a long walk down to the sidewalk, and too many angry folks with cameras down there."

Quinton crossed his right ankle over his left knee. "No worries."

"Judge Blaylock tells me you're a top-notch lawyer. He also says you've had a checkered past and a lot to overcome."

"Something like that. Not sure about the top-notch. I'm building my solo practice."

"Got the scoop on you from Silver Jamail, as well. She says you're great in a courtroom, and you know how to keep your head in a crisis."

"I hope so." *I've had enough experience doing it.*

"Good to hear."

"Silver's firm was a great place for me to get my legs under me after rehab. I assume you've heard that I had addiction issues if you checked me out." Of course, the issues Quinton was referring to were Q's problems, but no one else still alive knew that. *Except maybe the note writer.*

"Yes. I knew you went through a lot and your father helped you out before he died."

"He did. I miss him every day." Quinton did miss Sirus Bell, but not in the way one might think. "Judge Blaylock said you're looking for someone to represent an orphaned child and her mother's estate."

"Correct. It should be an easy settlement by the eighteen-wheeler company, and maybe a bit of negotiation with the other victims and drivers and their insurance companies."

"What about the criminal element Judge Blaylock mentioned?"

"Yes, there will be charges brought against the truck driver for some form of vehicular homicide. I don't know if that will stick. The prosecutor is still working up the case. You won't have anything to do with that except monitor their progress as it crosses over with the civil settlements. All you have to do is watch out for the child and try to steer the other lawyers toward settlement as well."

"Sounds reasonable for my part of the representation, but I

don't know if I'll have any sway over the other attorneys involved. What are the particulars?"

"Let me fill you in. March of last year, an eighteen-wheeler owned by Tommy Joe Hobbs, towing a trailer owned by Speedy Transportation Services, one of the largest trucking companies in the United States, was involved in a pileup on Interstate 10, near Katy, west of town."

"I know Katy. I heard about the accident at the time."

"Okay. So, there were several initial vehicles involved that created an accident that led to a pileup. You can read all about that and the other drivers in the case file. Personal injury suits have been filed by several of those injured, and I'm in the process of consolidating all the lawsuits into one mega tort case."

"I see. Where do I come in?"

Judge Garzon pushed over a thick paper file. "A young mother, Charlotte Collins, was hit while driving a Toyota Camry with her seven-year-old daughter, Lily Collins, in the back seat. Ms. Collins was pinned under the steering wheel and the daughter was trapped in the car, listening to her mother's groans, during a long and painful death, before emergency services could get to them."

"Sad."

"Very. Lily lost her right leg, amputated above the knee."

Quinton rubbed his chin. "How awful."

"Needless to say, the girl is in mental and physical therapy. She has no known living relatives who can take her and has gone through Child Protective Services and into foster care. She's housed here in Houston with a couple, Kevin and Jess Matherly, who temporarily care for children during crises. I need to appoint a mental health guardian for purposes of decision-making during the trial. The Matherlys won't be providing that type of support, and I don't want the attorney of record in a dual role as guardian ad litem and guardian for health purposes."

"I understand. When do you plan to appoint the health guardian?"

"As soon as I find the right attorney to represent Lily Collins and her deceased mother's estate. I hope that's you. I had planned to set up the attorney ad litem and guardian appointment hearing later in the week. Get both done at once."

Quinton didn't respond immediately. He had been considering the case since his conversation with Judge Blaylock, so asking for time to think about it didn't seem appropriate. However, he did have reservations.

"I have handled complicated cases with multiple issues at trial. I'm sure I can sort it out, but so you know, I'm just starting my firm and I can't overload my office with pro bono work right now. I don't want to disappoint you or Judge Blaylock."

"The mother had a car insurance policy that can be used, in part, for legal services. We'll get you paid if you can keep it reasonable."

"Okay. I can knock ten percent off my usual rate and keep expenses down as much as possible. Will that work for you?"

"Sounds about right. Anything else?"

"Two-thirds my rate for a second chair if we should go to trial. I usually bring in Maureen Powers. She's with Silver Jamail at my former firm."

"I know Mo Powers. I don't see a trial happening, but that's fine."

"Standard investigator and paralegal rates, by the hour, if necessary."

"Also probably not needed, but that all works for me as well."

"When will I receive the file?"

Judge Garson pulled a small flash drive from his desk

drawer and handed it to Quinton. "Here's the crux of it. I'll have the hard copies delivered to your office tomorrow."

"Okay. I'll draw up a contract for services and send it over."

"Fine."

As Quinton left the office, he wondered what he was getting himself into.

6

As the days and weeks passed after the accident, local authorities pieced together, as best they could, what happened on that fateful day. There were no witnesses to the initial impact, except for the truck driver and the first cars in the pileup. It all happened so fast, it seemed that no one actually saw the cause. Each added a small piece to the puzzle as the police took their statements and combined them into one larger picture.

There were two witnesses who reported seeing a motorcycle weave in and out of traffic before the impact occurred. This caused police to investigate CCTV footage from a mile or two before the accident to see if any motorcycles were traveling along the route. They were able to find one biker, but unable to identify the make and model or read the license plate. In an effort to locate the witness, police ran a spot on the local news for a few nights, asking for anyone who had knowledge of the motorcyclist or information about the bike to come forward.

Jesse Peters and his lovely wife, Viola, settled into their quiet home, not far from I-10, where the accident had occurred, for a night of takeout and television. Peters' beloved motorcycle was safely parked in the garage. He was hoping Viola might want to go for a romantic moonlight ride after dinner. She didn't love the bike as much as he did, but she did love him, and knew how much he enjoyed tooling around Houston after the traffic cleared.

Viola, barefoot, in a tight pair of jeans and a baggy LSU sweatshirt, Peters' favorite look on her, walked into the living room. Viola picked up the remote and turned on the local news and flopped down on the sofa. Peters watched her and the television from the island in the kitchen where he set out plates and napkins while the pizza reheated in the oven.

Onscreen, Terri Emery, the blonde reporter from the crash site, delivered a somber message. "We have a breaking story tonight. During the historical pileup on I-10, when an eighteen-wheeler lost control, allegedly causing the accident, a motorcycle was possibly involved in the accident. The motorcyclist left the scene and did not give a report to local authorities."

The picture left the reporter and showed a fuzzy video from a distant CCTV camera of a motorcycle in front of Hobbs's eighteen-wheeler. The bike's license plate was obscured and partially unreadable. The make and model also indecipherable, but the first number of the license plate looked like a three or an eight.

The report continued voice over the video. "Police are asking for the driver of the motorcycle, or anyone who can identify this driver or bike, to come forward and help with the investigation."

Jesse Peters' heart skipped a beat as the report showed dramatic footage of the pileup from news archives, then the motorcycle footage again, and froze on the shot of the back of the bike.

Viola looked over at Peters. "Is that you?"

"It looks like my bike."

A wave of panic washed over Peters as he watched the plea for information, and realized he had unwittingly left the scene, escaping with his life intact, but oblivious to the potential catastrophe he had narrowly avoided.

Viola looked at his stunned face. "Is that the accident you said happened the day you were on I-10? I thought it was later, after you got to work."

"So did I. I had no idea it was right after I passed through there."

The weight of his actions bore down on him and he knew he had a moral obligation to come forward. But he'd done nothing wrong. What if the authorities tried to assert that he was somehow responsible for what happened, or that he had knowingly and intentionally left the scene of an accident? Why were they so desperately seeking him? What did they want that he didn't know and couldn't guess?

He and Viola stared at each other, neither knowing what to say nor do next.

For hours, Peters and Viola sat on barstools at the island in their kitchen. As they discussed the situation, the pizza grew cold on their plates before them. Peters moved to pacing the floor of the living room, wrestling with his conscience. Could he be held responsible in any way? The reporter said that police were seeking information, but didn't they always say that at first? What if more video surfaced and he was identified without coming forward? Wouldn't that be worse? Why did he feel so threatened when he'd done nothing wrong?

Doubt gnawed at him, but deep down, he knew what he needed to do. "I think I have to call them."

Viola looked frightened but nodded her head.

With trembling fingers, he picked up his mobile, put the call on speaker, and dialed the local police department's non-emergency number. He identified himself as the possible driver of the motorcycle and was transferred to a detective who took his statement. After the last question was asked and answered, the detective asked him to come in the next day for an in-person interview.

After he hung up, Viola hugged him. "It will be alright. You did nothing wrong."

"I hope so. Do you think I need to take a lawyer?"

The next day, Jesse and Viola Peters went into the designated police office to finalize and sign his telephone statement. Viola was asked to stay outside in the reception area, where she reluctantly agreed to wait. As she sat and worried, Peters started to regret not bringing an attorney with them but followed the officer down the hall.

Peters' heart pounded as he entered the interrogation room. It felt cold and unwelcoming. His heart raced as he recounted the events of the day of the accident. His voice was unwavering as he asserted emphatically that he had not been speeding and had not seen the accident unfold behind him. He did admit that he was in a tight spot involving an eighteen-wheeler and a white Toyota car, the model he couldn't recall. Peters provided all the details he could remember, including the time and location of the incident, the lane he was in, his traveling on after the event, and the fact that he had not heard the crash or anything sounding like an accident over the noise of the motorcycle.

Peters asserted that the white car was going slower than he was, and he was not speeding. He further asserted that the eighteen-wheeler sped up to change lanes and that's what caused him to shoot out of the situation and on down the road. He remembered because it had scared him a little.

When Peters returned to Viola in the reception area, he felt a mix of relief and anxiety as the officer thanked him and returned through the door they'd exited.

Peters looked at his wife. "They said they'd call if they need anything else."

Viola smiled weakly. "No one tried to make it about you?"

"No, just wrote it all down. I signed it, and they said they'd be in touch if they need me."

He had done the right thing, but the uncertainty of the consequences weighed heavily on his mind. He could only hope that his statement would help the authorities piece together the puzzle of that day or realize that he had nothing to add to their investigation.

Little did he know that his decision to come forward would set in motion a series of events that would not only reveal the truth about the accident but affect the lives of everyone involved.

7

———

While Quinton was waiting for the last of the furniture to be delivered to the new office, he interviewed several men and women for the manager's position in the firm. He needed someone who was a well-organized jack of all trades, with people skills, bookkeeping, and paralegal experience.

Several candidates came to Quinton by way of an ad in the back of the Texas Bar Journal. He had placed the ad because he wanted an arm's length, well-qualified, efficient office manager with whom he had no prior ties. He didn't want a referral that could further entangle him with his old firm or any sitting judges. That way, if something went south, he'd dismiss the person, or if things got really scary, he could leave without personal involvement. It also limited the chance of a breach of confidence due to familiarity with other people. The fewer strings attached, the better.

Quinton's top candidate was an experienced, no-nonsense but friendly woman named Anna Van Buren. She was middle-aged, well groomed, and wore a suit a bit on the conservative side of stylish, with low-heeled pumps. The contrast with Lacey could not have been more obvious, which suited Quinton particularly well.

Lacey and Dart had started to go a little overboard with the flirting, and Quinton was ready to get that element out of his office. One night he'd come back to the office to grab a file he'd forgotten and found them coming out of the conference room, disheveled and embarrassed. Dart said, "It won't happen again," before Quinton said a word.

During the interview, Anna Van Buren sat upright with her legs crossed at the ankles and feet tucked under her chair. Quinton looked at her resume before him on his the desk, then back at her. "It's important to me that professionalism and confidences be kept at all times. Even the slightest betrayal of trust would result in immediate dismissal."

"I completely understand. As you see on my resume, I worked for two judges, both now retired. I'll take things to my grave that shouldn't see the light of day from both of those jobs."

Quinton nodded and flipped through the pages again. "I also need someone who can hit the ground running."

"I may need some training on any unusual software you might select, but I have most of the common ones mastered. There's a list of my skills at the bottom of page two."

Quinton looked at the list containing Microsoft Word, Excel, PowerPoint, Lexus, and several others that would be useful. "Great. I'm willing to pay a good salary for an experienced person who can get things organized quickly."

Anna looked Quinton in the eye. "I can do that. Please talk to both of my last employers about my track record."

"I already did. This looks like a good fit."

A couple of movers came into the outer office and asked Lacey where the credenza and chairs should go.

Quinton started to go out to tell them when his mobile rang, he checked the screen and picked it up. He held up a finger to Anna and she nodded.

The movers were making noise in the outer office and Anna went out to see what they were doing. Lacey was now now nowhere to be found, so she took a look at the furniture and began to direct the men. "Put the chairs in the conference room over there." She pointed. "Put the credenza behind Mr. Bell's desk please."

They nodded at her as if she owned the place and followed orders. When the two men carried the credenza into Quinton's office, he pointed to the wall behind his desk and they placed it there. Anna signed the delivery slip, took possession of a copy, and escorted them out the front door just as Lacey returned.

"Are they finished already?"

Anna handed her the delivery slip. "Looks that way."

Anna listened for Quinton to finish his call then took her seat before his desk as if nothing had happened.

Quinton smiled. "Where were we?"

"Compensation. I've hit the ceiling on what I can make at my current firm, and the cost of driving and parking downtown has become an issue. That's why I'm seeking new employment."

"I understand."

She swallowed, then asked, "What salary do you have in mind?"

Quinton liked her take-charge attitude and no-nonsense approach. "I can go ten percent above your current salary with an additional ten percent increase after a three-month probationary period. Benefits and free parking in the building garage. Performance reviews once a year after that, assuming all goes well."

Anna appeared to be doing some mental math. "That's satisfactory."

"You'd be the one to evaluate insurance companies, set up benefits for me, my investigator, and yourself."

"No problem."

"Good. When can you start?"

"I'm supposed to give two weeks' notice, but I may be able to negotiate that down to one week if you need me right away."

"A week would be better, but we have Lacey, whom you met on the way in. She's a temp but can cover during the transition. She's going back to school but may continue part-time if we need her."

"I'll let you know when I can begin by tomorrow at noon."

"Excellent." Quinton smiled at her, looked at the credenza and smiled again.

8

Before the wreckage had been cleared on I-10 the ambulance chasers had been on the scene scooping up plaintiffs at the edges of the wreckage and in hospitals around the area. Some went so far as to copy down or shoot pictures of license plates, and use hackers, connections, and bribes at the Texas Department of Transportation to get the names and addresses of car owners.

One particularly aggressive lawyer, Matt Johnson, had rounded up the majority of the injured and was in the process of having a class certified in a class-action lawsuit. As word got around, mostly through Johnson's advertisements on television, more and more of the injured contacted his office. Some victims even fired their present counsel and joined the Johnson group when promised a better settlement and more dog in the fight.

Johnson was not a downtown lawyer or a loop lawyer. He was set up in the suburbs between Humble and Cleveland in a strip mall on Highway 59, where real estate was cheaper and his level of clientele felt most comfortable. He actually owned the entire strip mall, including a dry cleaner, all night diner, gentlemen's club, and bowling alley. That didn't mean he eschewed the trappings of wealth. His office was expensively furnished with chunky masculine furniture that made a statement more with bulk than style. He also spent a lot of money on shark silk suits, monogrammed shirts with cufflinks, and leather loafers, in order to impress his clients.

Johnson's younger half-brother, Alvin Anderson, called Double A, was his runner, or for the record, private investigator. He was small and wiry, with spiky bleached blond hair. Runners had one purpose, to act as middlemen to solicit business for unethical personal injury attorneys and sign up plaintiffs faster than the next lawyer's case runner. Solicitors were illegal in Texas and frowned upon by the State Bar, but that didn't stop many attorneys from using them under the guise of investigating.

Double A had nicknamed his boss The Hammer and told potential clients that the attorney hammered away for victims' rights. Johnson liked the moniker, used it in advertising, and eventually became famously known as The Houston Hammer and The Hammer Lawyer. He advertised his championing of the little guy against big corporations and insurance companies that would surely deny them their legal rights, and their much-deserved cash.

Double A was currently spending his time pulling crash reports, known as CR-3s from the Texas Department of Transportation website. A small fee, combined with proper identification of the crash and person involved, allowed him to order the documents, but not view them online, due to the confidential nature of the information. The reports had to be ordered by mail, and Double A filled out a form for that purpose, sending them to the address of the dry cleaner. It wouldn't be the first time the law firm circumvented public scrutiny to gather information, nor would it be the last.

While Double A sought out the remaining victims of the pileup, and got them under contract, The Hammer prepared the motion to certify the class. Both liked their jobs and thought business was good. Money flowed their way.

9

Dalton Cole found a small, but clean, motel with a kitchenette on the northwest side of Houston. He checked in with a weekly rate, found his room, and threw his luggage on the flowery spread on one of the two queen beds closest to the door. He brought up a second load with a hotel gym setup he'd created over the years to keep his trim five-foot ten-inch frame in shape. It consisted of three stretch bands, a chin-up bar that he secured in the bathroom door opening, and an ab roller wheel that he placed on the floor between the beds.

Apparently, there weren't many people who worked out of the Prestige Motel because there wasn't a desk or office chair. It was also not very prestigious. He'd bought a folding table from Costco and drug it up from his Ram pickup truck. He set it up as a makeshift office in one corner of the room and put his computer on it. He pulled over a dining chair from a tiny table in the kitchenette, dropped into it, opened his laptop, and was open for business. First thing he did was notify the Boss of the last day's activities around Quinton. His email was short and sweet as there'd been little happening since he'd arrived in Houston just that morning.

His job, for now, was to follow Quinton, establish a record of his usual practices, and regularly report to the Boss about it all.

"Subject in office, subject at the gym swimming at lunch time, subject visited his bank. On and on. Fairly normal existence for a lawyer. I've settled into a cash hotel a short drive from Quinton's office. Plan to start following him from his condo first thing in the morning."

Boring. Boring. He hoped the Boss planned to shake things up a bit, and soon.

Cole sent the email and thought of an old lawyer joke: Know why lawyers don't play hide and seek? No one will look for them.

10

——————

Detective Clive Broussard arrived at the Law Firm of Quinton Bell and walked into the reception area. Lacey looked up from a Houston Community College catalog she was intently studying. "May I help you?"

He smiled his spicy Cajun smile and said, "Yes, ma'am. My name is Detective Clive Broussard. I'd like to speak to Mr. Bell, please."

"Do you have an appointment?"

"No, ma'am. I don't have an appointment, but I think he'll see me." Broussard had a rugged appearance and was part spice and part crocodile.

Lacey smiled back. "One moment. Please have a seat."

Broussard sat on a black leather sofa next to two blue guest chairs in front of a coffee table covered in State Bar Journals. He flipped through one and tossed it back on the table. "Lawyers." Broussard preferred to look at Lacey.

Lacey sensed that Broussard might not be welcome, so she went into Quinton's office. She could feel Broussard's eyes on her curvy rear as she closed the door behind her. "A Detective Broussard is here to see you. Do we have a case with him?"

Shit. "No. I'll explain later. Show him in."

———

Escorted by Lacey, Broussard entered Quinton's inner office and looked around. The desk was positioned in one end of a long rectangular room featuring a wall of windows providing a view of The Galleria area, lush with fall foliage that was just beginning to turn colors. The other end of the room housed a large wooden conference table with six gray swivel chairs. A bookcase held a set of state and federal casebooks and binders.

Broussard looked around, then walked along the short wall at the back and looked at the spines of legal reference books and continuing education binders. "You read all this?"

"Most of it. Had to study up when I came out of rehab to reestablish my law license." Actually, it was Q's law license, but Broussard didn't know that, as he'd found the real Q dead about a year before, assuming it was Byron Douglas. There were so many twists and turns, it gave Quinton a headache to think about it, so he didn't.

Quinton pointed to one of the two guest chairs before his desk. "Take a seat."

"Thanks. I'd like to ask you a few questions. I'm still investigating Judge Bell's drowning."

"Thought someone might be by about that eventually."

"Your father had a lot of irritation in his esophagus at the time of his death. The medical examiner thinks something was forced down his throat."

"I can't speak to that. When I dragged him out of the Gulf, I started CPR. Could that have caused it?"

"ME says no. More like a rag or sponge was pushed down there."

"Don't know," Quinton lied. "He was in the water, already drowned when I pulled him out. There were a dozen or more witnesses on the beach."

"I've spoken with them and read your statement. Do you have any reason to believe the judge would have killed himself?"

"No. I guess it may have been suicide or accident, but I don't know. He drowned, that's the only thing I'm sure of. The insurance company has already paid off on his death benefits. They had to pay under the policy whether it was accident, suicide, or murder. The judge had paid the premiums, and they seem satisfied. Probate court, too."

Broussard frowned. "He had a shirt on and was pretty far out in the Gulf for a casual swim."

"Yeah. He could have walked out too far and been swept out by the undertow. He had been drinking. I don't know which way it went. I just know by the time I got to him he was gone."

"Yeah? Death seems to follow you around. First Byron Douglas, then Joanne Wyatt, then Judge Sirus Bell."

Quinton almost winced at the sound of his own name in the dead category. He felt a pang of guilt, and the trauma of the past year washed over him. Would Judge Bell still be alive if he hadn't come into his life? Would Q? Would Joanne? He'd never know.

"That's a low blow, even for you, Broussard. Besides, I put Joanne's death on your shoulders, too. You were the one supposedly securing the courtroom during the trial."

"Yeah, right. You keep telling yourself that. I'll get in touch when I decide how this goes."

"You do that."

11

Quinton sat at his desk and inserted the flash drive he'd
received from Judge Garzon into his laptop and
unzipped a large file containing the Lily Collins case
pleadings and documentation. Before he began to unpack the
information, he dragged and dropped the file onto his desktop,
made a duplicate, and parked the copy in Dropbox. He used
the invite tool to advise others and included Dart and the new
office manager, Anna Van Buren, to share the information. He
reasoned he could add Mo Powers later, if needed.

There was no need to include Lacey, as she had moved to
part-time, two afternoons a week, and would not be working on
the case. Quinton had admonished Dart to stay out of the office
on those two days unless absolutely necessary. He could see her
on his own time if he wanted to.

Quinton began to pick apart the data in the files. There
were multiple folders about the accident scene and subsequent
criminal case against the truck driver, Tommy Joe (TJ) Hobbs.
Quinton popped open a folder marked Photos and viewed the
gruesome scene through the lens of the Houston Police Depart-

ment, Texas Department of Transportation, and Harris County Sheriff's Office.

Next, Quinton opened a folder marked Videos and found a lot of blurry, after the fact, streaming that was labeled from various witnesses' mobile phones and social media sites. There were several shots of cars piling into one another behind the initial collision, but he did not see a video of the actual eighteen-wheeler crash in progress. He reasoned it would have happened before anyone had time to get out a phone with a camera and react.

Law enforcement had also taken some video of the jaws of life removing Charlotte Collins from her Camry, the steaming eighteen-wheeler on the side of the overpass, and an overview of the post-accident scene via helicopter. A video of Lily Collins showed her being removed from the back seat of the Camry, after the roof was pried off with the jaws of life. She was eerily silent, staring straight ahead, and not responding to questions by a burly police officer who carried her to the back of an ambulance.

Further exploration revealed a folder containing the criminal court docket on the Hobbs vehicular manslaughter charge. The felony indictment did not include depraved indifference leading to homicide. It would be highly unlikely, and impossible to prove, that Hobbs intended to kill seven people, maim a child, and pileup the entire Katy Freeway. Quinton assumed that's why the authorities chose to prosecute reckless vehicular homicide instead of murder. The file indicated that Hobbs was out on bail.

Quinton saw folders marked with additional names of people who were involved in the primary crash, a general folder marked Pileup and one marked Police Reports.

Quinton composed an email to Dart instructing him to look further into the criminal aspects of Hobbs' arrest, the Pileup folder, and Police Reports folder for anything that might shed light on the primary accident. He also directed him to a file marked Possible Witnesses to be explored later, if needed.

Quinton saved the primary accident files for himself, including the Collins files and the one marked Allison Parker, Deceased, to review later. An alert on his calendar told him he had one hour to get to the courthouse for the guardian appointment hearing with Judge Garzon. Quinton had not been clued in about who he or she might be.

12

When Quinton arrived at Judge Garzon's courtroom, there was no child in the gallery, so Quinton assumed he would not be meeting his new client, Lily Collins, at least for now. Several people were seated and standing around the room, so there was no way for Quinton to guess which person might be the new guardian. He hoped it would not be a hard ass, as he was going to have to work with him, or her, for up to a year while things were sorted out in the case.

The bailiff called the court to order. "All rise."

Everyone stood, then everyone sat when the judge told them to.

The bailiff called the case. "In the matter of the Estate of Charlotte Collins and the Guardianship of Lily Collins. If you have business with this honorable court, stand and be heard."

Quinton stood and faced Judge Garzon. "Quinton Bell attorney for Lily Collins and the estate of Charlotte Collins."

A handsome young couple sitting in the first row stood and the husband introduced them to the court. "Kevin and Jess

Matherly here. We are the temporary custodial parents of Lily Collins."

A gray-haired attorney in a brown suit stood next. "Tom Patton representing State General, Charlotte Collins' automobile insurance carrier on her Toyota Camry."

A striking young brunette woman in a smart blue suit and black leather pumps, sitting behind the Matherlys, stood. "Channing Ward, licensed psychologist working with Lily Collins."

Judge Garzon nodded at each in turn. "Please move to the front row and be seated." When the participants had all found a seat, the judge continued. "Lily Collins is about to go through a long ordeal surrounding the loss of her mother, her mental and physical injuries, the establishment of a home, and the securing of her financial future. It will take each of you on the team to safeguard her wellbeing and her mother's estate."

The crew straightened in their seats at the magnitude of their responsibilities. The judge went on. "The purpose of this hearing is to finalize the appointment of the attorney ad litem and the guardian for Lily Collins. Mr. Bell has agreed to represent Lily's legal interests, and Ms. Ward has agreed to safeguard her mental and physical health."

Quinton knew that guardianship is a legal process intended to safeguard people who are unable to care for themselves. In Texas, if the guardianship has not been established by a parent prior to incapacity, such as in a will, the other parent is usually entitled to be the guardian. Guardians, usually appointed by the court, as in this case, might have broad or limited authority depending upon the mental and or physical limitations of the incapacitated person, known as the ward.

Judge Garzon expounded. "Lily is not of age to be married. Since her mother had designated no guardian, because she died intestate, and her father is unidentified, it falls to the court to appoint an objective third party to protect her interests."

Quinton fully expected a financial institution such as a bank or investment company to be appointed later to manage any money he recovered for Lily. For now, he and Channing Ward would be looking out for Lily's interests.

The judge continued. "By my signature on this order, I hereby appoint both Mr. Bell and Ms. Ward to these statutory positions." The judge signed two documents that the bailiff set before him. "You may obtain certified copies in the clerk's office later today. Thank you for your assistance with this delicate case." As those in the room watched, the judge left the bench through the rear door to his chambers.

That was fast.

Tom Patton, legal representative from the car insurance company, introduced himself to Quinton, but didn't stay around for further pleasantries, and made a quick exit. Quinton turned to the Matherlys who were standing beside him and offered his hand to Kevin. "Mr. and Mrs. Matherly, nice to make your acquaintance."

Quinton next shook hands with Jess who said, "Call us Kevin and Jess."

"Great, call me Quinton. If it's okay with you, I'd like to set a time to meet with Lily."

Quinton then offered his hand to Channing Ward who had joined them. "With your permission, of course, Ms. Ward."

"Please, call me Channing." They shook hands and held for a moment. For Quinton, something felt familiar.

13

A few days later, Quinton and Channing met at the home of Kevin and Jess Matherly in Memorial, an affluent neighborhood west of downtown Houston and east of the Energy Corridor. It wasn't far from Kincaid, Byron and Q's former private school. That seemed eons ago, and Quinton tried not to think about his deceased friend. The guardians each parked on the street and paused on the walkway to the front door.

"Quinton." She smiled.

"Hello, Channing." Quinton shuffled his briefcase to his left hand and extended his right.

She smiled, then took his hand and held it. "Good to see you again. Don't expect too much from Lily. She's still severely traumatized and may not be able to communicate with you."

"I understand."

When they were admitted to the home by Jess, they saw a young girl, with a pink bow in her curly hair, sitting at the kitchen island, writing in a notebook with a schoolbook spread open before her. Sadly, only one leg dangled from the stool and ended in a black patent leather Mary Jane shoe. A metal crutch with forearm support was propped against the end of the island.

Jess escorted them through the living room to the kitchen. "We're trying to do some homeschooling while Kevin is at work."

Channing turned to Quinton. "We don't think Lily is ready to go back to class yet. Let me introduce you."

"Lily, this is Mr. Bell. He's been appointed by the judge to represent you."

"Hello, Lily. Please call me Quinton." She did not respond and continued to work on the homework, eyes down. "I understand you are seven years old."

She kept her focus on the homework. "I just turned eight."

"I understand." Quinton picked up a pink marker from the island and wrote Quinton Bell and his phone number on a clean piece of art paper. "You can reach me at this number any time you want to talk to me." He then took a yellow marker and drew a smiley face under the number.

Lily looked at the page, then at Quinton. "Are you a lawyer?"

"I am. I'm your lawyer." He took his bar card from his wallet and showed it to her. "See, here's my name, Quinton Lamar Bell." *Lying to her already.*

Channing looked impressed with Quinton's approach and didn't try to intervene.

Lily took a separate clean page, selected a purple marker, and wrote her name, drawing a heart for the dot on the I in Lily. She wrote the number eight under her name, then pushed the page toward Quinton and went back to her workbook.

Channing and Jess smiled at each other, then at Quinton.

14

C ole gave the Boss an update, delivering the latest
information on their target, Quinton Bell. "Went to
court, back to the office, visited a client, all the lawyer stuff." He
then awaited instructions with an air of anticipation. The next
set of orders came through loud and clear.

"Let's step up the cat and mouse game and tease him just a
bit. Let him wonder who's out there. Don't reveal yourself. Try
to get me some video," the Boss instructed, revealing a sinister
desire to further toy with their unsuspecting prey.

"Will do." Cole concealed his mixed emotions behind a
facade of loyalty, while enjoying the bizarre and twisted world
he'd been drawn into as his profession.

*Like to watch, you crazy bastard? Some people have more money
than sense.*

Quinton parked in the garage of his office building and
grabbed his briefcase from the back seat. He had learned his

lesson about leaving it in the car during the Wyatt murder trial, and never did it again. He didn't bother with the go bag, the contents could easily be replaced, but it gave him comfort to know it was there. He slammed the car door and clicked the lock with his key fob. He looked over toward the stairwell entry and saw a man in a dark hoodie slip through the door and out of sight. It felt creepy, and Quinton never ignored his gut.

He walked over to the door and looked through a milky glass rectangle. No one was there as far as he could see, so he opened the door and looked inside. He still didn't see anyone, but there was the dark hoodie hanging over the stair rail. He could hear another stairwell door slamming a floor or two away, which direction, up or down, he wasn't sure because of the echo. He climbed up a floor, opened the hallway door, and saw no one, then he climbed back down and farther down another floor and did the same. Seeing nothing, he went back up to his floor and looked around again.

"Creepy," he said to no one, and headed toward the elevator.

Quinton slid into the open elevator and the doors closed just behind him. He thought he was alone, but realized there was another person in the corner of the car. A scrawny, short little boy-man in a set of brown coveralls, slumped against the far wall. His name tag had 'Van' stamped on a white rectangle on his chest. He had on a tool belt with a hammer, flashlight, and a big ring of dangling keys.

Quinton nodded, not sure if the little guy was friend or foe. *I'd hate to be whacked with those keys.*

"Hey, Mr. Bell. How's it going?"

"Did you see someone enter the stairwell just now?"

"No. I came through the garage."

Quinton studied the young face with a few whiskers trying to grow here and there. "I'm sorry. Have we met?"

"Sure, Mr. Bell. I'm Van." He pointed to his name on the tag. "I changed the burned-out lightbulbs in your office for Anna. I was up on a ladder, so you might have just seen my shoes." Van guffawed a long loud yuck of a laugh as if it was the funniest joke ever told.

Quinton couldn't help but laugh too, not at the joke, but at the comical antics. He was surprised by the big noise coming out of the little guy and forgot all about the hooded man in the garage. "I do remember the ladder and the uniform. Nice to meet you, Van. Is that a family name?"

The elevator door opened on Quinton's office floor and both men walked out.

"Yes, sir, Mr. Bell. My grandma was a hippie back in Austin. She loved Van Morrison, so she convinced my mama to name me after him."

"Van the Man."

"Right." The guffaw started again.

Quinton chuckled. "See you later, Van."

"See ya later, Mr. Bell."

Van walked toward one end of the hall and Quinton walked toward his office on the other end singing *Moondance*.

Van, hearing the song, laughed his quirky laugh all the way down the hall.

When Quinton entered his office, he saw Anna sitting at her desk in the reception area and nodded her way. She stopped talking midsentence and looked at Quinton with wide eyes.

He proceeded through the room to his inner office as he heard Anna say in a hushed tone, "I'll have to call you back later."

His gut started talking to him again. *Am I imagining things or is this just a strange day?*

15

Luke Parker, Allison Parker's brother, became the face of the class action group formed by Matt Johnson's law firm. Luke was selected by Johnson, The Hammer, because his sister had been killed, therefore he had the highest damage claim. Plus, he was young, attractive, and likable. He appeared to be about thirty years old and did not have an arrogant air. Today, in The Hammer's office, he looked a bit unkempt, his brown hair shaggy and oily.

The Hammer looked at the scruffy kid. "We need to clean you up. Image is important in this type of trial."

"No problem. Tell me what you want me to look like and that's what I'll be." Luke had already started spending the settlement money in his mind. Not that he hadn't loved his sister. He had. But she was gone and he'd lost his job in the process of his grief and caring for his mother. Money was tight, and they were in need.

"Double A will get you a list of grooming requirements and help you select some appropriate clothing."

"Good. I was told that you could advance some of the

money from the settlement proceeds, just enough to help me get by. I moved back in with my mother and she's on Social Security. Not much coming in."

"Sure. But just this once." The Hammer knew that when the advances started, it was never just once.

Luke smiled. "I understand."

"Double A can help you with that, too." The Hammer had been advancing money to clients for years. It was a good way to keep them attached to the firm and had become standard practice with most personal injury lawyers. He had a small red lockbox in the receptionist's desk full of twenty- and one-hundred dollar bills for just this purpose and an old-fashioned receipt book for quick signing.

"Thanks, Mr. Johnson."

The Hammer put on his best fake smile. "Sure."

Quinton and Dart found a spot ion the second row of the courtroom on the plaintiff's side in order to observe the representative for STS, Jacob Hollingsworth, and Matt Johnson, The Hammer, at work. Since Quinton was not joining his clients to the class, he was not a party to the proceedings today.

The Hammer had filed the petition to certify the class when he had reached one hundred plaintiffs involved in the pileup on I-10. That many were not specifically required, but it was a nice round number, and he expected more clients to join the class as Double A beat the bushes every day for more of the injured. Today, Judge Garzon was holding a hearing on the argument that the class should or should not be certified.

Next to Johnson sat Luke Parker, all cleaned up and ready for the show. They had styled, dressed, and coached him to appear sweet, like a brother should be. It didn't take much. He was already a likable guy. Johnson went first, after being prompted by Judge Garzon.

"Your Honor, as you can see from the motion before you, the group of plaintiffs that my firm represents share the elements required for the creation of a class, namely commonality, numerosity, typicality, and adequacy. Each of the defendants was in the pileup behind the defendant's eighteen-wheeler crash on the date shown. In addition, it would be a burden on the court to try each of these cases separately, as the same witnesses and experts would be duplicated in each case. Furthermore, it would be burdensome on most of the defendants to bear the costs of a separate lawsuit when their interests are so closely aligned with those of my client, Mr. Parker."

"Anything else?"

"Yes, Your Honor. As attorney with an overwhelming majority of clients in the class, I request that the court appoint me managing attorney for the class."

"That would entitle you to an extra fee, Mr. Johnson."

The Hammer smiled. "Yes, Your Honor, and extra work as well."

"So it would seem. Anything else?"

"No, Your Honor."

"Okay. Be seated, Mr. Johnson. Does defense counsel wish to speak?"

"Yes, Your Honor."

On the defense side, representing STS, and opposing the certification of the class, was Jacob Hollingsworth. Quinton and Dart perked up, as this was their first encounter with the lawyer in full showboating stance. He could not have been more different than The Hammer. Hollingsworth was almost regal in his posture, wore a conservative Brooks Brothers suit with tan Oxfords and a muted tie. When he spoke, his articulation and enunciation sounded one step removed from a British accent.

Quinton leaned over to whisper to Dart, "I wonder what his billable rate might be."

Dart whispered back, "I wonder if he has a stick up his ass."

Quinton stifled a laugh.

Hollingsworth turned toward the judge. "Your Honor, if it please the court. My clients, Speedy Transportation Services and Tommy Joe Hobbs, enthusiastically oppose the certification of the class represented by Mr. Johnson and his client, Mr. Parker. Upon reflection, I'm sure Your Honor will note that each person driving a car involved in the accident was acting in a different manner on the day in question. Some drivers may have been distracted and others may have been pushed from behind into other cars. Each driver has a unique set of injuries that could not possibly be called common. Some were killed, some are still in rehabilitation, and some were barely injured and went to work the day after the accident. It would be impossible for the court to establish a fair distribution of settlement funds to each plaintiff."

Johnson stood up. "May I address this point, Your Honor?"

"Alright but be brief."

"Yes, sir. As you and Mr. Hollingsworth are aware, courts have established different levels of injuries in many cases in class-action suits. Level one plaintiffs are those with property damage and little to no physical injuries. Level two plaintiffs have property damage and severe physical injuries, and level three plaintiffs have property damage and loss of life or limbs, or use of limbs. As you see in my motion, we do not think we will have any problem setting up a sliding scale to allocate funds once a settlement or trial award is reached." The Hammer took a breath and started to speak further.

"I said brief, Mr. Johnson."

Hollingsworth was on his feet again. "May I speak, Your Honor?"

"I think I've heard enough from both sides, and I've read your briefs. The plaintiffs in this action are best served by an appointed representative of the group. I'm going to certify the class contingent upon the submission of a proposal of allocation of funds based on level of injuries and possible fault if a settlement is reached or award granted by a jury at trial. Court dismissed."

Quinton jerked when the gavel came down. Dart looked at him. "You jumpy?"

To Quinton, it sounded like gunfire. "Distracted."

Quinton sent Dart on ahead and waited for Hollingsworth outside the courtroom door. "Allow me to introduce myself, I'm Quinton Bell. I represent Lily Collins and her mother's estate."

Hollingsworth shook Quinton's extended hand. "I know who you are. I've expected a call any day now."

"I'd like to set up a settlement conference. I can request it through the court if you're opposed, but I'd rather keep it informal for now and just negotiate a date."

"Why isn't your client going to be part of the class action?"

"Judge Garzon has appointed me to protect the interests of the child. I think she's best represented on her own."

"No need to make it formal. We can set a date. How does a conference in two weeks sound? Assuming I don't get my summary judgment granted."

"I assumed you'd be filing a motion for one."

"Yes, it's standard. My clients expect it."

Quinton didn't mention the fact that it ran up legal fees. "I'll check in with you if it's denied."

"Sounds good. Then, we'll see if we can hammer something out."

"Hammer is the other guy, but I appreciate the sentiment. I'll have my paralegal call your office."

Johnson exited the courtroom and approached the two outside the door. Quinton held up a finger to hush Hollingsworth. "Here comes The Hammer singing the *Greenback Boogie*."

Quinton and Hollingsworth stopped talking.

"Don't let me interrupt. I'm Matt Johnson." He extended his hand to Quinton. "I think our interests are aligned. Care to have a chat about it?"

Hollingsworth looked at the two. "I'll be going now. Mr. Bell, we'll expect your call."

After Hollingsworth walked off, Johnson said, "You planning a settlement conference?"

"Thinking about it."

"I'd like to join in."

"I don't know if it's in my client's best interest to align with the class. She has special circumstances."

"How so?"

"You know she lost her leg and her mother died right in front of her."

"My client's sister was killed, too. So were seven others in various circumstances."

"Yes, but he's a grown man and wasn't at the scene. The other seven had relatives in similar circumstances. Lily Collins will need care for the rest of her life, and supervision until at least her eighteenth birthday. Maybe longer if she goes to college. It's a whole different ballpark."

"Maybe, but you still have more in common with my clients than Hollingsworth's."

"That's true. I'll think about it." Quinton walked off.

"You do that."

16

Quinton was working late one night in his office, coat off, tie undone, going over other client files that were behind because of the Collins case, when he heard a tap on the outer office door. It made him jump. Anna and Lacey had both gone for the day and Quinton was hoping for some quiet hours to get his head around the issues confronting his clients. No such luck.

He went through the reception area and looked through the glass doors to see Detective Clive Broussard standing in the hallway. Quinton reluctantly unlocked the right door and let him in, relocking the door behind him.

Broussard laughed. "I guess I'm trapped."

"No. Just avoiding drop-ins, which you are one. What do you need?"

"Could we sit for a moment?"

Quinton walked back toward his inner office door. "Sure. Come on in." He sat behind his desk and Broussard took a seat in one of the guest chairs.

"I wanted to let you know that we have cleared the Judge

Sirus Bell case as an accidental drowning."

Quinton let out a small breath he hadn't realized he was holding. "What took so long?"

"Me. I know there was something going on around that whole case with Joanne Wyatt that ended in your father's death. I just can't prove it. But frankly, I don't see anyone being harmed by my letting the case go. I have a lot of other fish to fry. Whatever you were up to, it can be your little secret."

"That sounds sensible. I'm the only one left, and as you can see, I'm working my ass off to get this firm going. I don't have time for any shenanigans right now."

"I spoke to Silver Jamail. She said that you gave all Judge Bell's money to charity in one fashion or another. Doesn't seem as if profit was your goal if there was wrongdoing."

"Haven't I lost enough? Been punished enough? First Joanne, then my father. Not to mention my childhood friend, Byron. Why can't you just leave me alone?"

"Well, that brings me to the second reason I'm here. I need to hire a lawyer who's good at criminal defense. I was hoping you'd look at the case."

"What?"

"I want to hire you for a case."

"You what?"

"Are your ears full of gumbo? I need a lawyer for my nephew, and I'd like for you to look at the case and see if you think you can help him."

Quinton stared at Broussard for an eternal beat. His mind did flip-flops around staying in touch with Broussard, who was the one person who knew the most about Q's death as Byron, or putting as much distance as possible between them. Keeping him close might be a good idea, but right now, Quinton just wanted to run as far away from him as possible.

Quinton folded his hands on his desk. "I don't know. We've

not exactly been friendly."

"Well, I know that, but I'm not friendly with any criminal defense lawyers, so I might as well hire a good one, and I heard you are. Good, that is."

"Thanks. I think. What kind of a case?" *Maybe it would be a good idea to have an HPD detective owing me a favor. Maybe.*

"My sister's son has shit for brains. He and his buddies broke into a store in Galveston and some goods were looted."

"Is he over eighteen?"

"He's nineteen."

"Was the theft over five hundred dollars in value?"

"Yep."

"Well, as you know, that's grand larceny. Carries a sentence of up to a year and up to four thousand in restitution."

"Unfortunately, it was over fifteen hundred in value."

"Less than twenty thousand?"

"Yep."

"Okay, in Texas that's considered a state jail felony. He could face as much as two years of imprisonment and up to ten thousand dollars in fines."

"I know, but there are extenuating circumstances and I hope you can get him out of trouble or at least negotiate a deal for him."

"What extenuating circumstances?"

"Look, he's a good kid. He makes good grades. Plays sports. I'd like for him to come in and talk to you. Tell you what happened. You up for that?"

"I don't know of a 'good kid extenuating circumstance' defense, but maybe I can come up with something. You guaranteeing payment?"

"Yes. My sister plans to pay the bill, but if she doesn't, I'll pay it."

"Okay." *I guess.*

17

Quinton climbed into his rented Audi SUV and started driving toward his condo near the Houston Medical Center. He waited for the connection light to come up on the phone, then spoke into the car's microphone. "Call Alcott Wyatt, mobile."

Alcott was Joanne Wyatt's brother and the manager of her estate. Joanne, unbeknownst to Quinton, until after her death, had added a codicil to her will during the course of her murder trial. She had left Quinton one hundred percent of her assets, excluding her trust, which could not be bequeathed, and went to Wyatt. It was not a small sum, as her home and real estate holdings alone were worth millions of dollars, plus cash in her accounts. Quinton had not felt that he could keep any of that money after what had transpired in the courtroom, leading to her death. He was also motivated by the fact that he was not actually Quinton, and although Joanne knew that at the time of the codicil, he didn't want to open the transaction to scrutiny. His guilt was so great, he had Alcott's attorney draw up a document allowing Quinton to waive the bequest and leave the assets in the corpus of the estate. In essence, he gave it all back to Alcott.

Quinton had vowed to keep in touch with Alcott after the courtroom shooting, but he'd not been doing a very good job. The execution of the documents and the news about Judge Bell was a good excuse to call.

"Alcott Wyatt here."

"Alcott, this is Quinton Bell calling from Houston. Since we haven't spoken in a while, I thought I'd check in. I've executed the waiver of inheritance and had it notarized. My office manager overnighted it to you yesterday morning."

"Good of you to call, Quinton, and thanks for the update. I received it first thing today."

Quinton cleared his throat. "I guess I'm also missing Joanne and just wanted to talk to someone who also knew and loved her."

"She's in my thoughts every day."

"Mine, too. It would be great to see you. The date has been set for the groundbreaking and gala for my father's wing at South Texas College of Law. I've put you on the invitation list. I hope you can attend if you're in town."

"I'll watch for the invitation and see what I can do. If the estate's been settled, I assume there weren't any problems with the investigation?"

"Well, that's another reason I called. I also wanted to let you know that the police have designated my father's drowning as accidental. The investigation into murder or suicide didn't have much merit and was mostly a formality by Detective Broussard."

Quinton had kept Alcott current on the news about the investigation during their rare telephone conversations over the last few months.

"I remember Broussard. He's the one who didn't protect my sister in court."

"Right. He didn't. I didn't protect her either, Alcott. I feel guilty every day."

"You would have won her murder case. Byron Douglas is the one to blame for bringing those thugs into her life. I know she loved you, Quinton."

Quinton gulped so hard, his Adam's apple moved up and down. He was sure Alcott could hear him swallow over the phone. He was guilty of bringing danger to Joanne's door. If not for him, she'd still be alive. Fortunately, Alcott only knew him as Quinton Bell.

"Thank you."

"I'm glad to hear that you're getting some closure around your father's death. As much as possible, anyway."

"Thank you, Alcott."

"I'll let you know if I fly south. I need to run. Keep in touch."

"It was good talking to you. Let me know if you get to H-Town and I'll buy you a steak at Vic and Anthony's."

"Take care, Quinton."

18

As planned, Jacob Hollingsworth, attorney for the defense, requested a hearing on his motion to dismiss the lawsuit of Lily Collins and all the members of the class action plaintiffs.

Quinton arrived early and had a quick chat with Channing Ward prior to the hearing. She looked particularly lovely in a simple blue dress with her dark hair in a shaggy bun at the nape of her neck. Her long legs, ending in a pair of black open-toed slingbacks, were particularly appealing to Quinton. It wasn't necessary for her to attend the hearing, but it was nice that she was there. *Could it be she had come to see him?*

She smiled. "Hello, Quinton. Good to see you."

"You as well, Channing."

She seemingly unconsciously adjusted his tie then patted his chest. "There. You don't think Judge Garzon will take this motion to dismiss the case seriously, do you?"

Quinton swallowed hard at her touch. "Well, one never knows, but I don't see it happening. The deal was pretty much set when the judge signed the class action certification order, but I guess Hollingsworth was obligated to try. How's Lily?"

"She's making slow progress. I'd hoped she'd be further along by now. Would you like to see her again? It might have a positive impact on her to know you are fighting for justice for her mother."

"Absolutely, let me know of a good day for you and Lily. Late afternoons are best. Want to have dinner afterward?"

"To talk about the case?"

"Yes, to talk about the case and Lily and things in general." Quinton almost winked at her.

Channing smiled again, as did Quinton.

Judge Garzon's bailiff called the court to order, and both sides argued their motions for and against the dismissal. As Quinton had thought, the judge denied the motion to dismiss and set the court date. It was a long shot, but fairly common in this type of lawsuit. How could he grant such a motion? There were too many parties and details to sort out. The plaintiffs must have their day in court. He did, however, give a short speech at the end of his ruling encouraging settlement.

Good, that's what I want too. The sooner the better. Quinton looked over at Channing. *Maybe not too soon.*

19

Quinton felt the stress associated with the transition: The new firm, the Collins case, Broussard's nephew, looking for a house to buy, and most of all the duplicitous person who'd sent the note. He had not had another traumatic flashback since he'd been in Judge Blaylock's courtroom but was on high alert for it to happen again. Small tensions and distracting moments told him the emotions were just beneath the surface. He had gone through the stages of grief over the loss of Joanne Wyatt, but he still missed her and thought of her every day.

Quinton felt that old pressure building up, and it was time for a swim and a think. After work, he drove downtown to his athletic club, parked in the garage, and went to the reception desk.

"Hi, Kristen." He swiped his card on the reader.

"Hello, Mr. Bell."

"I've moved my office out by The Galleria and am looking for a house out there as well. Can you recommend a swim club similar to this one near the Loop? I'll need to give up my membership here. It's a month's notice, right?"

"That's right, Mr. Bell, but you don't need to give up your membership. You can use the swim club on San Felipe, right by The Galleria. Your membership is good at all three locations. The Woodlands, too."

A man wearing a dark sweatshirt was hanging around the weight room, turned away, but listened to their conversation.

Quinton smiled at Kristen who seemed to be flirting a little. "Is the lap pool as long as the one here?"

"Exactly the same length and one lane wider."

"Excellent. I'll give it a try." It had been months since Quinton had been with a woman. He hadn't desired anyone but Joanne, since her death, but that might be changing as he felt a small stir while watching Kristen move around in her black yoga pants and tight cropped tank top.

She smiled at him again. "All the addresses are on the website. Or just call me any time. Any old time."

He smiled back. "Thanks."

Quinton went into the men's locker room, changed into his blue Speedo, and passed through to the pool area. Two lanes were free, and he chose the one closest to the middle. He noticed someone open, then close the door to the men's locker room, without entering, as he slid down the side of the pool and into the water. He pulled on his goggles and began a slow steady breaststroke, dismissing the person behind the door as probably lost or touring the club.

Once his focus was on his stroking, the door opened again and a man watched him go back and forth, back and forth. Cole then walked over to Quinton's towel and patted it, found nothing underneath such as a cell phone or car keys. He dropped the towel onto the wet floor, then drop kicked it into the end of the pool.

Oblivious, Quinton made the turn at the wall of the pool and started back to the other end.

20

Quinton had very little time to research the assets available for his client prior to the settlement conference with Hollingsworth. The date for the meeting was set after Judge Garzon denied the defendant's request for summary judgment.

Quinton's primary concern was to nail down the insurance limits for each of the parties. As a general practice, the policy limits would be the starting point for each of the companies' lawyers to work toward in the settlement. The key to getting a good settlement was knowing what the other side had to work with. Sometimes that involved the net worth of the company, but with small claims, it involved insurance. No need trying to get blood from a turnip, and no need pushing anyone into bankruptcy, in which case, he'd get nothing. The insurance limits may or may not be confidential, so he'd have to go through the judge to get what he might know, have Dart dig up what he could, then use his intuition in the settlement meeting after he saw the opening offers.

Quinton did have legal authority to contact Charlotte

Collins' insurance company, as the attorney for the estate, so he picked up the phone and started with Tom Patton at State General Insurance. Low-hanging fruit.

"Hello, Mr. Patton. This is Quinton Bell. I represent Lily Collins and the estate of Charlotte Collins."

"Hello, Mr. Bell. I remember you from the guardianship hearing."

"Right. I was hoping that we could discuss the policy on the Collins' Camry. I don't have a copy of it yet. Would you send one over?"

"Of course."

"Mind sharing the policy limits now, so I can get started?"

"Not at all. I'll spare you the boring details, you can read that in the policy. We basically have coverage at one hundred thousand, plus three hundred thousand for bodily injury. Fifty thousand for property damage. Collision coverage is one hundred thousand. Uninsured motorist coverage is fifty thousand."

"That's not a lot."

"Fairly basic. Lastly, medical payment coverage depends on the medical bills, but is capped at one hundred thousand."

"Hmm. Any deductible?"

Patton paused and Quinton could hear pages flipping. "Looks like five hundred dollars."

"Okay. Hang on a sec." Quinton looked at the notes he'd been scratching on his legal pad and did quick mental math.

He thought through all the angles. "Doesn't sound like there's a lot to work with. What are you thinking?"

Patton cleared his throat. "Well. We were going to monitor the settlement meetings and see who has what, but if you want to save us some time and attorney's fees, we could offer the replacement cost of the Camry and maybe another ten thousand or so for a full release upfront."

"I'd have to put a condition for more in case none of the other parties' insurances cover the medical bills, but there are deep pockets everywhere. I doubt I'd have to come back to you later for that."

"Understood."

"We wouldn't be able to guarantee no one else in the pileup won't come after the bodily or property coverage; you'd have to deal with them separately."

"Also understood."

"If that's all okay, I could settle for the Collins at fifty thousand if I could get it this week. I need some operating cash to work the other settlement claims, pay my investigator, and all that."

"The car wasn't worth that, but kicking in the attorney's fees would get us to that ballpark. Let's do it and get this file off my desk. Fifty K."

"Great. Send over the policy, release, and a check and I'll get the judge to approve the deal."

"I guess you can't effectively consult with your client on this one."

"No, since Charlotte Collins is not with us, and I'm not sure Lily Collins knows what insurance is. Unfortunately."

Patton didn't have a response for that.

Dart joined Quinton at the office and they moved the boxes of Collins files to the conference room, spread out the documents, and poured steaming coffee from a carafe into mugs left for them by Anna.

She had sorted the files by plaintiff and defendant, and color-coded the ones most applicable to Lily's case with red stickers. Most of the information had been scanned to folders and placed in Dropbox, but Quinton liked to visualize the case with hard copies at various stages. This was one such stage. He needed to get into his mind, clearly and concisely, each defendant, their liability, their insurance company, and his best guess at policy limits.

That's where Dart came in. He rolled a white erase board to the end of the conference table and marked off several columns, creating a grid on the board. First was a list of each defendant, including STS, Hobbs, Collins' Camry Insurer, Texas Department of Transportation, Allison Parker - Deceased, and the two vehicles that had secondary collisions with the Collins' Camry. In the second column was the name of each defendant's insurance company and their attorney of record. In the third column were the policy limits, if known, and the best guess, if unknown. Finally, the last column was for the amount that Quinton hoped he could settle for, per defendant. For now, it was empty.

Dart pointed to the coverage column. "I've looked into each of these people and companies and researched average coverage for the type of vehicle they were driving, just like you asked."

Quinton joined him at the board. "I settled for the max on the Collins' Camry, so let's take that off the list." Quinton took a different colored marker and drew a line through that defendant, for now.

Dart nodded.

Quinton addressed the board again. "The insurance companies for the pickup trucks that sandwiched the Collins' Camry have pled all of their coverage into the court registry. They say they owe it, they just don't know to whom. They'll collect from STS and Hobbs on the back side if they can."

"Yep. I checked them out. Renters, not homeowners,

without a pot to piss in. Plus, they were pushed into her car by the pileup."

"Right, no real liability, no use suing them. We'll ask for the full amount of insurance coverage from Judge Garzon, but he'll likely spread it around a little. For now, I'll just put a guess of fifty thousand dollars in the settlement column."

Dart studied the white board. "How about the highway repair crew?"

"TxDOT has statutory limits covering all claims. There are caps on the damages that can be collected set at two hundred fifty thousand for each individual involved in the incident and five hundred thousand for each instance of bodily harm or death. Problem is, their attorney is denying all liability on the part of the agency."

Dart nodded. "From watchin' the video, looks like they did everythin' by the book to me, but what do I know about highway construction?"

"We might want to get an expert opinion on that, just to make sure we haven't missed anything."

"Maybe they're liable just for being in the way. I'll see if I can find us one of 'those kind' of experts."

"You can try the back of the Texas Bar Journal out there on the coffee table. Experts advertise there. If you don't see anyone, I'll check around with some other insurance companies for referrals."

"The Hammer might do the work for us. If he can't find a mistake, we probably won't either."

"Good point. Check the TxDOT file when we're finished with the list, and if his discovery is not there yet, make a note for Anna to ask for it in our next set of interrogatories and production request."

"Want to guess a number for now?"

"If they were to settle at all, they might toss in attorney's fees to keep from going to trial. Otherwise, unless we find a big mistake, they're going to deny liability and fight all claims. So, for now, I'm putting in a question mark with less than five hundred thousand in parentheses."

"Sounds good to me."

"The next easiest one is Allison Parker's Estate. What did you find out about her family?"

"Buzz is, her brother, Luke Parker, is borrowin' money from The Hammer until the trial is finished. He's livin' with his mama and she's got nothin' too."

"Good to know."

"According to the info from The Hammer in the class action docs, her car insurance was 30/60/25 coverage."

"That's the lowest allowed by law in Texas. The class action hasn't filed suit against the Parker Estate, since Luke Parker is the class poster boy. She did contribute to the cause of the accident, but in a minor way, so we can assume, for now, we'll get some of that for Lily."

"Right. I'm surprised she had insurance at all." Dart took another colored marker and wrote 30/60/25 in the settlement column.

"We're going to run out of colors." Quinton laughed. "Would be nice to write something in black and white."

Dart laughed too. "This is just a fancy game of poker, way I see it."

"That's exactly what it is. You check the cards you've been dealt, trade some for others, guess who's bluffing about settling or going to trial, and hope for the best on the river cards."

"So far, we ain't got no millions up there."

"That's where our two main plaintiffs come in, Speedy Transportation Services and the driver, TJ Hobbs. I'm sure Hobbs has a healthy insurance policy on his truck and his own liability, and STS is worth millions if not billions."

"How we gonna get soma dat?"

"That's the interesting part of the game. No luck getting information on the policy limits?"

"Nope. Not a single clue dat I could find."

"Expected that. I'll have to do some more research on those two and nationwide averages. Let's go through the files and see if we have any clues."

Dart sat down and pulled over a stack of files. "It's always a laugh a minute wit' you."

Quinton laughed, then faked a big yawn, and covered his mouth with his hand.

21

Quinton parked his rented Audi SUV in his designated spot in the garage of his office building and vowed one more time to go out and buy himself a car. Soon.

He grabbed his briefcase off the back seat, as always, and headed to the elevator. When he stepped inside and turned around, he saw a man sitting in a dark Ram pickup at the end of a row of cars. The driver wore a baseball cap and had what might be a camera or phone pointed toward the elevator. The doors closed before Quinton could identify exactly what he was seeing or press the hold button. Was he being paranoid? Maybe the guy was just looking at his phone. Maybe it was nothing at all, but his instincts told him it was more. By the time he pressed the button to return the elevator to the garage, the man was gone. His gut said the guy had been watching and photographing or videoing him.

MANNING WOLFE

Quinton went to his desk and opened the browser on his laptop. He contemplated who might be following him and why. His past life in New York seemed a distant memory, but he knew that the Irish mob didn't forget. He was pretty sure they thought he was dead, but he'd fooled them before and they'd caught up with him. The head of the mob, Tua Dannon, had been prosecuted and imprisoned, but Dannon's right hand, Seamus Devlin, had disappeared as far as Quinton knew. Being in jail would not stop the mob boss from running his cartel; in fact, it might make it easier. Devlin could be working for Dannon on the outside, or he might have run to Mexico and left it all behind. No sense speculating. It was time to update his information.

He typed Seamus Devlin into his search engine and found an article in the *New York Times* about Tua Dannon's prosecution on murder and RICO charges, and the fact that the FBI was still looking for Devlin as a co-conspirator and material witness. The article was a few months old. That was the last reference he could find on Devlin, although he tried different spellings and references to locate additional information, so it appeared that Devlin had not been caught and was still in the wind. Could he be back in town?

One of Dannon's appeals had been denied, so it appeared the mobster might never get out of jail, or at least not soon. Could Dannon have sent someone else to check up on Byron? But why? How in the world could Byron be important enough to continue to pursue, especially since there was documented proof that he was dead?

Hell, maybe he was being paranoid and no one was spying at all. Why would Dannon or Devlin still believe he was alive, and if they did, what good would it do them to follow him around? Vengeance? Making an example? Believing he had information that he didn't have? What could they possibly

102

think he knew that was important enough to track him? What did they suspect his former client had told him that could be much worse than what the FBI already knew?

It didn't seem their style to send taunting notes. If they wanted something, why didn't they just ask for it? And, if they wanted him dead, and knew he was really Byron Douglas, he already would be.

Quinton slammed the laptop closed and contemplated his next swim, or better yet, a card game.

22

As it often happened, when swimming didn't fully relieve the pressure, Quinton started thinking about a card game. At first it was a slight itch, like a whisper. But, if unanswered, the urge became stronger until it preoccupied his mind and demanded a release, as it did today.

Quinton had identified several gambling establishments around Houston, most of them well advertised and open to the public. He never went to those. He found the private clubs more interesting, with better quality players and higher stakes. His favorite spot had become The Dog Pound on the northwest side, but he was reluctant to go too often. He didn't want it getting around town that he was a player, especially since he'd recently been fully reestablished with the State Bar as Quinton. Although most of the players were part of a conspiracy of anonymity, there was no guarantee of confidentiality, so Quinton didn't introduce himself or try to make pals.

When he had time, Quinton went to Kinder, Louisiana, a two and one-half-hour drive away, to the Coushatta Indian Reservation Casino. At that distance from Houston, and in his disguises, he felt safe there. If time was short, and he'd been to The Dog Pound too frequently, he'd gamble on the offshore casino boat out of Galveston.

Today, he wanted a quick fix, so he decided to risk it and went to the strip center where The Dog Pound was located. He circled the parking lot behind the building, recognized no vehicles, didn't sniff out any trouble, and backed into a spot at the end. He pulled on a blue and white Rice Owls baseball cap and a pair of tortoiseshell Ray Bans.

As usual, Quinton went through the empty kennel area that smelled like wet dog and approached the door at the back. He gave the entry signal at the small glass window, upraised fist turned into peace sign, and was admitted. He was hit with the smell of a card room, stale beer, smoke, and stress sweat.

He mumbled his traditional lucky mantra under his breath, "Baby needs a new pair of shoes."

He walked into the back of the poker room, checked out his favorite table, didn't recognize anyone, sat down, and placed ten one-hundred-dollar bills in front of the dealer. He was rewarded with an assortment of chips and used one to ante up.

He didn't notice anyone watching him and didn't recognize any of the other faces in the room. Quinton played for about five hours, leaving at 3:00 a.m., eight hundred dollars richer, a low night for him, but feeling more settled and focused. He drove across H-Town to his condo near the medical center and slept like a baby in his king-size bed.

He had no idea his follower had been in the parking lot at The Dog Pound or in the car behind him on his way home.

23

Quinton had called Channing to ask if she'd like a ride out to Lily's temporary home. She had accepted and they were on their way out the I-10 Freeway to Memorial. She looked especially attractive in a short red dress that rode up a little when she'd climbed into his SUV. Not slutty, but just enough to pique his interest.

"Channing, are you a native Houstonian?" Of course, Quinton had checked her out online, but he wanted to know more. The basic bio was there, undergraduate at Bryn Mawr College for Women in Pennsylvania, then graduate work in Social Sciences and Psychology at Northwestern University in Illinois.

"No, I've only been here for about five years. I grew up in the Midwest and went to college there. I got a job in the medical center which brought me to town, then I opened up my own shop last year."

"Do you like being on your own?"

"Pros and cons. I have a lot more freedom this way. More

consulting, expert testimony, and guardianship. Less couch sitting with patients."

"Get tired of listening to the angst and the daily grind?"

"Somewhat, but mostly, I like being around the courtroom. If I could do it over, I might have gone to law school instead of graduate school."

"It's never too late."

Channing laughed. "That's what I tell my patients. And you? I looked at your website, so you can skip the boring parts."

Quinton laughed. "I'm an open book. Everything you saw on there, plus a lot of long hours getting my new practice going."

"I was sorry to hear the news about your friend and client, Joanne. My condolences."

"Thank you."

They grew silent for the last few minutes of the drive.

When they arrived at the Matherlys' home, Kevin came outside to greet them. "Lily had an incident this afternoon. I just got home, and Jess has had her hands full. It was a full-blown temper tantrum followed by over an hour of inconsolable sobbing."

Channing looked sympathetic. "That's understandable as she experiences the loss of her limb and her mother. Life as she knew it is over."

Quinton kept quiet as this was all somewhat new to him.

Kevin turned toward the door. "Come in, but please remain very calm and follow Jess's lead before you ask any questions."

"Absolutely." Quinton followed Channing up the sidewalk.

When they entered the living room, Jess was sitting on the floor with Lily between her legs with her back to Jess. The foster mother had the child in her arms, loosely restrained, in case she went off again. Lily's face was streaked with tears, and she appeared to be calming down from a hard cry.

The stump of her missing leg was hiding under her skirt. Channing had told Quinton that Lily wasn't willing to wear shorts or pants yet. Months had passed since the fateful car accident that forever changed the young life. The emotional toll was immense, and she called out for her mother frequently. Physical pain was another part of the struggle. Phantom pain, PTSD, and frequent bouts of terror haunted her days and nights, making it seem as if there was no escape from her own mind.

Lily finally collapsed back against Jess. She clutched a plush pink teddy bear, a gift from her dead mother, tightly against her chest. The soft fabric seemed to bring her some comfort.

Channing gently stepped into the room, as Quinton hung back by the door with Kevin. The counselor had a calming presence that Lily seemed to find reassuring. Channing had been working with Lily since before she was discharged from the hospital, guiding her through the challenging journey of recovery.

"Hey, Lily," Channing said softly, sitting by her side. "How are you feeling today?"

Lily hesitated for a moment, then whimpered. "I'm scared, Channing. It wakes me up at night. It's like my leg is still there, hurting, but it's not. It hurts all the time." Jess smoothed back her hair on her forehead and nodded understandingly, her empathy evident in her eyes.

"It's entirely normal to feel this way, but remember, you're not alone in this. Have you tried any of the relaxation techniques I showed you?"

"I tried, but when I think too much, my mind keeps going back to the accident," Lily confessed, her voice trembling.

Quinton could not keep his eyes from tearing up at the sight of the poor girl. He hadn't cried since Michael's death and his emotions threatened to flood in. He knew this was not the time or place, so he thought of the court case and how he could help her that way.

Channing placed a gentle hand on Lily's shoulder. "Let's try something else today. Close your eyes and take a deep breath. Focus on the sound of my voice and no other sounds. Imagine a peaceful place, somewhere you feel safe and loved. Can you do that?"

Lily followed Channing's instructions as Jess held her. She closed her eyes and took a deep breath. She expressed a sense of calm enveloping her, if only for a fleeting moment.

"Now, let's try some mindfulness exercises," Channing continued. "Pay attention to the sensations in your body without judgment. Focus on the feeling of the floor beneath you, Jess's arms around you, and the softness of your teddy bear. Acknowledge your emotions but let them pass like clouds in the sky."

As Channing guided Lily through the mindfulness exercises, they all could see the tension in the young girl's body begin to ease. "Lily, keep your eyes closed and remember this is a slow and gradual process. The more you practice, the more you'll be able to separate from the overwhelming emotions. And, you can always call on any of us to help you calm yourself if you can't do it alone."

Quinton did not approach Lily when she opened her eyes, only smiled and waved a small acknowledgement from across the room. Quinton found a new appreciation for not only what Lily was going through, but the invaluable support offered by the Matherlys and Channing.

A quickly whispered conversation with Channing and Kevin in the hallway confirmed that it was not the day for Quinton to talk about the case. When they said goodbye to Lily and left, he stopped and took a deep shuddering breath outside the door.

By the time Quinton and Channing arrived at Trattoria Sophia, an elegant Italian foodie spot in the Heights, they had discussed Lily and her circumstances and calmed their own nerves. The restaurant was located in a charming old building on West 11th Street. It promised to be a memorable first date when Quinton checked them in for their reservation and escorted Channing, with his hand at the small of her back, through the restaurant, behind the maitre d'.

Quinton gallantly pulled out Channing's chair when they arrived at their table, a cozy spot out back in the secret garden that was drenched in candlelight and smelled like the freesia on the tables.

Channing adjusted her seat. "Thank you. It's pleasant out here. I'll have to be on my best behavior."

"You're welcome. I assume they taught you proper etiquette at that fancy college you went to."

Channing put her napkin in her lap. "Oh, so you googled me as well."

Quinton chuckled a lusty laugh. "Caught me."

Channing winked at him and opened her menu. "I hope so."

The comment left Quinton speechless so he took a sip of water and opened his menu as well.

As they settled in, Quinton couldn't help but admire her green eyes. It was the second thing he'd noticed about her in court. He tried not to think about the first thing. After all, it was their first date.

A waiter, in her black-and-white uniform, approached the table, prompting Quinton to ask, "What do you say, Channing? Cocktail or wine?"

"Wine, I think."

"Red or white?"

She teased him with a sly smile as the waiter poured water. "Well, you're the lawyer here, Quinton. I think you should make a compelling argument for both, and I'll be the judge of your taste."

Quinton chuckled, accepting the challenge. "For the defense, we have a robust Cabernet Sauvignon, rich in flavors, with hints of blackberry and dark chocolate. It pairs well with savory dishes and might just win you over with its boldness. Or, one of my favorites, a Tuscan red blend, equally full bodied and a bit jammy. Great with lamb or beef."

Channing played along, nodding thoughtfully. "Interesting choices, Counselor. But on the defense side, I present a crisp Chardonnay, elegant and well balanced. Its subtle notes of apple and vanilla will dance on your palate and complement seafood dishes to perfection."

He was thoroughly enjoying their banter. "You're quite the wine connoisseur, I see. Alright, you decide."

"Red, of course, with all this great looking pasta. I was only kidding about the white wine."

"Trickery, already?"

She smiled sweetly, sealing the deal. "Yep. I have a knack for fooling handsome men."

Quinton ordered the Italian red, and the waiter suggested warm olives with citrus, spices, and rosemary as an appetizer.

"Agreed," they said in unison, then laughed.

As they sipped their wine and delved further into conversation, the chemistry between them was palpable. They didn't notice when a basket of baked bread magically appeared on the table. Quinton learned more about Channing's challenging career as a social worker, helping adolescents in need, which impressed him deeply. Quinton's admiration for Channing's work and Channing's respect for Quinton's dedication to his clients only deepened their attraction.

"I must say, Channing, what you do is truly admirable," Quinton said, affection evident in his eyes. "It takes a special kind of person to make a difference in the lives of the young and injured."

Channing's eyes sparkled with appreciation. "Thank you, Quinton. But I've noticed you don't shy away from difficult cases either. The way you related to Lily was charming."

"Thanks. Sad that's she's having such a tough time, but who could blame her."

"She'll be okay. She has a great deal of support. Having a long-term income will help her a lot."

"Just let me worry about that. I won't let her down."

Channing touched his hand on the table. "I know you won't. The judge seems to think a settlement is imminent."

"I hope so, but there are a lot of legal interests and they don't all line up. We'll see."

Channing asked a few more questions about the case until the waiter interrupted with more questions. The evening flowed effortlessly, filled with laughter and engaging discussions of work, food, and travel. They seemed totally compatible. They laughed, flirted, and shared stories, forging a connection that went beyond their professional roles. Quinton didn't mention his gambling habit, but he did tell her about the benefits he enjoyed from swimming for maintaining his sanity.

After another starter of wood-roasted beet and pear salad, that they shared, they followed with pesto bucatini for her and lamb ragu for him, accompanied by the rich red Super Tuscan. Channing ate with the appetite of a linebacker, regardless of her petite size. Quinton admired and marveled at how much food the little lady could put away. He wondered if her sexual appetite was as grand but let that thought drift on by. *Too soon.*

The night unfolded seamlessly and their bond grew stronger with each passing moment. Quinton and Channing found themselves engrossed in each other's company. Their laughter and shared moments made the night feel magical as they left the restaurant together, hand in hand, sparks flying. It was evident that this first date was just the beginning of something wonderful, and slightly dangerous. But what?

When Quinton drove her home, not far from the restaurant, and walked her to the door, she leaned in and kissed him. The moment evolved from a nice touch of the lips to something much deeper and more passionate as the kiss developed.

Quinton pulled back to catch his breath. "Well, maybe not such proper etiquette after all."

Channing laughed. "Want to come in for a nightcap?"

Quinton leaned in, a playful glint in his eyes. "I must admit that I hoped you'd ask, but may I take a raincheck?" The whole thing was moving a little fast for Quinton. "I have court early in the morning. I'd love to see you soon, if you have a night open."

She fluttered her eyelashes at him. "Okay, as long as you promise that it won't be too long."

He flirted too, enjoying the subtle back-and-forth. "I'll gladly accept that invitation, Channing."

She smiled; her cheeks slightly flushed. "You never know, Quinton. Maybe I'll surprise you."

"I don't doubt that for a minute."

Things are looking up in the dating department, Quinton thought as he watched her go in the door, enjoying the view of her nicely shaped bottom and the backs of her legs, but something didn't feel right. It was the memory of Joanne.

In the car, on the way home, all he could think about was Joanne. He felt like a traitor dating someone already when she had been gone less than a year. They had not been engaged, or even living together, but the bond they had was strong and he felt her absence. He felt guilty for enjoying the company of another woman when Joanne couldn't experience anything ever again. The night soured and he went home to an empty bed.

24

TJ Hobbs grew more resentful by the day as his attorneys groomed him for the upcoming depositions leading to trial. He was out on bail, he didn't have an eighteen-wheeler to drive, he was suspended pending the outcome of several investigations involving his license, and his insurance company was unwilling to advance him any funds until his personal negligence was proved or disproved. He had passed a sobriety test at the scene and was up-to-date on his driving record book, so what did they think they were going to find? So far, he had not ratted out STS about the overweight load or the unsecured cargo. They were footing the bill for all of the trial defense, his and theirs, and he didn't want to go it alone.

Hobbs was sick of the lawyers, the insurance adjusters, the sitting around and waiting. All of it. His focus and resentment turned more and more toward Quinton Bell and Matt Johnson, The Hammer. Hobbs deceived himself into thinking that if it weren't for those two greedy assholes filing paper after paper and always pushing and pushing for money, his worries would end and he'd be back in the driver's seat doing his part to keep the country supplied with all its material needs. He saw himself as a modern form of Robin Hood, delivering from the rich to the poor. The everyday man needed him to provide, and he was good at it. Now, because of a series of unfortunate circumstances culminating in the accident, he was out of work and may never drive again. *Fucking lawyers.*

Hobbs set his sights on Quinton Bell on Mondays, Wednesdays, and Fridays and on The Hammer on Tuesdays, Thursdays, and one day of the weekend, to be determined each week. Today was Wednesday, and he was sitting outside of Quinton's office at 5:00 p.m., waiting for him to leave for the day.

Hobbs had a mental checklist. His first task was to follow each of the lawyers and find out where they lived and stopped most frequently, where they shopped, and if they had a girlfriend or wife. Some of these answers he found online. Quinton was single and The Hammer was married. He read that Quinton Bell had lost his girlfriend in a courtroom shoot out. Very interesting reading. He found Mrs. Hammer, or Mrs. Johnson, was a homemaker who liked to garden and do charity work. Not much interest to him there.

Each time he gleaned a bit more information about the two, their habits, families, and friends, he added it to a small spiral notebook he kept in his pickup truck's console. He hadn't decided what he might do with the information, if anything, but it gave him something to do and relieved his anger in a macabre yet satisfying way. He'd keep it up until he got tired of it, or the trial was over, whichever came first.

Today, he waited at the office until well after seven, almost giving up and leaving, when Quinton finally drove his Audi out of the parking garage and headed toward downtown. Hobbs followed him until he reached a high-rise condo near the medical center and Rice University. When Quinton pulled through the garage gate, after entering his security code, Hobbs made notes in his little book. He assumed the lawyer was in for the night, so he headed to his neighborhood bar across town near his own home. He liked drinking as close to home as possible so he could walk or Uber if he felt he'd had too much, which occurred more often than not. No sense giving the licensing board more ammunition with which to hang him.

Over the next few weeks, he learned that Quinton Bell never left the office at 5:00 p.m. unless he had a meeting somewhere. He rarely got home before eight and often went by his gym if he left the office at a decent hour.

On the days that he followed The Hammer, Hobbs learned where he lived and all of his haunts too. He worked even longer hours than Quinton but had a chauffeur most of the time. Johnson's step-brother, whom he learned about from one of his own lawyers, was the driver and runner for The Hammer's law office. Just looking at that kid, called Double A, made him back off a step or two. He didn't think he'd like to take him on. Besides, Hobbs's hatred for Quinton was stronger and easier to focus on as he lived and officed in town.

Hobbs made sure from the first day forward that he had a pint of Wild Turkey stashed in his glove box for sipping, in the event that he couldn't get a drink in a bar for a while. By 10:00 p.m. each evening, regardless of where Quinton or The Hammer might be, Hobbs would call off the watch and head for a real bar and a real drink. The drinking didn't help his depression over his state of affairs or his ongoing blame game. So far, his actions were only stalking related, but his anger grew daily and his boiling point was coming.

It didn't take long for Cole to realize that he was not the only one stalking Quinton. After a few Monday, Wednesday, Friday encounters with the F-150 pickup truck, Cole began taking notes on not only Quinton but Hobbs as well, although he did not yet know his name. For now, he called him Hillbilly and reported on him to the Boss along with his reports on Quinton.

One night, Cole watched Hillbilly sipping his bourbon and tapping the steering wheel to some kind of twangy music he could barely hear. He tried to assess the situation with this curious interloper. Cole had been following Quinton, his subject, for weeks and he couldn't let this drunk hillbilly ruin anything. He watched for a while longer, until he became bored. He decided to mix things up a little and create some excitement. The thought gave him a rush of adrenaline as it might actually make the job more interesting and give him something extra to report to the Boss.

Cole moved closer to the pickup to observe Hillbilly until he could hear the country and western music twanging out the open window. Hobbs sang along, then drank more, then began muttering to himself. Cole crept up on Hobbs, reached in the open window, and grabbed him by the throat from the side. Hobbs tried to turn his head to see who it was, but Cole firmly held his face and eyes straight forward.

Cole growled. "What are you up to?"

Hobbs gurgled. He could not speak, but Cole wasn't really after an answer, he was just messing with Hobbs. Cole took out his cell phone with his free hand and snapped a picture of Hobbs from the side as he continued to hold his throat. Next, he smashed Hobbs's head into the steering wheel, knocking him out, and left him slumped over. He reached in and grabbed Hillbilly's wallet and snapped a picture of his driver's license. His name was Tommy Joe Hobbs.

"Sleep it off, asshole."

Cole sent the pictures he'd taken of Hobbs and his driver's license to the Boss with a note that he was looking into who he was and why he was also following Quinton. He did some online research on his iPad and discovered that Hobbs was a defendant in a case that Quinton was handling for a deceased mother and her injured daughter, both named Collins. The twist was interesting enough for him to call the Boss back and fill him in on the details.

"So far, our boy's been very predictable. He goes to work, to court, to swim, then home. The most interesting thing this week is the guy I choked and photographed in the garage. He goes by TJ. He's a semitruck driver who ran into a bunch of cars and caused a pileup on I-10. Quinton is representing a dead woman and her daughter, who got maimed in the accident."

The Boss chuckled. "This just keeps getting better and better."

"Yeah. When he visited the daughter, a girl I now know is named Lily Collins, he and the psychologist on the case went out afterward on what looked like a first date."

"Already?"

"Yeah. They went to a candlelit place in the Heights for Italian food and wine. When I followed them to her door, it looked like a mugging, they went at it so hard on the goodnight kiss." Cole exaggerated, knowing it would not please the Boss that Quinton was enjoying himself.

"Really? That just pisses me off."

"What do you want me to do about it?"

"Let's give him a little scare."

"Anything in particular?"

"Use your imagination, but not too severe."

"You got it."

Cole located and drove to a nearby Walmart, picked up some staples for the motel, including bottled water, Hot Cheetos, and microwave ramen. He went through the home goods department and selected an assortment of four different can openers, checked out, and left.

When Cole returned to Quinton's office garage, the Audi was still parked in Quinton's designated spot. Cole avoided the security cameras, that were a joke for real security, and went to the back of Quinton's SUV. Wearing gloves, he removed the packaging from the can openers and methodically scraped each one down the back, then sides and hood of the SUV until each, in turn, was too dull to be effective. He dropped them one by one on the concrete as their usefulness was played out. By the time he'd finished with the fourth can opener, the SUV was a mess. He parked himself in his truck, out of view, got ready to video the discovery for the Boss, and waited for Quinton to leave work.

When Quinton left his office for the night, he discovered the can openers and the vandalism of his SUV and looked around the garage for anyone who might be the perpetrator. Not seeing anyone, he called the police and reported the damage. He also called building security, more like glorified receptionists, who had nothing to offer, except call the police and complain about the cameras to building management.

Quinton drove the scraped SUV to his condo and realized he could no longer put off buying a new car. He notified the rental agency of the issue, thankful that he'd bought the maximum insurance coverage, and arranged to return the Audi as soon as he could get a new vehicle.

25

The next night, Quinton worked late in his office and tried not to think about the blemished SUV in the parking garage. He sorted through the files of several new clients and then began work on details for the settlement meeting on the Collins matter. The trial was moving forward, at the prompting of Matt Johnson and his class-action suit. Although Quinton was obligated to do all of his work independently, he was being dragged along at a fast pace because of The Hammer's rush to set trial dates, thereby pushing discovery motions through the court like Lucy's chocolates on a conveyor belt.

Hobb's and STS' attorney, Jacob Hollingsworth, seemed to be forthcoming, but Quinton was suspicious of the cooperation, as the defense bar had a habit of hiding the ball. Both sides had exchanged documents, and by reading them he hoped to have a better understanding of the sorts of arguments that the other attorneys would present at trial, just in case they wound up there.

The boxes of paperwork were daunting, but Quinton had to go through them and gritted his teeth in preparation for the upcoming grind. Quinton knew there would be more documents to come but now might be a good time to settle before the defense spent much more time on attorney's fees and expert witnesses. To be ready for settlement, he needed to be informed and have a solid idea of what was coming his way in terms of witness testimony and the defense's legal arguments. Those would emerge as he plowed through the discovery boxes.

He took a big swig of coffee and dug in for a long night.

Before the settlement conference began, Quinton met with The Hammer to strategize. They used a small secondary conference room outside of the main meeting place. Quinton and Johnson were the primary attorneys for the plaintiffs, with the most at stake, because each represented a deceased client. The Hammer, of course, with his class-action suit had the more powerful position in terms of numbers, but Quinton won the sympathy battle hands down with Lily. There were a few other plaintiff attorneys, with a handful of clients each, but they'd been drawn into the class action with The Hammer as court-appointed managing attorney for the class.

Quinton spoke confidently, "I believe settling with one defendant first will set the tone for the rest that we are more interested in settling than going to trial. It'll give us the financial leverage we need to take on the rest of the defendants to settlement as well. I have some funds in escrow already. I intend to use them wisely."

The Hammer considered this. "Maybe we'd rather take a stronger stance that we are more than willing to go to trial, to keep the settlement talks on a higher level."

"I disagree. I think we have one willing to settle for one

million dollars. We take that, then see if that's the train that pulls the others along. If not, we can show the others we mean business. Also, let's not forget the financial strain this case has already placed on some of our clients. This one million will help them while we keep pursuing the others aggressively, if need be."

"One million? That's hardly enough to cover the damages these people have suffered! We should fight for more and make an example of these defendants."

"The million is just a starting point for one defendant. We don't have to settle that low with all of them, just use it to push the others along."

"I've been doing this a long time, and no offense, but you're new to this type of practice. I think we keep the pressure on and have them come to us individually with settlement offers." Quinton had handled several cases of this nature in New York, as Byron, but that wouldn't show up if The Hammer had researched him, which he obviously had.

"Doesn't that defeat the whole purpose of a settlement conference?"

"Maybe, but we don't have to give them what they're expecting. Let's let them stew on the idea of a jury trial for a while longer."

"I don't have the cash to finance a full-blown trial on the merits. I also, as you say, don't have the experience with tort cases that you do." Quinton figured if The Hammer was going to use his lack of experience, he would too.

"I need to fill the coffers with at least attorney's fees from the first settlement so I can finance anything else that comes up. I know we're looking at video productions, accident reenactments, expert witnesses, on and on. That costs, as you know. Plus, the judge has indicated to me that a settlement is his preference. He doesn't want us eating up the plaintiffs' awards with attorney's fees."

The Hammer shook his head. "It's not the judge's decision. All judges would rather have a settlement than the work of a trial. I'll finance my cases if we have to go to court, but I think they'll all eventually settle, just for more."

Quinton scratched his chin. It was his tell when he was playing poker, and it arose here. "I can't align my case completely with yours. We may be competing for some of the same funds in the case of defendants with caps on what they can pay. My client might be the only truly innocent party in the whole mix. Almost everyone else was driving a vehicle. I can't gamble with my young client's future with a jury trial."

"I disagree. My lead client wasn't driving either, his sister was. I have no intention of going to trial, but there's always a place for defense lawyers to search for more settlement funds if they have to."

Quinton shook his head. "Let's go in, take the temperature of the room, and see where we stand. Just don't blow it up until we can confer again. Okay?"

The Hammer walked away. "We'll see."

The air was tense as Quinton and The Hammer joined the other lawyers in the oversized conference room. Multiple attorneys gathered for the settlement conference in the litigation involving STS, Hobbs individually, the eighteen-wheeler insurance company, and multiple cars in the pileup. The primary defense attorney, Jacob Hollingsworth, along with the other lawyers, had organized themselves in various power positions around the table and were assessing their competition as Quinton and Johnson sat down.

In such settlements, not only did the defense attorneys jockey their position for staying under coverage caps, indicating the maximum amounts to be paid, the plaintiffs knew that the pie was only so large and each wanted the biggest piece they could get. Insurance was a controlling factor for most of the attorneys. Making sure they didn't bust the coverage caps in settlement was their primary goal.

Hollingsworth opened the discussion by letting everyone know that some attorneys representing the defendants were willing to settle to avoid the uncertainty and costs of a prolonged trial. However, they would need a comprehensive settlement package to move forward. All or none. A piecemeal settlement wasn't in their best interests. It was apparent to Quinton and The Hammer that they, too, had held a pre-settlement strategy session.

A lawyer for one of the insurance companies said, "I've already offered up our one-million-dollar insurance policy. That still stands if the rest of you join in."

Another seasoned attorney from the defendant's side spoke up, "We're willing to settle too, but the amount has to be reasonable for both parties."

Quinton started working through his spreadsheet on his laptop which reflected the research he and Dart had done in the office on the white board. "How much coverage do you have?"

"We have five million."

Hollingsworth and the defense counsel rolled up their sleeves and also started to crunch the numbers on their computers.

Hollingsworth, obviously the leader of the group, threw out the first number, a healthy thirty million. "That's for all of us. We'll apportion who pays what between us."

Quinton scratched his chin. "We can look at that, but that's a bit low. We'll need to counter." He knew that if Hollingsworth was willing to start at thirty million, his client was worried about liability, and they also had plenty of cash to supplement the other smaller defendants.

Johnson had a more aggressive negotiating style. "You bet we will." The Hammer was not accustomed to making a deal before he fully pushed the limits. As the discussion continued, he showed resistance in the form of nasty comments and distrust of the statements made by the other attorneys as to their policy limits and clients' ability to pay outside of insurance coverage. His antagonistic approach caused ruffled feathers among the defense lawyers and ignited an argument between a few of them. The discourse spread, until all became entangled in a finger pointing exercise with each accusing the other's clients of fault and negligence in causing the accident.

Quinton and Hollingsworth tried to continue negotiations, but tensions remained high. Finally, Quinton offered to take the single offer of one million dollars from one company, hoping to regroup and get back on track.

However, it had the opposite effect and other attorneys balked at the piecemeal settlement strategy.

Hollingsworth shook his head. "All or none, we said."

The Hammer sat quietly at this stage with a smug look on his face. He had achieved the discord and outcome that he'd desired.

Finally, as the comments deteriorated further, the attorney offering the one million stood and said, "My offer is on the table. If you want it, give me a call." He then left the room and slammed the door behind him. The attorneys remaining in the room closed their files and laptops and began to depart.

Quinton looked frustrated and blew out a long breath.

The Hammer smiled a sly smile.

26

Detective Broussard brought his nephew, Jaden 'Sonny' Selcik, to Quinton's office for an initial conference and evaluation of his case.

Anna escorted the two Cajuns into the conference room, offered coffee, and designated seats at the long table where Dart was already seated. Quinton finished a phone call at the other end of the room and joined them, sitting at the head of the table and taking charge of the meeting.

Quinton sized up Jaden, turned to Dart, and shared a look that said: This might be just a kid in trouble.

Broussard shook hands with Quinton and gestured at his nephew. "This is my sister's son, Jaden Selcik. We call him Sonny."

"Would you rather I called you Jaden or Sonny?"

"Sonny is fine."

"You look pretty athletic, Sonny. What sports do you play?"

"I'm on the baseball team at the University of Houston. I play short stop."

"Go Cougars." Quinton laughed. "Are you any good?"

"That's what they say."

Broussard joined in. "He's good. Great at bat. Has a full ride scholarship."

"That's impressive. Let's talk about your case. Your uncle tells me you were at the wrong place at the wrong time and got caught."

"Yes, sir. I shouldn't have been hangin' with those guys, but we were at the beach, drinking beer, and things got a little out of hand. I only knew two of the guys. The rest sort of showed up and drank our beer. We ran out and one thing led to another. I didn't know they were gang members."

"Breaking into a store and looting is more than a little out of hand. We don't specifically have a looting law here in Texas, it all falls under burglary or larceny."

"Yes, sir. I wouldn't have done it without having a few beers. I was there, but I didn't steal anything. I just watched."

Broussard grimaced. "Sonny and his buddies had more than a few beers."

Quinton nodded. "You're not twenty-one yet, Sonny. Using the breaking of one law to justify the breaking of another is not a very good strategy."

Sonny looked scared. "Yes, sir."

Dart looked at Quinton and seemed sympathetic. He had certainly had his share of being in the wrong place at the wrong time, more than once.

Quinton turned to the young man. "Well, Sonny, we looked into your file and I think I can talk to the prosecutor and try to work something out, but you won't get a clean walk away from this. I don't know how hard they will be on you. It could go either way."

"Yes, sir."

"Maybe we can minimize the impact on your scholarship, but no guarantees. Should I proceed with your case?"

"Please. Mr. Bell, please get me out of this mess."

Broussard's shoulders dropped. "Cher."

27

Quinton had decided a few months before to clean up Q's credit, which was now his credit. Before Judge Bell died, the judge had paid off most of Q's debts, but the credit reporting agencies still showed a low credit score because of all the slow pays in Q's history.

In order to buy a house, Quinton needed a hefty down payment, which he was quickly accumulating, and a loan from a mortgage company or bank. He could have paid cash by cleaning out his offshore account, but then he'd have no 'Plan B' money in the event he had to run again. Best to get a mortgage. It would also help to solidify his persona as Quinton and further develop his credit.

He knew the fastest way to up a credit score was to borrow money and repay it in a timely manner, so he applied for several more credit cards as Quinton Bell, and used them every chance he got. He set up auto pay from his bank account to make sure he was never late on a single payment.

Another way he planned to build his credit was to turn in the, now ugly, leased Audi and buy a car with a regular loan. He browsed the websites of several brands of SUVs, including BMW, Mercedes, Volvo, and Range Rover. He'd always loved the imports but had no idea what Q drove or would have bought. He settled on two models and decided to test drive them, rolling his eyes toward heaven.

"Thanks for the credit, Q."

When Quinton arrived at the Mercedes Dealership at Greenway, just a few minutes from his condo, he didn't notice the car that had followed him or the man in the hoodie entering the showroom a few minutes after him. Quinton circled the different sizes of SUVs, opening doors and examining features, and asked the salesman if he could test drive the full-size model in the G Class. Cole heard his request and quietly left the showroom.

While Quinton drove the Mercedes, Cole waited in his car, eating junk food and listening to sports talk radio, until Quinton returned and gave the keys back to the salesman. They shook hands and Quinton went to his rental.

Cole started following him again when Quinton left the Mercedes dealership and drove to the Land Rover dealership near the 610 Loop. Quinton repeated the same series of actions. Cole went inside when Quinton returned from the test drive and surrendered the keys. Cole eavesdropped on the conversation with the salesman. Quinton apparently decided on the Range Rover because he asked to apply for credit. All this was overheard or discerned by Cole, who left the dealership floor with a salesman chasing him and offering to show him a car, while Quinton went into the credit department.

Cole got rid of the salesman, returned to his car in the parking lot, and watched the door of the dealership for Quinton to wrap up the visit. As he waited, he speed dialed the nursing home where his wife was being cared for. He called at least every other day to check on her and make sure she was doing okay. Getting a positive report, as much as there could be, he turned his attention back to the job.

Next, Cole called the Boss and reported in.

"Our boy is buying a new SUV. Range Rover. Nice one. Loaded. Dark gray."

"Is that so? I guess he doesn't like driving the scratched one." The Boss laughed.

Cole laughed too. "New office, new car, new employees. Yesterday I followed him to his club again for a better look. He's an impressive swimmer."

"I'll bet."

"After that, he went to a local under-the-radar gambling spot called The Dog Pound. I couldn't get in, but he was there all night. The fuckers have some kind of secret handshake. I'm working on getting an invitation in case he goes back."

"Gambling? Really? I'd like to know more about that."

"On it. I'll check in again tomorrow."

28

Quinton drove down to Galveston early on a Friday morning and dropped some groceries, liquor, and a few extra clothes at the Bell Victorian beach house. He was dressed in his usual office attire, suit and tie, although he hadn't gone there before he left Houston.

He had an appointment with Gordon Rhodes, in the Galveston County Criminal District Attorney's office. Rhodes had filed the case against Jaden 'Sonny' Selcik in the Galveston County District Court, not county court, and Quinton was wondering why such a small case would be bumped up to that level.

Quinton had read the report filed by the local police that led to the indictment and it seemed to reflect stupid boys doing bad acts, and nothing more. *What gives?*

When Quinton had called for the appointment, he'd assumed he'd meet with one of the assistant district attorneys and was surprised to find that the DA himself was handling the case. He had researched the Galveston County website and found that Rhodes headed a larger department than Quinton had imagined. He was first elected as DA about fifteen years before, and then reelected two times for three four-year terms. Prior to that, he had been a prosecutor in the Harris County DA's office in Houston. He now ran a team of about forty assistant DAs, five peace officers, and twenty-five staffers. They purportedly prosecuted about ten thousand criminal cases a year.

Impressive. Quinton considered looking for more criminal clients in Galveston and going back and forth to Houston. Maybe even get in a little surfing between cases.

Quinton left the Victorian and drove toward the Gulf then right on Seawall Boulevard. No matter how many times he drove down the street along the ocean, he never grew tired of it or took it for granted. He listened to vintage Rolling Stones for a while, then turned over to the local fishing report while he drove. Apparently, redfish bite was up around areas where good current flow had bait up against the shorelines and grass lines. Quinton made a mental note to try to find the time to go fishing soon.

He turned right on 59th Street, located the building, and as he parked readied himself for battle.

He entered the DA's office, checked in with the receptionist, and handed her his business card.

"I'm here to see DA Gordon Rhodes, please. I have an appointment."

Only part of her head showed above the counter behind the glass of the desk, protection left over from the Covid epidemic, so all he could see of her was curly brown hair and brown eyes.

"Please have a seat." Quinton tried to tune out the flat elevator music that filtered through the speaker system. He identified a slow watered-down version of Tina Turner's *What's Love Got To Do With It*. To Quinton it was unforgiveable to annihilate such a great song.

After a polite wait, Quinton was escorted to the conference room, somewhat sterile and municipal, and met with a man who was anything but boring. He looked like a scarecrow in a suit with a ZZ Top style beard, but neatly trimmed. Quinton wondered if he was recently ill or if he was just naturally gaunt. Either way, he immediately liked his easygoing manner and friendly posture.

After introductions were made, hands shaken, and coffee offered, the two attorneys sat at the table and got down to business.

Quinton started, as he swiveled in his chair. "I hope we can work something out for this kid."

Rhodes raised an eyebrow. "Why would you think that?"

"Well, he's a first offender and more like a kid in the wrong place at the wrong time than a hardened criminal."

Rhodes shook his head. "I hate to tell you this, but your baby-faced client is a troublemaker."

Quinton looked surprised. "What do you mean? I thought we were discussing a plea today."

"We can discuss a plea, but you need to see something first. You'll get it in discovery anyway, might as well show it to you now."

Rhodes opened a laptop, pressed a couple of keys, then turned the screen toward Quinton. He watched CCTV footage of a gang of young men smashing the glass of a building, running in to collect the merchandise, then running out again with their arms full of loot, including beer. On the screen, clear as day was his client, Sonny Selcik in a University of Houston baseball cap, smashing glass with a Louisville Slugger.

"I had no idea. Is that all of it? Did my client actually go in the store and steal anything?"

"We don't have the full scene captured, but I think it's safe to assume he did. I think a jury would think so."

"He says he didn't loot. It's hard to believe, I know, but I'd hate to see this kid's life ruined for something like this. He has a full ride at U of H. Supposed to be a great baseball player."

Rhodes gestured at the screen with Sonny's face frozen in a cocky grin and enlarged. "Well, obviously he can bat."

Quinton frowned. "I'd laugh if it weren't so tragic. Do you believe in second chances?"

Rhodes considered. "I do in some cases, but what's to keep this kid from doing this again, or something worse, if he's not taught a lesson? The other young men are all being fully prosecuted."

Quinton considered his own second chances. "Maybe we can come up with something that will satisfy you. His uncle, who brought me the case, is a Harris County police detective, Clive Broussard."

"I know Broussard. Reputation only. He's considered a good cop. Put together a proposal and I'll look it over, but the kid can't skate on the whole deal."

"I understand. Let me work with Sonny and Broussard and I'll get back with you."

The next day, Broussard and his nephew, Sonny, were once again sitting in Quinton's office in Houston. Quinton placed his laptop on the table before the two and cued up the CCTV footage that the prosecutor had given to him during the plea conference.

"Looks like you did a little more than go along for the ride, Sonny."

Broussard jerked his head around and looked at Sonny. "What did you think you were doing?"

Sonny's face fell and he didn't meet the eyes of either of the men.

"I got my pants pulled down in that meeting. You told me you had revealed everything that happened that night. From this video, it looks like you were the ringleader. Two of your new friends have given statements that you started it and broke the window with the baseball bat."

Sonny looked up at Broussard. "I'm sorry, Uncle Clive. I know it was stupid. I just got caught up in the moment, but I didn't start it. I was drunk, and the guys dared me to do it. The baseball bat thing, because of my skills, but I stopped short of stealing."

Broussard's face turned bright red. "Dared you? Dared you! What are you, three years old?"

Quinton stepped in. "Let's see what we can salvage of this. If you'd told me the truth in the first place, I might have done better for your plea. Now, I'll need to develop a defense for trial unless you want to plead guilty and just take your punishment. Rhodes has left the door open for a plea deal, but it probably won't save your scholarship without a miracle."

Broussard looked at Quinton. "Is there a defense? His entire future is at risk. What can I do to help?"

Sonny pointed at the screen. "That's not the whole story."

Quinton looked skeptical. "Well, what is the whole story? This time, I want all of it."

Broussard frowned at Sonny. "If you leave anything out, I'll be on you like white on rice."

"Okay. That video just shows me hitting the glass, I broke it through with one hit, but the guys broke the other window first with a big landscaping rock from the parking lot. See that boulder-looking thing on the floor there. That's what broke the other window. And I never went in. The other guys looted the store."

Broussard flared again. "You think that makes you innocent?"

"No, sir."

"Hold on." Quinton closed the laptop. "Let me get my investigator on it. See if we can get more footage or conflicting statements from the other guys. I want you to stay out of it, Broussard. No poking around or agitating his friends. Got it?"

"Mmhmm."

Quinton stared at Broussard as if to say: I mean it.

29

Q uinton and Channing attended the celebration of the new wing of the South Texas College of Law, made possible by the Sirus Lamar Bell Trust that Quinton's inheritance had funded. The ribbon cutting at the law school campus had been earlier in the afternoon, complete with dignitaries, politicians, alumni, board members, and of course, the press. Quinton and Silver Jamail, Quinton's co-trustee, had held onto the huge faux scissors and let the ribbon fly while reporters covered the story. That was the official part, tonight was the fun part.

The gala and fundraiser were being held in the heart of downtown Houston in the historic Julia Idelson Building with its distinctive, elegant Spanish Renaissance-style architecture. The 1926 treasure, Houston's library from 1926 to 1976, stood out amongst the contemporary buildings surrounding it. It had recently been remodeled and offered to the community for special events such as this one.

Quinton looked dashing in a black Tom Ford tuxedo that looked like it had been tailored to fit him perfectly, and it had.

But Channing was the real showstopper, in a red Marchesa floral embroidered off-the-shoulder tulle gown. It had a fishtail like a mermaid, and looked like a cat had scratched the fabric across the dress, making it jagged and fluffy in the most remarkable and attractive way.

All eyes turned toward the handsome couple as they plucked champagne glasses from a tray and glided over to chat with Silver Jamail, hostess for the evening. She wore a more classic black Etro wrap front tailored gown. Her jewelry was set off perfectly against the black fabric, her ivory skin and silver-gray hair.

After introductions, air kisses, and mutual compliments, Silver said, "I miss being on your father's arm for events such as this."

Quinton lowered his gaze. "I miss him, too."

Channing slid her hand into Quinton's and held it.

Silver smiled. "He'd love this. It's just exactly the kind of showy evening he never missed."

Quinton smiled. "He left plenty of money to fund it, and a good cause too. A lot of students will be helped by this."

"Thanks to your generosity, Quinton." Silver smiled. "Let me make the rounds, and then we'll take a few press pictures."

"Sounds good." Quinton turned to Channing as Silver slipped away and the orchestra began to play a slow sexy ballad. "Want to dance?"

She looked at him all google-eyed and they walked toward the dance floor. Eric Clapton's *Wonderful Tonight* was the perfect song for the perfect moment.

Cole, dressed in a rented tux and holding a whiskey neat, skulked at the edges of the party. He didn't look totally out of place, as he also wore cowboy boots that fit the style of the Texas rural millionaire. He occasionally looked at his phone as if he was receiving a text but was actually photographing Quinton and Channing as they twirled gracefully around the dance floor.

The Boss is going to eat this up.

After he'd grown tired of watching them, he slipped out the door as if going to the men's room but took a sneaky detour past the front entrance and down to a side exit to his vehicle. He started the truck, drove around the corner, pulled off, and sent the footage, attached to an email, to the Boss with a few brief sentences of explanation about how Channing Ward behaved and how she was the same female from the first date.

Cole thought but didn't email: *Our boy has good taste in women.*

30

Dart took the CCTV footage of Sonny Selcik's drunken night in Galveston and dissected it frame by frame. He had received a list of the other young arrestees from Quinton, who'd gotten it from Broussard, who'd gotten it from Sonny. Dart's task was to identify each of the other defendants and work up a resume on each. Quinton wanted to know, according to the footage, which ones actually entered the store and which ones had carried out loot. He also requested a search on which perps had criminal records.

Once Dart isolated a new face, he took a screenshot of it, saved it in a file, and sent it to the printer. It was a gnarly bunch compared to the clean-shaven, braces-perfect smile of Sonny Selcik.

He then worked up an online one-page summary of what each one had apparently done on the night in question, what evidence there was, and left a space at the bottom for inputting the current circumstance of the perpetrator, whether a student, gang member, homeless, etc. On an additional page, he carved out space to input the criminal record of each. He needed some help to track all that down, and that he'd do another day.

Quinton had indicated his hope to differentiate Sonny from the other bad actors and provide a reason for the prosecutor to see him differently. If that didn't work, and trial was imminent, the plan was to show the presiding judge that the Sonny Selcik trial should be severed from the rest of the gang, giving Sonny a better chance at an acquittal or suspended sentence.

Dart wrapped up the research and made a list of all the names for Quinton in a separate email and hit send. As he stood to leave the office, he dusted his hands to signal job done.

The next day, Broussard crashed into Quinton's law firm and didn't bother to stop at Anna's desk for permission to breach Quinton's inner office.

"Hey, Bell. You said we were going to settle Sonny's case. What's all this about going to trial?"

Anna walked in behind him, Quinton nodded at her, and she quietly closed the door. Quinton reached back to a small speaker on the credenza and turned down a Beatles mix he was playing on SiriusXM.

"I tried to settle it, but there wasn't a deal that would allow him to keep his scholarship and not have a felony record."

"So, you'll trot him out in court and that will keep it all quiet?"

"I hope we aren't going to fight, but the best way to get a good deal is to set the case for trial and make the prosecutors think we'll go all the way. You're a cop. You know how the game is played."

"That's not how I play. He deserves a break more than most."

"Maybe he does, but the prosecutor sees him as a criminal and we have to get him to look past the charges and actually see the kid. That takes a little time and some leverage. His buddies have all been charged with felonies as well."

"Some of them have records and they're not his buddies. I've been riding him like olives on a muffuletta since his arrest. He can't breathe without his mother or me knowing about it."

"All the more reason to separate him from the pack with the prosecutor. And, it might help that his uncle is a decorated police officer who's willing to stand up for him in court."

Broussard calmed down a little with the compliment.

Quinton handed him the list of names that Dart had compiled from the CCTV footage. "We could use some help with the criminal records on these guys if you don't mind bending the rules a bit. We also need their addresses and education level if you can find it."

"No problem."

"Don't forget to double-check Sonny's arrest record as well. I know you say he doesn't have one, but we don't need any surprises in that regard."

"Okay, but he doesn't have one."

"Just check it, okay?"

"Yep. I can't risk that kid going to jail or having a felony record. He's the bright spot in our family. All our hopes and plans revolve around him. We have to figure this out."

"We will." *I hope.*

31

Quinton followed the rather robust bottom of Lydia Fields up the sidewalk to the fifth house of the day. Lydia, his realtor, located and selected by Anna because of her great reputation for deep research, inside deals, and fast sales, waddled a little as she took the steps up to the front door. Her gray hair was curled tightly, and her neck was wrapped in several strands of oversized beads. Matching balls flopped out of her pierced ears.

"This is the only un-remodeled house on the market in this neighborhood."

"I can see why."

"This neighborhood is called Afton Oaks." It was just inside the loop, about ten minutes from where his office was located. The outside of the house had deteriorated. Paint peeled off the siding and the brick was an ugly mottled brown. The roof sagged a little around the gutters on the north side, and the front yard was overgrown. A rusted metal mailbox bent over with grocery sales flyers hanging out.

"Okay, it looks horrible, but try to keep an open mind for ten minutes."

Quinton looked around at the other perfectly manicured homes. "How are they getting away with this mess in this neighborhood?"

"The owners have been warned and fined several times by the Homeowner's Association, but they just tell them they'll pay the lien when they sell. A couple of middle-aged children of elderly parents inherited it when their father died. The HOA has been mowing it and keeping an account."

"Hmm."

Lydia saw the look on Quinton's face. "You did say you were open to a fixer-upper."

"Yes, but I also said I'd like to live in it while I remodeled."

"I heard you, but that's a terrible idea. Sawdust in your bed and all your pockets. Water off when you're needing to shower for the office. Noise on the weekends. Just keep the condo you're renting and get this re-done quickly. Then move in."

Quinton pulled at the doorbell hanging out by the wiring by the front door. *Bossy, but probably right.*

Lydia unlocked the arched, heavy wooden door, which did add a bit of character, but it was orange, and not the good kind. The two stepped over the threshold and a wave of stench hit them in the nostrils.

Quinton took a step back. "What the hell is that?"

"Just ignore that. Water damage. First thing you'll want to do is have the whole place cleaned out, take down a few walls, rip out the carpet, get a new roof."

Quinton followed her through a long rectangular living room, into the kitchen, then the dining room. The arch theme continued inside between the rooms. "It's very segmented."

"Yes, but the arches mimicking the front door are charming." Lydia pointed to the wall in the dining room. "That wall should come down."

"Is it load bearing?"

"I don't know. An architect and engineer would be needed on this one. That is, before you hire a contractor to do the remodel."

"Whoa. I was thinking of a little paint and some new floors. Maybe an updated bathroom. This might be too much for me."

"You might not say that when you see the back yard." Lydia walked over to what might once have been French doors and pulled hard on one side causing the wood to scrape along the buckled flooring. Quinton took over and pulled harder, as neither of them was going to fit through the small opening she'd managed to create.

When they stepped out carefully onto a littered concrete patio, before them was an overgrown but secluded oasis, cool and mossy. The yard was fenced, and filled with weeds, but it was totally private, and best of all, it had a small kidney-shaped pool a few steps from the patio. Now, half filled with green water, but the potential was obvious.

"Wow."

"See what I mean? This could really be something with the right design. And, it's a steal. No one has wanted to take it on, but you could. You're young and ambitious. Just hire the right people and you'll have a beauty right here in the middle of Houston."

"Why not just tear it down and start over?"

"It would cost even more, and the permitting would take forever. This way, you keep the same footprint, bypass all that architectural board approval, and go straight to the easy permits. The city takes forever if you try to add a single square foot of concrete or change the outside character of a property.

Just imagine this yard with blue water, beautiful flowers, trees swaying in the breeze."

Quinton caught her vision, walked around the pool, then, holding his nose, back into the house and through the three bedrooms, two and a half baths, and small study.

He laughed. "I thought it might be haunted, but it feels pretty good in here."

"And it can all be yours."

Quinton spent most of the weekend and part of the next two weeks getting bids from architects and contractors and assessing the total cost of the project after the work was done. He had a house leveling company go out and make sure the foundation was solid and not shifting or cracking. An engineer gave him a report on which walls could be removed easily, and which removals would require beams to support the house. The foundation was the one thing that did not need to be replaced, besides the outer brick.

When the bids for demo, wiring, plumbing, drywall, and all the other things needed to beautify the home were in, he did the math and called Lydia.

"If I can get the house for under six hundred thousand, I can do all the work, spend the necessary funds, and come out even with the market. If not, we'll have to keep looking."

"Let me do my magic and I'll get back with you."

Quinton closed on the house with a low interest rate loan based on Q's credit. The sellers filed all their documents with the title company by Federal Express. Only Quinton and Lydia were at the closing, she taking charge of the title agent, and Quinton reading every document carefully before signing.

When all the paperwork was executed and he was handed the keys, Lydia popped the cork on a bottle of mediocre champagne. Quinton didn't know if they were celebrating his purchase or her commission, but he was happy to be putting down roots. His days of running and hiding were over. *Home.*

"Salud!"

"Cheers!"

32

Quinton looked over the conference table at Dart as they both flipped through paperwork on the Lily Collins case. "If we can't work this out in some type of settlement, we'll need to have all the documentary evidence, witness testimony, and video footage ready to go for trial, so keep everything organized as if we'll wind up in court."

Dart nodded. "Got it. How long does a trial like this usually last?"

"It could be from a couple of days to a few weeks. One of this size, maybe longer, then the jury will take additional time to deliberate before presenting a verdict. We do want to try and settle."

"I don't see what makes this so complicated. Big truck hits a bunch of cars and should pay for it. Right?"

Quinton closed the file he was scanning. "The cost of a truck crash is like an iceberg: While some of it is visible, the bulk of it, and the biggest dangers, are hidden below the surface. Some insurance industry veterans say the indirect costs of an accident are generally four times the direct costs, no matter who is at fault."

Dart was wide-eyed. "Really?"

"It's a specialized area of the law. Some attorneys make an entire living off nothing but eighteen-wheeler accidents."

"I seen the TV ads."

"There's also an entire industry around automobile safety consultants who testify as expert witnesses in truck-related accidents. It's very expensive to defend one of these cases."

"So, we want to settle, but we'll be ready to go to court, jus' in case."

"Exactly."

Quinton made a quick exit from the conference room, heading for the restroom, and ran directly into Anna. She was leaning against the doorjamb, just out of sight, and appeared to be listening to their conversation.

"Excuse me, Anna. I didn't realize you were there."

She appeared as if a deer in headlights. "Sorry, Quinton. I was just going to see if you two needed more coffee."

"Coffee?" Quinton could tell she was avoiding a direct answer.

Anna didn't respond, she just turned and walked to her desk, sat, and appeared to be looking at the computer screen.

Dart came to the door and saw the look on Quinton's face. "What was dat about?"

"Coffee."

33

P hil Lyme entered the Law Office of Quinton Bell and
stood before Anna at the reception desk. She immediately bristled at his nasty grin and rumpled sports jacket. He
sported a day's growth on his chin which was specked with gray
between the brown stubble. His brown hair was shaggy and
looked like it had been recently dyed as the color was not
anything found anywhere in nature that Anna could recall.

"I'm here to see Attorney Bell."

"Do you have an appointment?"

"No, but he'll want to see me. It's about the Lily Collins
case."

"Yes, sir. What's your name?"

"Phil Lyme."

"Please have a seat, Mr. Lyme, and I'll see if Mr. Bell can
work you in."

Lyme sat in one of the guest chairs and looked around at
the tastefully decorated office. A private sneer crept across his
face.

Anna returned to the reception area, slipped behind her

desk providing a barrier between them, and said, "Mr. Bell will be happy to see you." She pointed to Quinton's office door.

When Lyme entered, Quinton felt the atmosphere shift to that of tension and uncertainty. Quinton stood out of habit, but did not offer his hand, and pointed to one of the guest chairs before his desk.

Quinton sat. "You referred to my client, Lily Collins? How may I help you?"

Lyme lounged in the leather chair; his body hung over the arms like a sea animal without bones. He exuded an unsettling confidence, or was it arrogance? Quinton couldn't be sure, but he knew it was not going to go well, either way.

"My name is Phil, Philip Lyme, and I've got a proposition for you, Mr. Bell." A crooked grin played across his lips which exposed yellow teeth.

Quinton raised an eyebrow. He'd met this type before, many times in New York. He pegged Lyme as half swindler and half bully.

Lyme leaned forward as if sharing a dark secret. "See, I was common law married to Charlotte Collins, Lily's mother."

Quinton's eyes narrowed with suspicion, but he did not comment. He knew he wouldn't have to wait long for Lyme to reveal what he wanted, but Quinton was pretty sure money would be involved.

"Lily is my stepdaughter. I am her legal guardian."

"Is that so?"

"Yes, and I have rights."

"Actually, the court has appointed me her guardian, and in Texas, that's what makes it legal, and Lily has the rights."

"That's why I want you to represent me, too. Since I'm also a beneficiary of the lawsuit, my interests are the same as Lily and her mother's estate."

"Even assuming I would want to do that, there are several

hoops you'd have to jump through before you would even have standing in court. Common law marriage requires more than just words, Mr. Lyme. The court would require concrete evidence."

Lyme produced a worn photograph from his shirt pocket and slid it across the desk toward Quinton. The image depicted Lyme and a woman who looked a lot like Lily in what seemed like happier times, their arms wrapped around each other, both smiling.

"Here's your proof. We were as good as married, just never made it official. We were very unconventional, ya know?"

"A picture may speak a thousand words, but it doesn't guarantee legal validity. There are statutory requirements in Texas to prove common law marriage."

"Yeah. That's why I want to hire you. You can prove it up for the court and put me in your lawsuit. We had friends who can vouch for what I'm saying. Those people knew we were together. We just need to track them down. There'll be more money for you and some for me, too."

"Is that right? I assume you've not seen Lily."

"No, I don't know where she is."

"Would you like to know how she's doing?"

"Uh yeah. Sure. How is the kiddo?"

"She's suffering terribly. She lost her mother and one of her legs in the accident. She's under the care of a psychologist and is having a rough time of it."

"Well, I'm sorry to hear that. She was always a cute baby. Her mother was a real babe."

Quinton recoiled and shot a sarcastic response at Lyme. "You must be overcome with grief."

Phil's grin widened. "Well, we hadn't kept in touch. Charlotte was always headstrong and when Lily got older, she went on without me. That doesn't change the fact that we were married and I'm entitled to some of her estate and to be Lily's legal guardian."

"I don't think I'm going to be able to help you, Mr. Lyme. I suggest you hire an attorney to represent you if you feel you have rights and standing in the case."

Lyme's demeanor shifted; his arrogance momentarily replaced with frustration. "Fine. If you won't help me, I'll find someone who will. Lily's my stepdaughter and I'll do whatever it takes to be recognized as her rightful guardian, and Charlotte's heir."

Quinton stood. At over six feet, he was intimidating. "I'll need you to leave my office now."

Lyme stood, took a menacing posture, then retreated toward the door, leaving Quinton to add another headache to the list that came along with the Collins case.

Quinton sat at his desk, getting organized for the day, when he received a notice of hearing in his inbox from Judge Garzon's court. It had been filed by Johnson, The Hammer, and asserted that Philip Lyme was now his client and was the common law husband of Charlotte Collins. It demanded that the court acknowledge his standing as Charlotte's widower and Lily's stepfather and appoint him guardian of her and her estate.

Quinton was taken aback. He had not trusted The Hammer from the beginning, but was hoping they would stay in alignment in order to make a stronger case for their clients who shared mutual issues in the suit.

So much for being on the same side.

Quinton appeared in Judge Garzon's court, on the appointed day, for the hearing on the common law marriage of Charlotte Collins and Philip Lyme. Hollingsworth and his entourage were not present, but Channing was there, looking fine to Quinton, as usual. She sat on his side of the courtroom a few rows back from the attorneys' tables. The Matherlys had been notified of the hearing, but apparently had decided to stay home with Lily and let the attorneys sort it out.

The Hammer looked dapper, as always, making his client, Lyme, appear even more shoddy than he might otherwise. Both sat at the opposing table and for the first time the new lines of battle were drawn between Quinton and The Hammer. Lyme smiled at Quinton who turned his eyes straight ahead and showed no emotion.

After Judge Garzon took the bench and dispensed with the formalities, he instructed The Hammer. "Mr. Johnson, you requested this hearing, please proceed."

The Hammer stood. "May it please the court. My client, Philip Lyme, has presented photographic evidence as well as affidavits from three witnesses who have sworn that he was married to Charlotte Collins approximately three years ago. Since they were never divorced, and neither remarried, the plaintiff requests that the court first, recognize the common law marriage as legitimate, and second, declare Mr. Lyme the legal guardian of Lily Collins."

Judge Garzon nodded. "Continue, Mr. Johnson."

"As Your Honor is no doubt aware, in Texas, if a guardianship has not been established by the deceased, the spouse, if qualified, may be entitled to be the guardian."

Judge Garzon studied Lyme, as this was the first time he'd laid eyes on him. "Mr. Lyme, have you kept in touch with Lily Collins? Sent her birthday cards or gifts at Christmas?"

The Hammer nudged Lyme to stand. "No, sir. Her mother

didn't want to see me, and that kept me from seeing the girl, too." The Hammer cringed at the poor wording of the response.

Judge Garzon was obviously unimpressed. "I see. You may be seated. Mr. Johnson, you are familiar with Section 2.401 of the Texas Family Code which outlines how to prove a common law or informal marriage in this state."

"Yes, sir. I have quoted it in my motion and shown how Mr. Lyme has met each of the requirements."

"For the record, a common law marriage may be proved by evidence that the couple agreed to be married. Further, after such agreement they must have lived together in this state as husband and wife and represented to others that they were married."

"Yes, Your Honor, and I have addressed each of those requirements in my motion."

"I see that. And, Mr. Bell, do you have a statement to make?"

The Hammer sat and Quinton stood. "Yes, Your Honor. As guardians of Lily Collins, Ms. Ward and I request that the court use the strictest standards to ascertain the validity of the common law marriage asserted by Mr. Lyme since Charlotte Collins is not here to testify."

Judge Garzon nodded.

"Further, we assert that even if the marriage is found to be legal, that Lily Collins' interests remain best served with us as her continued representatives. Lily has not seen Mr. Lyme in many years. She does not remember him and does not wish to see him. Ms. Ward can verify that Lily is in no condition to handle the insertion of a stranger from her past into her current situation."

Judge Garzon addressed Channing. "Ms. Ward, do you concur with Mr. Bell's assertions?"

Channing stood and smoothed the front of her dress. "Yes, Your Honor. I spoke with Lily about this situation. Indeed, she does not remember Mr. Lyme and has no wish to see him at this time."

Judge Garzon nodded at Channing. "Thank you."

The Hammer stood. "May I be heard, Your Honor?"

"Speak."

"How do we know that Lily Collins has made such assertions? We have not had access to her and do not even know her whereabouts other than an address for the Matherlys in the file."

Quinton, still standing blurted, "How do we know that the signatures on your affidavits relating to the common law marriage are valid? We have not been able to cross-examine those affiants."

Judge Garzon raised his hand. "All right, gentlemen, that's enough of that. I will assume that each of you can be taken at your word for purposes of this hearing. If a lawsuit needs to be filed by either of you, we'll take it up in that event. Mr. Bell, you may proceed."

Channing sat and Quinton continued. "Thank you, Your Honor. You have tasked us with the protection and representation of Lily's best interests. Ms. Ward and I both assert that those interests are best served without a personal relationship between Lily and Mr. Lyme. In the future, if Lily wishes to see him, she may contact him. No harm will be done in delaying the interaction of the two, regardless of the outcome of this hearing today concerning common law marriage."

Judge Garzon paused for a moment. "I would tend to agree. My holding here today is that Mr. Lyme did indeed have a common law marriage with Charlotte Collins and may assert his rights in the lawsuit as her widower. He may further assert his rights to a portion of her estate in probate court if he so chooses. However, he may not serve in any legal capacity for Lily Collins, and Mr. Bell and Ms. Ward will continue in their current capacity as court-appointed guardians."

Lyme's sly smile crept across his lips, and The Hammer looked pleased.

The judge slammed down the gavel, and that was that.

34

Quinton arrived at the courthouse an hour before a hearing in the Collins case, so he could stop by Judge Blaylock's office and say hello to Bailiff Grant. The morning sun spilled through the courthouse windows, casting a golden hue on the polished floors as attorneys and litigants shuffled in and out of various offices. Quinton adjusted his tie and started down the long corridor to Judge Blaylock's offices and Bailiff Grant's desk.

As he rounded the corner to enter, he saw Hollingsworth coming down the hall from Judge Garzon's chambers. There were several other chamber entrances at that end of the hall, so he couldn't be sure it was Garzon's door that Hollingsworth was exiting. Quinton had used the back exit down that same hall when avoiding the press, but there was nothing going on in the courthouse today that drew reporters. Maybe Hollingsworth had a special parking spot back there.

Quinton was diverted by Bailiff Grant who opened the door to Judge Blaylock's chambers for him and asked how he was doing.

"Great, George. My practice is going gangbusters, and my office is all set up." Quinton looked back toward the door as Hollingsworth passed by, a moment that wasn't lost on Bailiff Grant.

"I didn't know Judge was expecting you today." He sniffed the air. "Tacos?"

Quinton laughed. "You've got a nose like a bloodhound. I'm not here to see Judge Blaylock. These are for you."

"Me?"

"A thank you for helping me out the other day. I really appreciate it."

"Thanks, Quinton. I better hide these or Judge will make me share."

Quinton laughed. "Better eat fast." He turned to go.

"Have a good day, Quinton, and remember, if your gut tells you something is going on, it probably is." Bailiff Grant walked off before Quinton could quiz him further.

A disappointment for Quinton occurred when The Hammer added Lyme to the class-action suit as Charlotte's widower. He was claiming pain and suffering at the loss along with all the other plaintiffs, although he wasn't aware of the accident until long after it had happened. Quinton knew there would be more trouble from Lyme, and just waited for the other shoe to drop. He didn't have long to wait.

Quinton, The Hammer, and Hollingsworth were back in court before Judge Garzon on a motion for pre-trial depositions. The attorneys had been squabbling since mediation, each accusing the other of withholding their witness lists and preventing those witnesses from being deposed. Finally, Quinton and The Hammer had filed a motion with the court to compel the defense team to comply.

After calling the court to order, Judge Garzon stared down at the attorneys. "I thought you were going to settle this mess and get it out of my courtroom."

No one responded. All three just stood at their respective tables, tongue-tied.

"As you know, I have the right to require at least an honest attempt at settlement or mediation before going to trial. I don't think you've 'attempted' well enough for me, honest or otherwise."

Quinton found his voice. "Your Honor, the case has become so contentious that settlement does not appear to be a promising path."

The judge scowled. "Is that so?

Hollingsworth stood. "We'd be happy to try again, Your Honor, if you would give some direction and structure to our settlement conference."

Quinton had never heard of an attorney asking for structure for a settlement meeting. It was awkward and bizarre to pull the judge further into the negotiations. He was supposed to be fair and impartial. The purpose of the hearing today was for the judge to compel discovery under the Texas statutes.

The Hammer stood. "May I be heard, Your Honor?" His voice was silky like honey.

"Speak, Mr. Johnson."

"Thank you, Your Honor. My take on it is this paltry sum offered by the defendants is not going to get it for my clients. The opening bid was so low, it didn't even merit a counteroffer. We are under no obligation to settle, and we want to go to trial. We'll let a jury decide what's fair."

The judge was obviously enraged at the arrogance of The Hammer's statement.

"This is not a television commercial, Mr. Johnson, neither is it a movie scene. You know better than grandstanding in my courtroom."

The Hammer remained standing. "Ask Mr. Bell. He wasn't interested in taking their measly offer either."

Quinton was caught. "Your Honor, I did not think it a fair settlement, but I was willing to work toward a fair number for all involved. Negotiations fell apart and there was nowhere left to go with it."

Judge Garzon glared at Quinton. "Is that so?"

Quinton had rarely felt so misunderstood. He didn't know how to respond.

"Let's see what you think is fair when your own money is at stake. You're off the hourly and on your own. If you stay on the case, it's on a percentage basis, just like your buddy Johnson."

"But, Your Honor, we have a contract."

"Within my discretion, and my discretion is if you want to play, you pay. Let's see if that gets us to a settlement."

And just like that, Judge Garzon pulled the fee agreement and put Quinton on a contingency against winnings from the case.

Both Hollingsworth and The Hammer showed a great deal of delight in the new scenario, each obviously for their own reasons.

Quinton was dumbfounded. *Now, I'm a tort lawyer, just like The Hammer.*

Quinton went back to his office and, after everyone was gone for the day, thought long and hard about whether to stay on the

Collins case. He still had about twenty thousand of the car insurance money he'd settled for on the Camry, but that would be gone in a quick minute if he was to take on all the expenses involved with defending the tort case. He kicked himself for not having billed his hours more frequently. Of course, he'd send a bill to Judge Garzon for his time up to the date of the court hearing when his ticket was jerked, but he had no idea if he'd get paid for the outstanding balance. *Probably not.*

He thought he had a good case, and with The Hammer pushing for big bucks, it could go either way. The Hammer could drive them toward a good settlement offer, or he could drag them into court and force him to spend hundreds of thousands to defend Lily's claim. He'd invested so much time on the case already, he was reluctant to cut and run if a paycheck was right around the corner.

And what about Lily? If The Hammer took over her case, which is probably what would happen, she might be forced into a settlement for pennies on the dollar along with all the other members of the class. If, by chance, Judge Garzon found another lawyer, in lieu of The Hammer, would he stand up for Lily in the face of the pressure to settle?

Can I live with myself if I abandon her?

He heard a gentle tapping at the outer door and went out to see who might be trying to get his attention. It was Channing. Quinton opened the door and smiled. "You're a sight for sore eyes."

"You, too." She kissed him on the cheek.

"Come in. May I offer you a glass of wine or coffee?"

"Wine would be great."

"Go on into the conference room. I'll be right there." He returned with two glasses of pinot noir in large glass wine balloons, purchased by Anna when she'd stocked the break room.

Channing stood at the window gazing down on the lovely lights all around The Galleria and Post Oak Boulevard. "Great view."

"I had planned to show it to you at some point. Have a seat. What brings you by?"

"I heard about what happened in court today with Judge Garzon pulling your meal ticket."

Quinton winced. "Word gets around fast."

"Thought you might need some moral support."

"As a matter-of-fact, I was just mulling it over. Pros and cons, you know."

"And?"

"I haven't decided. Do you have an opinion?"

"Not really." She studied his face. "I do wonder if it's worth the risk and the headache."

"What about Lily?"

"I'll be there for her. You could visit at some point in the future if you felt so inclined."

"So you think I should get out?"

"Only if you want to. I'd just hate to see you stay in because of guilt. Best business decision, right?"

Quinton sipped his wine and thought for a moment. "I don't know. I don't want to run from a fight. Especially one I think I can win."

Channing sipped her wine and swiveled in her chair to stare out the window. Her reflection showed Quinton that she was not smiling.

35

Quinton Bell was now pretty sure he was being followed and watched. All of the hairs on the back of his neck stood at attention, and his heart thudded in his chest. He had been living under his assumed identity, and watching over his shoulder for so long, he had thought he was just being paranoid. Now, he had to admit that he could feel someone back there.

He had been expecting a blackmail note or some other form of threatening contact, but instead the person lurking behind the curtain of his past had remained silent. The feeling of being stalked and hunted cast a dark cloud over Quinton. All of the excitement he was feeling about his new office and his budding relationship with Channing was being eroded by this constant shadow. He stewed and fidgeted. He started to rub his chin and jerked his hand away from his face. He was getting lazy about his tell.

He pondered the possibilities of what might be happening to him. If the follower was not a blackmailer, and didn't want money, what did he want? And who is it? Is it the same person who left the note calling Byron out by name? How could it be anyone else? The follower seemed to be growing bolder by slipping out of sight just as Quinton exited his car or turned down a hallway. Did he want Quinton to feel the pressure of his presence? Who would care to torment him in this way?

There were a few loose ends involving Judge Bell's orchestration of Byron's transition to Quinton, but those involved would not have known his name or why they were doing the work. The Judge's contact in the medical examiner's office who had swapped the fingerprints and some of the other forensics evidence did not know whose fingerprints they had handled. Of course, they could have discovered that with simple research, but to what end? They were committing felonies and surely didn't want a paper trail between themselves and the offense they had helped to perpetrate. Judge Bell had asserted that those involved had scattered to the four winds, each taking a job in other jurisdictions.

There were the calls that Judge Bell had made to the chief of police in an attempt to protect Joanne, prior to her arrest. But those were buried deep, and no one had a reason to be suspicious about Judge Bell's interest in helping his son's childhood girlfriend. The police chief had moved to Florida to run the Miami police force. Surely, he had better things to do than to torment Quinton.

Maybe it had something to do with his current caseload. Litigation attorneys were always challenged with protection from disgruntled clients and the families of victims on the other side of their cases. But, how would any of them know of his former life as Byron Douglas?

Quinton was developing a headache and he was no closer to understanding what was happening to him. He hated feeling like a victim but could think of nothing he could do unless he was able to catch the follower in the act. He could hire security, but they added another person or persons who might learn of his past identity. And, it would appear strange to his colleagues. This wasn't New York.

Quinton had Anna call building management again and complain about the security in the garage. It was becoming a joke how many excuses they could come up with for not spending more money on it. Apparently, no one else had complained, or so they said.

In the event that he had to run again, Quinton added even more money to his offshore account. It gave him a small amount of comfort knowing that he could grab his go bag and head to another continent, to hide from his past, if it rose up to threaten his life as Quinton.

Of course, that would be the end of his career as a trial lawyer, which was the true love of his life. Sure, he could make it a go somewhere, doing something, but he was deeply connected to, and proud of, his courtroom skills. He did not fool himself into thinking he'd get a third chance at developing a successful and high-powered legal career.

He fingered the dive knife in his pocket and hoped he would never have to use it.

At the gym, Quinton didn't find any relief in swimming. All he could think of was being watched. It threw off his stroke and ruined his ability to reach the zone.

He decided it was time for a night of poker. He drove home, all the while watching the lights in his rearview mirror. He went through his closet, pushing aside his geek disguise, and settled on a pair of jeans and a polo shirt. He was going to play in the judge's game that he'd been invited to several times by the bail bondsman he used for his criminal clients, but never attended. Why not? He was hiding in plain sight, why not play poker in plain sight? No one could threaten to report him to the bar, as the game was not legal, and half of the board was going to be playing. He didn't plan to make it a habit, but it was too convenient, and he needed it too much to resist.

He opened his door and looked down the hall. Seeing no one, he locked the door and headed for the elevator to the parking garage.

Taking a chance, just this once. Right.

Cole followed Quinton out of the parking garage of the condo and trailed him downtown. Hobbs must have taken the night off because he was nowhere to be seen. He'd been a lot more scarce since Cole had knocked him out and taken photos of his identification in the parking garage.

When Quinton drove to the courthouse, Cole wondered, *What's our boy doing in court at this hour?*

When Quinton drove on by the building on Fannin and turned right onto LaBranch, Cole was even more puzzled. Quinton finally stopped at Acme Bail Bonds and turned into the surface parking lot, found a spot, and backed in. Hmm. *Quick getaway planned?*

Cole waited for Quinton to approach a side door with the scales of justice stenciled on the side. He saw Quinton say something to a guard, enter, and disappear when the door closed.

Gambling again? What's wrong with The Dog Pound?

It had cost Cole a hundred-dollar bill to bribe the doorman at The Dog Pound for the peace sign turned fist, and now he couldn't use it.

Damn.

As he'd been instructed, Quinton went through the side door at Acme Bail Bonds and told the password to the guard: *Intrare nostro periculo.* Latin for 'enter at your own risk.'

He went down a short dimly-lit hall with a series of closed doors and entered a large room with four round green felt poker tables and a self-service bar along one wall featuring a beer keg, three bottles of bourbon, and a stack of red plastic cups. There was no bartender, as this wasn't a moneymaker for the house. It was just a friendly group of like-minded jurisprudence junkies getting together for a drink and a game. He drew a beer, letting the brew float down the side to limit the foam, put five dollars in a Mason jar beside the tap, and went to find a table.

It was a group very similar to the one he'd played at in New York with judges and lawyers mixing it up after dark, just a little less formal. He joined one of the tables with the bail bondsman, the only person in the room he knew. He recognized a few faces from around the courthouse but didn't remember any names.

There were no official dealers. One of the players shuffled the cards and dealt them around a pile of greenbacks in the middle of the table. Quinton ante upped ten bucks and looked at his hand. He felt better immediately.

36

Quinton called his former firm associate and co-counsel, Mo Powers, and asked her if she had time to talk over a trial he was working on. He wanted to warm her up to an idea slowly, like a frog in water, not put her in all at once and scare her out of the pot.

They met for lunch near her office in the tunnel, twenty feet down and six miles long, beneath downtown H-Town. Mo had chosen Otto's, beneath Pennzoil Place, as they were known for their good BBQ, burgers, and fast service. She wasn't one to dawdle.

After they had ordered and found a semi-clean table, Mo said, "What are you up to, and what does it have to do with me?"

Quinton laughed. "Right to the point. You haven't changed a bit."

"You want some small talk? How's the new office?"

"Great. How's the rodeo circuit?"

Mo had been barrel-racing since she was a youngster and still boarded horses just outside the city.

"I won a new buckle a couple of weeks ago. Haven't been out to practice since, but Abby and I are going out to ride this weekend."

"So, you're still together? How is she?"

"She's fine. We're great. Stop stalling. What can I do for you?"

"Okay. You got me. I'm going into trial on a tort case, and I need a second chair."

She nodded as if she'd expected as much. Quinton filled her in on the case and they were still talking long after their food had been eaten and plates pushed aside. She clearly was interested in the case. Mo didn't need work, she had a thriving law firm with two other partners, but she had an itch for trial work that she didn't scratch often. This was just the type of case she relished.

After all the details of the case had been laid before her, Quinton sat back in his chair and waited. Mo seemed to be chewing it over in her mind.

"Let me get back to the office and make sure the firm will support the decision, but if they do, I'm in."

Quinton and Mo met at his office the next night to strategize the case. He escorted her into the conference room, after giving her the nickel tour and grabbing two cups of coffee on the way through the break room.

Mo admired the décor. "Well, it's not the thirty-ninth floor at our office, but I like it."

Quinton laughed and guided her through the conference room door. They sat at the conference table, in what was now the war room, amidst the boxes of trial materials. Quinton passed over a document.

"I've gotten some bad news since we first discussed the case. The defense team is now asserting contributory negligence on the part of Charlotte Collins, our client."

"Unexpected?"

"A little. Adding contributory negligence to their defense strategy is not surprising if there was a smoking gun or witness, but I don't see either of those here."

"I remember something about that from torts class in law school. Give me a refresher."

"The law school version goes something like this: A truck driver is set to haul a load of pottery from Pennsylvania to Chicago. He secured the load at his client's terminal and decides to spend the night at home and leave the next morning. He drives his big rig to his house, where he needs to back it into his driveway. He stops on the two-lane road and gets ready to back the trailer in. He sees no traffic, and he's done this a hundred times before."

Mo nodded. "Got it."

"Meanwhile, heading in the opposite direction is a young mother with her two children in the rear seats, coming back from baseball practice. She's speeding, about forty-five miles per hour in a thirty, but is not tired and not under the influence. She has been down this road hundreds of times before and doesn't expect anything unusual."

"Uh-oh."

"Right. She sees headlights in the other lane. No problem, she thinks, until she catches a glimpse of something in her lane and slams on the brakes. But it's too late. The upper half of the car is torn back as the vehicle plows into the side of the truck's trailer and half goes under. None in the car survive. What's happened, of course, is that the woman saw the truck's headlights in the other lane and thought it was an oncoming car.

What she didn't see was the trailer stretching across her lane of the road."

"So, nobody was reckless, but the results are tragic."

"Right, and who's liable?"

"So that gets us back to comparative negligence."

"Correct. It's an affirmative defense that the accused must plead in court. It's a reason given by the defendant for why the plaintiff should not win the lawsuit, even if what we say is true. In our case, the truck did cause the damage but says Charlotte Collins was speeding and could have avoided the accident."

"Why did you just find out about this?"

"The allegation that Charlotte Collins contributed to the accident came out of left field. How could anyone know, much less prove, what she did or didn't do that day?"

Mo nodded. "They didn't have to plead it in court?"

"Normally, an affirmative defense, such as this, must be asserted at the beginning of the case or they risk not being able to use it later. It's covered under Rule 94 of the Texas Rules of Civil Procedure. Judge Garzon has the discretion to allow it in, and he has."

"What do they assert she was doing?"

"The truck driver now says she was speeding and swerving on the highway and caused the accident."

"Convenient."

"Right."

"So, the jury has to believe Hobbs, or not."

"Correct. It's all on him."

"What kind of a witness will he make?"

"He's not unlikable. The defense will trot him out as a hardworking truck driver just trying to make a living. A Texas good ol' boy with bills to pay."

"Sympathetic with most juries."

"Correct."

"Do they say she caused the entire thing?"

"No, but by definition, in some states, if the plaintiff is found one percent at fault for an accident and the defendant is found ninety-nine percent at fault, the plaintiff recovers nothing."

"All or none?"

"In Texas, we call it comparative negligence. We follow the fifty-one percent bar rule, allowing a party to recover damages only if their fault in the accident is fifty percent or less. If Charlotte is found fifty-one percent or more at fault, we cannot receive any compensation."

"Do we have any evidence either way that she was or wasn't speeding?"

"Not really. She had a good driving record, and no health issues that we could find that might cause her to drive recklessly or pass out. Nothing in her system at autopsy."

"Then how can it be proved or disproved?"

"The court will consider actions leading up to and during the collision. Unfortunately, she's not here to defend herself."

"Any CCTV footage?"

"Yes, back when Charlotte first entered the freeway. She was not speeding and was driving normally at that stage. Unfortunately, there's nothing of record exactly at the time and place of the accident."

"If it's not all or none, how does comparative negligence work?"

"The system allows assigning percentages of fault to each party. If we convincingly argue that Charlotte's actions contributed minimally, or not at all, to the collision and Hobbs bears the majority of the fault, we win."

"What if both parties were at fault?"

"Then the jury will allocate the percentage of negligence by each party and the monetary award will be divided by that percent."

"You mean if Charlotte was ten percent negligent, she gets ninety percent of the judgment?"

"Correct, or whatever other percent the jury might find, up to fifty-one percent, where it then flips over."

"What the hell kind of law is that?"

"Well, I agree, but it comes out of a long history of tort cases and seemed to some judge at some point like it was the best way to allocate responsibility. Regardless, that's what we have to work with."

"Any chance for settlement?"

"I've tried, but every time we step up to the plate, something goes bad. The Hammer has scuttled the boat a couple of times. The fact that Hollingsworth wants no piecemeal settlement is a big problem, too. He's tied all the smaller plaintiffs to his case."

Mo nodded. "I've heard he wields a lot of power in the defense bar."

Quinton stood and stretched. "I thought the case was a slam dunk until Garzon allowed them to add the comparative negligence defense. It's muddying the waters, and a jury is not going to like that."

"I can see why. It's he said, she said, and she's dead."

"Exactly. And, most importantly, how do we prove a negative? If she wasn't speeding, how do we show that? How do we show someone was not doing something?"

37

Quinton met Curtis Buzzy at the house in Afton Oaks for a walk-through in hopes of a bid that wouldn't break the bank. The realtor, Lydia, had located Buzzy through contacts that highly recommended him and his construction company. Buzzy Remodeling, LLC, known for doing good work, on time, and under budget. He was a big burly guy with a gut that indicated a lot of beer drinking. He wore a blue one-piece jumpsuit with his logo, a yellow bee, on the pocket and steel-toed boots with paint speckled all over them. Quinton, in his gray suit and tie from work, could not have looked more different.

They started at the front door, went through the interior, and finished at the pool and the back fence. Buzzy took several pages of notes on his bid sheet, then dropped into a rusty lawn chair that creaked under his weight.

"Whew! This is a whale of a project. I'll have to get some bids on the landscaping and some of the handmade woodwork inside. You sure you don't want to just tear it down and start over?"

Quinton laughed. "I've thought about it, but I'd like to live in something with character, and I'm told keeping the footprint will speed along the process."

"Well, that's true, the city doesn't like it when you start pouring concrete in these older neighborhoods. Let me put a calculator to it."

Half an hour later, Quinton reviewed the bid thoroughly. The primary quote covered gutting most of it, replacing all of the insulation and sheetrock, and adding a beam so the wall dividing the kitchen from the living area could be removed and the space opened up. After that, all manner of fancy woodwork, arches, and a new mantle were envisioned. By the time they went through the whole thing and Quinton signed the contract, he was sweating and Buzzy was smiling.

"I'll need a deposit to order materials, and I can get started next week."

"Sounds good. I'll have the bank wire the first payment to the account in the contract."

"Great."

"Great."

The sales pitch by his realtor was a distant memory in the face of the task ahead.

What have I gotten myself into? Quinton felt a sense of déjà vu. He'd been saying that a lot lately.

38

Hobbs continued to follow Quinton but became more careful in order to avoid the mugger who'd photographed his license. He hid his vehicle and went in on foot or, if in his truck, hid behind barriers and away from Quinton's designated parking spot near the elevator door in the garage.

As he observed from a distance, he realized that Quinton was already being followed by some guy in a Ram pickup truck. One day, Hobbs realized the other guy had been on Quinton's tail all day long and had split off when Quinton returned to his condo. Hobbs assumed Quinton was in for the night, abandoned his watch over him, and tracked the follower in the Ram truck to a cheap motel called The Prestige on the northwest side of town.

Hoping it might be something to help his case, he started to look into why someone else would be after Quinton. At first, he'd thought it was a bodyguard, watching and protecting. Maybe he was the guy who took the picture of his driver's license, possibly for Quinton. But, based on his behavior, he didn't think that Quinton was aware of the follower's presence.

Hobbs wanted to tell his attorneys about the follower, but he knew he was breaking several laws in stalking Quinton, and wanted more to report before he exposed his culpability. Besides, his truck driving license was suspended until after the criminal investigation linked to the accident, so what better did he have to do but follow Quinton, brood, and seek revenge?

Hobbs blamed the lawyers for all his current worries. He felt he'd done nothing wrong, had been a victim of the circumstances of the road on the day of the accident, culminating in a perfect storm that had actually caused the collision. After all, he was barely speeding and just trying to change lanes and get away from the girl in the parked car.

He felt he had little to no blame for the loss of those who had died and felt persecuted and demeaned by the press and social media. His attorneys had told him the storm would die down after a while, but it had not. Video of the aftermath of the accident and footage of the little girl, Lily, limping around on one leg was too juicy for bloggers to resist. He resented them for the position he was in, but mostly he blamed the lawyers.

Those damn fucking lawyers.

After a week or two of intermittently following Quinton, Hobbs began to drink heavily. Again. He had stopped drinking, except on weekends, when he'd obtained his professional driver's license and bought his truck. The motivation to stay sober was no longer there, and he dropped into the bar by his house on the way home on most days.

In his quiet time, he ruminated on the day of the accident. He replayed each element of his driving, the accelerated speed, the rush to get out of town, the car on the side of the road, and the motorcycle squeezing between him and the cars when he'd moved into the other lane. Had he really caused it all or was he a victim of the circumstance as well? He'd never admit the former to himself, so it must be the latter.

He missed the open road, he missed the power of controlling the beast of a machine that his eighteen-wheeler represented to him, and most of all, he missed the money. His insurance company was covering his attorney's fees, but he had to pay the mortgage on his mobile home and other bills. He'd cut into his small savings account until he feared he might run out of funds before he got back on the road. Plus, the bar bill almost every day didn't help his financial situation.

He'd tried to work out a plan with a buddy to drive for him for a route or two a week under the radar, but the buddy had gotten cold feet at the last minute and called off the deal. All money out, and no money in.

I'll have another drink.

39

Cole called the Boss and reported that Hobbs must have been scared off because he hadn't been around lately. He also told him about Broussard and how he and Quinton were getting chummy.

"A cop?"

"Detective."

"Hmm. I remember him very well. Be careful. He's no dummy."

Cole had no idea how the Boss knew so much about Houston people, but he took the warning to heart. He'd been getting away with all types of risk taking. So far, Quinton, nor anyone in his entourage, had spotted him. But he knew his luck wouldn't hold forever. He had too much experience to think he could stalk someone indefinitely and not be noticed.

The Boss cleared his throat. "We need to up the ante, cause some bigger threat and destruction around Quinton. Wake him up a bit. Rain on his parade."

A wicked grin spread across Cole's face. *I'm going to enjoy this.*

"Sure, Boss. I'll think of something and let you know how it goes. Quinton Bell will be very unhappy by this time tomorrow."

"Good. I'll be expecting results, but no slipups. If they find you, you don't know me."

"Understood," he said, ending the call.

Cole had been carefully observing Quinton's every move for some time now. He needed a way to get under his skin without exposing himself. He loved his work. He got to creatively aggravate and often physically harm people and get paid for it. The job suited his evil mind perfectly.

What to do? What to do? He pondered.

———

That night, Cole crept, under cover of darkness, into Quinton's Afton Oaks house. It was very late, and all of the workers had been gone for some time. He didn't turn on any lights, just used the flashlight on his phone to look around.

He saw mostly open studs with walls being added. The kitchen was a skeletal space with a small microwave and a mini fridge on a sawhorse with boards, but no sink or running water. Take-out debris cluttered folding tables near what would become an island.

With a chilling sense of purpose, Cole set about the assigned task of destruction. He commenced in the living room, ripping out the insulation that had recently been placed in the walls. He also tore out most of the wiring and electrical boxes. In the bathroom, he used his boot to push over the toilet which had not yet been seated. It hit the side of the old tub, crashed, and broke into several pieces.

He methodically tore apart every room, leaving a trail of devastation. The serenity of the night was shattered by the cacophony of chaos he created, a stark contrast to the tranquil neighborhood that surrounded the Afton Oaks house. He listened to make sure no neighbors or dogs were activated by the noise. No one seemed to notice, or if they did, they didn't care or respond.

After he ravaged the bedrooms, he made his way to the back yard. There wasn't much there to destroy, so he threw some old chairs, carpentry tools, and debris into the empty pool. He pulled a few plants out by the roots and threw them in as well.

A noise and reflecting headlights from around the house disrupted his actions. He froze, his heart pounding as he listened to the looming threat. Someone had pulled into the driveway. He heard the door of a car open, then slam shut.

Cole didn't have time to get back through the house before whoever it was cleared the distance to the front door. The fence around the back yard was very tall, and he could not easily climb it because of the flat wooden slats. The part where the fence was falling down had thick vines and roots creating a barrier. He looked back through the open patio doors and saw the front door of the house open. He looked around for a means of escape as he heard a male voice yell, "Son of a bitch!" It was Quinton discovering the destruction in the living room. He must have sensed movement in the back yard because he came running toward the open patio doors.

Cole spotted a wheelbarrow tilted upright against the side of the house. He grabbed the handles and rolled it over to the side fence. He climbed onto it and leveraged himself over the fence, his breaths ragged, just as Quinton reached the outside pool decking.

Cole charged through the neighbor's yard and sprinted down the dimly-lit street of the charming neighborhood that lay out before him. As he raced around the block, he heard footfalls behind him, getting closer.

Finally, he reached his pickup truck, concealed in the shadows of a nearby tree-lined street. With trembling hands, he opened the door, jumped in, and pressed the start button. The engine cranked, and he pulled away from the curb. As he sped away, he stole one last chilling glance through the rearview mirror at the silhouette of Quinton running behind him down the middle of the street. He waited until he turned the corner to turn on his headlights, hopefully preventing Quinton from seeing his license plate.

He could not hear Quinton yelling after him, "You son of a bitch!"

40

Quinton returned to the house and turned on all the lights in order to assess the damage. It was a total disaster. Everything that could be destroyed had been.

He knew he needed help, but how could he tell anyone that he thought he was being stalked? Someone was after him, that was clear, but how could he explain the threat without revealing his true identity? And, he had to file a claim to collect his insurance, which meant he needed a police report.

Broussard. He knew enough but not too much. Quinton decided to stay overnight in the house and call him the next morning.

When the sun rose over Afton Oaks, it cast long shadows on the freshly demolished house. Quinton's dream of the perfect home was reduced to a tangled mess of wires and debris. He called Broussard and waited for him to arrive at the scene.

When the detective walked in, his sharp eyes quickly took in the wreckage of the house while Quinton recounted what he had discovered upon his arrival the night before.

"So, not kids or drug addicts?"

"I don't think so. It was one man, about average height or more, and fit based on his sprint to the truck."

"So, a deliberate intent to destroy. Any idea who would want to do such a thing?"

"I'm not sure, but I got a threatening note at the office recently."

"Did you keep it?"

"No, I didn't," Quinton lied about the note locked in his office desk drawer.

"What did it say?"

"Something to the effect that the sender was coming after me."

As Broussard continued his investigation, he couldn't help but sense that this was a more personal attack than it appeared at first glance. The destruction was too systematic, too methodical, to be the work of a mere vandal.

"This looks like it was done by someone enraged. Are you sure there's nothing else you need to tell me?"

"I'm sure."

Later that night, at HPD, as Broussard was reviewing the evidence from the vandalism scene at Quinton Bell's house, he received a call from one of his officers. "Detective, we've analyzed the fingerprints on the fence from where the intruder jumped over. There were no prints inside. Looks like he used some type of metal rod or tire iron and taken it with him."

"What do the prints from the fence tell us?"

"We've seen this guy before. They match those of a man who's been on our radar for a while and is on the federal IAFIS data base."

Broussard's brow furrowed. "Okay, what's his name?"

"We don't have an ID on him, but his prints show he's been involved in some serious criminal activities. A habitual offender. Maybe even murderer. He's slippery and has gotten away from some fairly experienced investigators over the years. We've got a notice out that if someone with his fingerprints is picked up, or if they show up in another case, we're to be advised immediately."

"Wonder what he has to do with Quinton Bell."

"Maybe a disgruntled client? He does work with the evil side of life."

"Maybe."

"What's next?"

"Keep me posted." The motive behind the destruction of Quinton's house was still shrouded in mystery, but one thing was clear. They were dealing with a dangerous individual and he was now on their radar.

41

The Sonny Selcik criminal matter had been stewing in the background for weeks as the court docket in Galveston slowly crawled toward the case. Finally, the judge set a date to have a hearing on the severance of Sonny's trial from the rest of the gang.

Quinton was prepared to go to court, if necessary, but wanted one more shot at DA Rhodes before he put Sonny, and Broussard, through the hearing and a possible trial. He also needed to check on the Galveston Victorian, so he set an appointment with Rhodes. This time they met at the Pirate's Booty, hanging out over the water, for a beer and some oysters. He had a feeling, or maybe it was a hope, that if he got Rhodes away from the office, he might cave in and help young Sonny with a shot at redemption.

After they sat, ordered, and appreciated the view of the Gulf, Rhodes said, "I've looked at the chart you sent over differentiating your client from the others in the smash-and-grab gang. I do see that he is not the same, has no record, and has never been in trouble before."

Quinton chuckled. "Don't forget well educated and part of a law enforcement family. I told you he deserved a second chance."

Rhodes held up his hand. "Not so fast."

Quinton took a swig of his St. Arnold's. "Let me guess, you have conditions before you help him out."

"I do, and not just a few. Nothing easy either."

"Okay. Shoot."

"He pleads to a Class C misdemeanor in a closed document with my office. We'll keep it in a file until he meets all of the other requirements. That will be under the Texas Penal Code, 28.03."

"Isn't that the statute covering vandalism or malicious destruction of property?"

"Yes, it's the graffiti statute. Don't mess with Texas. But it also covers a laundry list of criminal mischief."

"Sounds good so far. What else?"

"His uncle, Broussard, agrees to be his monitor for a full year. Akin to a parole officer, but without the paper trail."

"No problem, he's already doing that. The kid can't go to the toilet without Broussard peeking in."

"Second, he pays a fine of five hundred dollars, the max for a Class C misdemeanor."

"Okay."

"Third, he works in the store that was vandalized, bagging groceries on weekends until he works off an additional five hundred dollars in salary. The owner is a friend of the Island and he'll do it if I ask him."

"Thanks. You've got yourself a deal if we can work around his school schedule."

"You can. It will just take a little longer if he misses weekends for baseball."

"Thank you so much. I'll have to clear it with my client, but I'm sure he'll be grateful." Quinton then gestured to the bartender for two more cold ones.

A new friend in Rhodes, and now Broussard owes me one. Cheers.

42

Quinton had invited Channing to the Galveston Beach house for the weekend following his meeting with DA Rhodes. He was still upset about the Houston house being torn up, but he didn't want it to affect the developing romance between them. He pushed thoughts of the violation aside and prepared for her visit.

She joined him on Friday night, after work. Quinton had been looking forward to this weekend for some time, even before he'd invited her. It was a chance to escape the chaos of their busy lives and spend some quality time together. See where it might lead.

As she arrived at the Victorian, the sun dipped below the horizon, painting the sky in hues of orange and pink that reflected on the stained-glass windows of the beautiful home. Quinton met her at the car and carried her bag in for her.

"Let me show you around."

Channing admired the architecture. "It's breathtaking."

Quinton closed the antique door, placed her bag at the foot of the stairs, and opened a bottle of wine to breathe while

Channing admired the view. He wanted to put her things in his room, but he didn't want to push her. He assumed there would be romance, but assuming could get him into trouble if she had different ideas. He decided to relax and let things play out naturally.

They started the evening by firing up the grill on the patio. Quinton expertly seasoned some red snapper fillets he had purchased from the local fishmonger, and Channing prepared a colorful salad.

She took a sip of wine and teased Quinton. "Red with fish. Tsk-tsk. What would the foodies say about that?"

"Like I care. They're not here, and we like red. It's a pinot, not a cabernet. Good pairing." Quinton laughed as they ventured outdoors, and he grilled the fish. With their plates filled, they settled down at the patio table and paused to listen to the crashing of the waves against the shore nearby. It provided a soothing and romantic backdrop to their conversation.

"Mmm. Quinton, this is delicious."

"We've been getting fish from Sampson & Son's at Pier 20 since I was a child."

"Did you come down with your family a lot?"

Quinton hated to lie to her, but this was not the time for a tell-all. "Yes. Judge Bell, Dad, was a great fisherman and he knew all the places to get fresh fish when he didn't feel like catching and cleaning anything."

Channing looked across the table at Quinton. His heart warmed by her presence. Her eyes sparkled in the fading light as they both forgot about the case, and the responsibilities in H-Town, only an hour away.

They talked about their dreams for the future, and as the night air grew cooler, they took a leisurely stroll on the moonlit beach. Hand in hand, they walked along the shoreline, the sand damp beneath their feet.

"This place is magical," Channing whispered, her voice barely louder than the gentle lapping of the waves.

"Even more special with you here." Quinton turned toward Channing and kissed her deeply and fully. The kiss transported him to a peaceful place that he hadn't experienced in some time.

When they returned to the house, Quinton picked up Channing's bag at the foot of the stairs with one hand and grabbed Channing's hand with the other. "Come with me."

They settled into his bed and slowly explored each other. Quinton knew that he had found something precious, something worth cherishing. Channing moaned softly as he nuzzled her neck and dropped his head to her breast.

After their lovemaking, they fell asleep in each other's arms, the promise of a new day and a bright future ahead of them.

43

When the trial against STS and Hobbs was to begin, Judge Garzon called Quinton in for a meeting with Hollingsworth and they broke some unfortunate news to him in the judge's chambers.

"Where's Johnson? We can't have a meeting without his being present."

Judge Garzon took a long pull, then tamped out a cigar. "Johnson and Hollingsworth settled this morning."

"Here?"

Garzon lied. "No, outside of court, of course."

Quinton looked at Hollingsworth. "Did you not think to include me?"

"We considered it, but Johnson and I felt we could work out a settlement without your clients involved. You do have the most sympathetic of the group, and your attorney's fees are not what Johnson was asking for."

"You made a deal with him on attorney's fees?"

Hollingsworth gloated. "Right, we worked it out for him to get sixty percent of the payout by adding his class action management fee and his attorney's fees together, plus expenses, of course."

"We?" Quinton looked at the judge. "Sixty percent? Did you approve that?"

"I did. I told you I wanted this matter settled. I do not want to go to trial on this case."

Hollingsworth gauged Quinton's reaction, then offered a thinly veiled bribe. "We're prepared to do something similar for you."

"You mean for my client?"

"No, I mean for you."

"And how would you propose to do that? I only have two clients, the estate and Lily. I don't represent a class."

Judge Garzon fielded the question. "I can approve just about anything you want. You two just have to pick a number."

"Are you offering me a bribe?"

Hollingsworth put on his best aristocratic air. "Of course not, but these cases can be expensive, and you need to be compensated for your efforts, plus all the costs of preparation and out-of-pocket expenses."

Judge Garzon nodded. "Right."

"Do you have a settlement number in mind?"

"We'll add five million more to the last offer."

"That's nowhere near the national average for these cases, and that will not compensate a young woman for the loss of her leg."

"You'd walk away with millions, and she'd be covered for the rest of her life."

"I have no intention of upping my attorney's fees and taking more than my client. I'll think about the settlement offer for her."

With that, Quinton left the room without a farewell to Hollingsworth or His Honor.

Quinton returned to his office and stewed all day about the end-run Hollingsworth and the judge had played on him. He was furious at The Hammer for settling without telling him and wanted to call him and give him a piece of his mind, but he refrained. What good would it do?

In the afternoon, he called Mo, put her on speaker, and asked her opinion. When he filled her in on the sandbagging, she sounded shocked. "I can't believe Garzon did that. There are ethical violations galore in his actions."

Quinton agreed. "Who's going to believe it? He's been on the bench forever, and no one's ever accused him of being in anyone's pocket."

"Maybe this is his big payday?"

"You think?"

"No way of knowing. Something is motivating him. What are you going to do about the offer?"

"If I take the settlement, I'll be leaving lots of money on the table."

Mo's voice came back. "And, if we lose at trial, she'll get less than she deserves from the other settlements, and nothing from STS and Hobbs. And, you won't cover your fees and expenses."

"Correct. It's a multimillion-dollar dilemma."

"And, you have an unfavorable judge."

"There's that."

Quinton looked over at the door and saw movement. The shadows that played across the floor indicated that someone was outside the door. He got up as Mo was talking, walked over, and looked out. Anna almost jumped out of her skin.

"You scared me."

She stood at the wall of bookshelves, full of knick-knacks and décor, with a duster in her hand.

"What are you doing?"

"The cleaning crew never gets to this. I can't stand looking at it anymore."

Quinton didn't know what to say, so he went back to his desk and finished the conversation with Mo, no closer to a decision than before he'd called her.

After Mo left, Quinton stayed late and alone at the office. He'd not made a final decision about the settlement offer, and he used the work on the trial to help him think it through.

Around eight, he heard a knock at the glass outer doors, went through the reception area, and saw Channing standing with a bag of take-out.

"I had a feeling I'd find you here."

He kissed her on the cheek and smelled the air. "Mmm. What's in the bag?"

"Chicken and funnel cakes from The Honey Hole."

"Any pimento cheese?"

"Not today. Have any wine?"

They walked into the break room and Channing began to unpack the containers from the bag. Quinton poured two glasses of wine, a full one for her and half for him. He opened a container and sniffed the fried chicken and confectioner's sugar.

"Oh my. Are you trying to spoil me?"

"Just take care of you a little. Bet you had a big day?"

"Where'd you hear that?"

Channing took a sip of her wine. "All your days are big days lately. Why? What's going on?"

They sat and loaded their plates while Quinton told her about the settlement offer. He didn't go into the details of the attorney's fees or the bribe.

"What are you going to do?"

Quinton took a bite of chicken. "What do you think I should do?"

"It's a lot of money. Lily could use that."

Quinton swallowed, then said, "Right, but she deserves more."

Channing nibbled on her food. "True, but a bird in the hand, as they say."

"That's the dilemma."

"What does Mo think?"

"That it's a dilemma."

"Well, pros, you get out of the case with a nice chunk of cash and Lily is guaranteed medical care for a long time. Maybe her entire life."

Quinton nodded. "And cons?"

"I can't think of any."

"Really? None? What about letting big business off the hook for negligence? What about Hobbs and his lying about Charlotte? What about letting them off for a song, and what does that do to the next guy who's hit by one of these trucks?"

Channing jerked her head up. "Are you in this to teach them a lesson or to get Lily covered?"

"I'm in it to win, for her and for me. This offer is not a win. It's a... It's a... thing I can't say in front of a lady."

Channing paused for a moment. "Hmm. Sounds to me like you're letting your ego get in the way of your good sense."

Quinton put down his fork. "Are you kidding me? Whose side are you on?"

"Lily's. I think she needs the guarantee, and you're the one who needs to win."

"What do you think Charlotte Collins would want me to do? What do you think her life is worth? You think I'm that selfish?"

Channing took a step back from the heat of the argument. "Of course not." She put her hand on Quinton's arm, and he pulled back.

"I've got more work to do." Quinton stood up and placed his wine glass, untouched, into the sink. "Thanks for dinner."

"I thought you wanted my opinion, so I gave it to you. I'll get out of your way."

"Right, I did." He sighed deeply. "It's been a tough day. May I call you tomorrow?"

Channing smiled her most charming smile. "I'll be disappointed if you don't."

Channing left Quinton working in the office and went down the hall toward the elevator that led to the garage. As she walked, she hit the speed dial for her contact at STS.

"I pulled out all the stops short of that nasty pimento cheese he likes and sex on the conference room table. He's not going to go for it. I don't think he'll settle."

"Maybe you should have tried the sex. We're paying you enough."

"I might have if things hadn't gotten so heated."

Channing stepped into the elevator as Van, unseen, stood in the stairwell doorway listening to her side of the conversation.

44

Quinton, Mo, and Dart arrived at Judge Garzon's courtroom on the morning of trial to a contingent of reporters and onlookers. Quinton was accustomed to the camera crews that big cases brought, but he was usually the big dog. Today, he was the underdog. What was worse, he and Mo were alone. He had not realized that he would ever miss The Hammer, but he did. The settlement by the tort giant had left Quinton to defend his client without help or support from anyone other than Mo and his small office staff.

He should have known better than to bet on a big tort case. He'd heard the stories his entire career from New York to Houston about law firms that mortgaged to the hilt to finance a big case, then had to bring in a financier who took half of their profits when the case was finally won, if they were lucky. Some joined with another firm, but the outcome was no better.

Quinton had the twenty thousand that was left from the settlement from the Camry insurance, but that was already promised, and more. He was fighting an uphill battle against a team of lawyers with deep pockets and clients with unlimited budgets. It was David versus Goliath in every sense of the word.

He and Mo took their seats at the plaintiff's table with Dart sitting directly behind them in the gallery area. Anna was back in the law office holding down the fort and sitting by the phone for any last-minute research or unexpected tasks that might arise.

The jury had been through voir dire the week before and sat empaneled and ready to pass judgment on all they witnessed in the court today.

As plaintiff in the civil case, Quinton went first with his opening argument.

"Ladies and gentlemen of the jury, today we are here to serve a young girl named Lily Collins and the estate of Charlotte Collins. Lily and her mother were harmed due to the negligence of the defendants. You see that Charlotte Collins is not at the plaintiff's table today because she was killed in the pileup that also took the leg and emotional wellbeing of her daughter, Lily. In one act of poor judgment by the defendant, their small family of two was devastated forever."

The jury was attentive to Quinton as he walked to and fro before them.

"Today we will show that Speedy Transportation Services and their driver, Tommy Joe Hobbs, negligently cut corners by rushing deliveries and put their profit over my client's safety. While the defense team will try to lay blame on my client, there is no proof that Charlotte Collins was guilty of any wrongdoing. In fact, there is no video or photographic evidence, and the only witness is one who has the most to gain by laying blame at Charlotte Collins' door."

Jacob Hollingsworth went second with his opening argument. He commanded attention by his very demeanor, dress, and style of speaking. Today, he was all peaches and cream as he greeted the jury and thanked them for their service. After all, he was on their side, the side of the consumer. How could the everyday man and woman afford to purchase what was needed for their homes and lives if exorbitant fees continued to be awarded to everyone involved in a semitruck accident?

Hollingsworth walked right up to the jury box, looked into the eyes of its members, most of them just making ends meet, and said, "Trucking companies are the backbone of the transportation industry. How can the trucking industry provide effective logistic services to thousands of businesses operating in the country, helping them move from one place to the other? In fact, a recent survey emphasized that about eighty percent of the US heavily relies on trucking companies for food, medicine, everyday goods, and other essential items. Heavy trucks carry millions of tons of these essential goods across the country every day."

Quinton exchanged a concealed look with Mo. They could tell the jury was eating it up. The money was virtually flowing out of their pockets as they sat and listened to Hollingsworth's silver tongue. Quinton had intentionally not used the word accident in his opening statement, while Hollingsworth threw it out repeatedly, reminding the jury that accidents happen often on the highway, and through no fault of his client.

"During the course of this trial, we will show through witness and video testimony that Charlotte Collins was speeding in her rush to get out of town with her daughter, Lily. While it is tragic that Lily lost her mother and her leg in the accident, it was just that, an accident. The cause of which can be directly attributable to Charlotte Collins and not my clients."

Outside the courtroom, as they walked to the elevator, Quinton, Mo, and Dart did a postmortem on the day's trial.

Mo wheeled a rolling briefcase full of files. "I think it went pretty well, don't you?"

Quinton lugged a large briefcase. "Seemed like a wash to me."

Dart carried a couple of large banker's boxes. "At least you put them on notice that they don't have a credible witness. That Hobbs is a liar."

Mo nodded. "But, will they see through his lies?"

Quinton pushed the button to call the elevator as they arrived at the door. "All depends on how well Hollingsworth preps him as a witness. He could sway the jury either way."

45

The follower called the nursing home where his wife was being housed. It was a vile place in his mind. Overcrowded, smelling of urine, with lousy food, and poor medical care, but it was all he could afford at the moment. He needed the big score to get her out of there. He was tired of the short-term gigs that only covered the medical bills and got him to the next job. He needed to stop working for a year or two and take care of her, nurse her back to health, give her some time by the ocean or in the desert air. Anything to prolong her life and make her final days more pleasant, restful, and what she absolutely deserved.

"I'm calling to check on my wife, Gracie. How's she doing today?"

"Uh. I'll need to get someone to tell you. Just a moment. I'll put you through to her floor nurse."

"Third-floor nurses' station."

"Hello, I'm calling to check on my wife, Gracie. I usually can get what I need from the receptionist. Did something happen?"

"Yes, sir. She was in the shower and stood up from her wheelchair. She slipped and hit her head."

"Was she left by herself?"

"Yes, sir, but only for a moment. She was told to stay in her chair."

"You know she doesn't remember things like that. Why was she left alone?"

"The orderly has been reprimanded. Your wife's doctor is coming in to see her later today."

"Does she need to go to the emergency room?"

"Obviously, we don't think so, or we would have sent her. The doctor will decide if she needs additional treatment. Right now, she's resting. We gave her a sedative because she was upset and disoriented."

"I want the doctor to call me the minute he leaves her room. I'll fly back tonight if I need to."

"Yes, sir."

Cole hung up the phone and flung it across the room. He had already moved his wife twice to different care facilities, and there seemed to be no improvement in the price range he was looking to pay. He needed something better. Something more hands-on. Something that would support her and ease her discomfort. She needed a full-time nurse. Someone with better training. She needed things that cost a lot of money. And, he needed to be with her. She would be happier with him. She would be better if he were home all the time, instead of chasing around the country looking for a quick buck.

Cole returned to Quinton's Afton Oaks house, still fuming from the conversation with his wife's doctor. A sinister resolve burned within him. He had unfinished business, and tonight, he intended to make a statement. It was a moonless night and the darkness enveloped him like a shroud as he passed the last streetlamp and approached the house.

He came with a plan and a deadly arsenal. In his hand, he held a small canister filled with a highly flammable liquid. It was a homemade concoction, a volatile mixture of gasoline and other accelerants that he'd used before and crafted for the purpose at hand.

He moved stealthily around the side of the house, broke a window , and climbed through, his senses on high alert. He knew the layout well from his previous visit, and now he navigated the open studs like a ghost moving through walls. The kitchen, still barren and lifeless, served as the starting point for his destructive mission.

He unscrewed the cap of the canister, and poured the deadly concoction onto the floor and along the wall studs. The pungent smell of gasoline hung heavy in the air, a harbinger of the impending inferno. He pulled another canister from this pocked and placed it on a sawhorse set up with a wooden plank supporting a saw, pulled out a cheap plastic lighter, and took a moment to light a cloth fuse hanging out of the other canister.

The flames erupted with a fierce roar, a chaotic dance of orange and red. Cole stepped aside and watched, his eyes alight with his rage, as the fire hungrily consumed the kitchen, devouring everything in its path. The wood crackled and splintered, the flames hissing and spitting in their destructive frenzy.

With grim satisfaction, Cole moved deeper into the house, his steps careful and deliberate. The fire followed him like a malevolent spirit, its tendrils licking the walls and ceilings. Smoke billowed through the open studs, into the living room, thickening the air with acrid fumes.

The bedrooms were next, and Cole spared no remorse as he watched the flames engulf the back of the house. The walls seemed to weep with fire, and sag under the weight of the inferno.

Cole kicked his way out the French doors in the master bedroom, onto the patio, and into the back yard as his satisfaction grew. He looked back at the house as flames danced across the windows.

He heard sirens in the near distance, and with a final glance at the roaring flames, went over the back yard fence, using the same wheelbarrow as before, and disappeared into the night once more.

Mission accomplished.

Quinton was called to the house by Broussard, but by the time Quinton joined him, the flames were all gone. The fire department was rolling up hoses and packing their truck as steam rose off the downed embers. Quinton was sickened at the pile of destruction that remained of the house he had so looked forward to making his dream home.

Quinton approached the detective who was standing in the back yard by the pool. "Any idea who's responsible?"

Broussard almost felt sorry for him. "Best guess is the same asshole who tore up the place came back to finish the job. Wasn't your contractor supposed to take some security measures?"

Quinton shook his head. "He was. I certainly paid him enough to do it."

"We still have a watch out for the guy who left the prints."

Broussard walked with Quinton back to his car parked on

the street. Quinton looked back at the money pit he now regretted buying.

"You'll have to handle this Broussard. I can't deal with this now. I have court in about two hours."

46

Dart came into the law office late in the afternoon on a day when Lacey was not working. They had become a little too involved for Dart, and he'd resolved to lessen the frequency of their interaction. Interaction was an interesting way to describe what they had going. More like two racing freight trains colliding on a regular basis. Fun, but dangerous. He sensed she was getting attached, and he didn't need any complications of a romantic nature.

Dart settled into the conference room, turned war room, and opened the box of files marked Tommy Joe (TJ) Hobbs. As usual, they were perfectly organized and color-coded by Anna. She'd added a couple of recent searches Quinton had instructed her to do, knowing that Dart was coming in to dig up dirt on the truck driver. Those reports had Post-it notes sticking out from the tops and marked with the date they were added, which was that day.

At first, there were the usual docs. Where Hobbs had lived, family, licensure to drive the truck, bank records showing a mortgage on the rig, and so forth. As Dart delved deeper, his eyes caught a familiar thread. Every year or so, there was a three- to six-month period without income. There was a truck storage fee that equated with the dates of the time off.

There was no obvious reason for the supposed vacations until Dart opened one of the new files marked Medical Insurance. Coinciding with the periods of time off were payments to various recovery centers and rehabilitation programs. There it was, a history of alcoholism spanning many years.

He opened a laptop and put the information into a spreadsheet for Quinton to use at trial. As he completed the timeline, the last two years showed continuous income and no signs of admission to programs or visits with doctors. Apparently, Hobbs had either given up or kicked the habit. The answer was hinted at in a release from the last rehab center showing a story of redemption by a man who had seemingly conquered his inner turmoil. A letter from his AA sponsor attested to the fact that Hobbs had been sober and attending meetings for about six months.

Dart leaned back in the office chair, causing it to creek under his substantial weight.

Gotta admire the guy.

He sent it all to Quinton in an email. "I don't think he's drinking anymore, but you can never tell when someone might slip. Regardless, attached is the proof of the past issue."

In the wood-paneled courtroom of Judge Garzon, the atmosphere hummed with activity, as the trial progressed. The trial became a test of the witnesses. Who would the jury believe?

STS asserted speeding by Charlotte Collins as contributory negligence and hung their hat on Hobbs's testimony. It was a delicate dance not to victimize the dead woman, but Hollingsworth had prepped Hobbs perfectly, and phrased his questions delicately. When Hobbs swore that Charlotte Collins was speeding and swerving, he could see that the jury believed him. He was one of them. A working man who was being gouged by the system. Finally, someone was on his side.

Next, Hollingsworth introduced a line of questioning that caught Quinton totally by surprise. Hollingsworth asked Hobbs if he'd ever had a drinking problem. Quinton looked at Mo who also looked shocked. It was their ace in the hole, the move they were going to make on Hobbs to discredit him on cross-examination. Now, Hollingsworth had stolen their thunder, and by the time he finished questioning Hobbs, he looked like a damn hero, conquering his demons and serving humanity in the best way he knew how to make up for years of sinful behavior.

On cross, Quinton tried to probe further into the alcoholism and did score a few points, but he didn't feel that he'd won the jury back to his side. The turning of the jury, along with some very questionable rulings by Judge Garzon, and Quinton lost his footing. Overcoming the alleged speeding by Charlotte Collins looked impossible. He did not know how he would get the jury back on his side. He decided that refusal of the settlement had been a mistake and asked to see Hollingsworth.

In the attorney's meeting room, down the hall from the courtroom, Quinton and Hollingsworth had a heart to heart. Quinton hated to eat crow, it was his least favorite meal, but he knew he had to do it.

"Is that settlement offer still good?"

Hollingsworth laughed. "Now that the tide has turned, you think you can still get that deal? I think not."

Quinton quipped. "Yes, I admit I lost some steam with Hobbs, but they still heard that he was a drunk. Once a drunk, always a drunk, so they say."

"Maybe. Maybe not."

Quinton frowned. "Then, what would you propose we do?" He hated showing weakness, but he had to see what he was dealing with in terms of a number.

"Well, I hate to be the one to tell you this, but my client, Hobbs, has decided he will not settle. He thinks the jury believes him, and I tend to agree. He thinks we have you on the run. So does STS. No settlement today."

The next day, Quinton sat at the plaintiff's table and waited patiently for his chance to be heard. There was no jury today. This was a hearing on Quinton's motion for a continuance. Across the aisle, Jacob Hollingsworth and his entourage whispered and gestured in a conspiratorial manner. Not much unnerved Quinton, but he was anxious about the continuance he had requested. He knew he didn't have a leg to stand on, but he was in hopes that the judge would have pity on him.

When the judge appeared and court was finally called to order, Quinton stood, his crisp suit and poised posture not reflecting what he felt inside. He made an urgent plea for the continuance of the trial to give him more time to prove that Charlotte Collins was not speeding. The defense had not raised contributory negligence in a timely manner, and the judge had ruled in their favor. He hoped that it was now his turn for a break.

"Your Honor, I must request a continuance for the trial. The complexity of the case demands further preparation and examination of additional evidence that has just come to light."

Judge Garzon peered down at Quinton from the bench with a look that hinted at impatience. He then looked over at Hollingsworth. "What do to have to say, Counselor?"

"To delay the trial places an additional and undue burden on my clients. Mr. Hobbs has been waiting to regain his ability to earn a living, and STS has been spending its time in preparation and paying attorney's fees and court costs during the entire preparation and trial. These expenses are difficult enough to bear without extending the length of the trial and adding to their burden and time commitment."

Quinton stood again. "Your Honor."

"Hold it. I've heard enough. The arguments of defense counsel and my pressing trial docket lead me to refuse the extension. We can't afford any further delay. The trial proceeds on schedule."

He gave the gavel a decisive tap.

<hr>

When Quinton got back to the office, he and Mo settled into the conference room for a strategy session. Quinton asked her to listen to what he was thinking.

"Is this going to require a glass of wine?"

"It might." Quinton hit the intercom on his desk and asked Anna to bring in a glass of Chardonnay for Mo and a cup of coffee for him. After she served the beverages, he rose and closed the door so that Anna could not hear them.

Quinton took a deep breath and told Mo the entire story of why he was brought in through Judge Blaylock to Judge Garzon, meeting Lily and her foster parents and guardian, the surprise of the contributory negligence allegation, and reminded her of the refusal of a continuance just that morning. Then, he listed each time in court where the defense team was prepared for his next move before he made it.

Mo sipped her wine and remained quiet, letting him finish his thoughts.

Quinton took a deep breath, "It's as if every step I take, the defense is one step ahead of me. I'm not accustomed to being outsmarted by attorneys that are not as experienced as I am, but also not as clever or intelligent."

"A bit of ego showing there, Counselor?"

"Yes, but it's you, Mo. I can speak freely. You know where I'm coming from."

"I do. Just razzing you a little. It does seem as if the opposition is reading your mail."

Quinton looked at the door. Was Anna listening outside? He shrugged it off but lowered his voice. She was loyal. Surely, she wouldn't feed information to opposing counsel. Her references were impeccable.

"Do you suspect someone in your office?"

Quinton felt guilty for even considering such a thing. "No. Well. I guess I'm just paranoid. A friend recently told me if your gut is telling you something's going on, it probably is."

"Good advice. Do we have an expert who can cover the comparative negligence issue?"

"My guy is an expert in crash sites and ordering the impact of each vehicle. She's also a speed expert, but what would she measure? There's nothing to compare her speed to except the eighteen-wheeler. There are no witnesses at the head of the crash. Almost all are in the rear, piling on."

"How about a new expert?"

"Same issue. What does the new expert use to calculate speed? Hobbs has testified that Charlotte Collins was speeding, and she's not alive to defend herself. Lily has no concept of driving practices, and no one else is in a position to know or testify as to what happened."

"What will you do? And, more importantly, how can I help?"

Quinton's heart sank. He had hoped that going over the case with Mo would give him a spark, some idea of how to proceed. It hadn't worked. His only option was to attack the veracity of Hobbs. How could he do that?

Quinton took a drink of his now-cold coffee. "For the first time in this case, I think I might lose."

47

That weekend, Quinton arrived at the house in Afton Oaks and was once again sickened at the site of the charred remains. He had arranged to meet his architect and contractor to discuss starting over and set a timeframe for new plans and completing the rebuild. Quinton and the architect walked the property along the outer perimeter of the concrete slab.

"As soon as I can get the debris removed, we'll have to start over. The bank is not going to hold the interest on my loan, and I only have so much insurance on the property."

"Let's look at the plans." The two men walked back to the front of the house and spread the architectural drawings on the hood of Quinton's Range Rover. The architect pointed to the portion covering the living room and kitchen.

"Since you have to start over, we can widen this area and leave no walls through the entire front space. We can also reconfigure the bathrooms to make them larger and include more closet space. We just need to keep the existing outer footprint to avoid a variance, same as before."

"Right." Quinton looked at his watch, wondering what was keeping the contractor. He looked at his phone and saw that there had been no texts or calls.

"I won't keep you waiting any longer. Can you draw up your ideas and let me run by your office when you get them completed?"

"No problem."

"I'll wait for the contractor for another few minutes and let you know of anything he needs to add."

Quinton called the contractor again and left another message, but he knew the guy was gone for good. He had been paid up to and including the work and materials to date in a draw from the bank, and he was ahead for the last phase. He had not provided security, as promised, and was probably afraid of being sued. He guessed the guy would keep the money and cut out. Buzzy had flown away.

Quinton's emotions swung between anger and depression. He'd see what his realtor had to say about the company she'd recommended, but he knew it was all for nothing. He would have to clean up and sell the lot or start over with a new builder.

48

The rain poured relentlessly, creating a rhythmic symphony on the roof of the cheap motel where Cole had set up his makeshift headquarters. The dim light of a single flickering bulb cast long shadows, adding an aura of secrecy to the room. The air was thick with tension as he paced back and forth, the gravity of his decision weighing heavily on his shoulders. He tried a few pull-ups on the bar at the bathroom door, but grew bored and opened a bag of Doritos.

For weeks, he had trailed Quinton, his every move meticulously documented for his enigmatic employer. But as the days passed, Cole grew disillusioned with the lack of excitement in his job. He had become a ghost in the shadows, a mere puppet dancing to the whims of a faceless puppeteer.

And now, Broussard was getting too close. That, combined with his realization that reaching his money goal was going to take a lot longer than he'd like, marked the culmination of his resentment.

Cole's jealousy burned deep. He hated Quinton for his ability to blow money on gambling, buy houses and cars, and live the good life. Cole wanted to escape. He wanted to live the life of another, without constant money pressures, without bosses who treated him like an errand boy.

He had been struggling to push past his income ceiling for his entire life. Without an education and no family backing, he had earned every cent he'd ever made, and struggled alone through every downturn in his financial situation. His wife's illness pulled the last penny from their bank account, and now she needed more. He needed more. He needed to control his own destiny. He was sick and tired of being a victim of life's circumstances and fate's whims.

It's time to do something.

There in the dingy room, he hatched a plan, a daring scheme that would sever the strings that bound him to his employer and give him the freedom he'd been longing for his entire life. He had gathered enough information, enough leverage to make his final play and disappear into the life he so craved and be with the wife he truly loved.

Since the Boss didn't seem to want money from Quinton, he'd make a play for it. If he worked it right, he surmised that he could get paid on both ends, first from the Boss, and a retirement plan by blackmailing Quinton.

How would the Boss ever find out? And, if he did, Cole reasoned he and his wife would be long gone by then. Maybe on a beach or in a mountain lodge. A quiet place where she could rest and recover, and he could spend his days with her. And, what if the Boss caught him? It wasn't like he could call the cops. The Boss would be in as much trouble as Cole.

To get some insurance, he planned to purchase a small recording device that connected to his phone and also rephrase his emails to read: Per your instructions, and as we discussed. That should give him plenty of ammunition in the event that the Boss caught on to what he was doing and threatened him. *Hell, he might even blackmail him, too.*

The referral system he'd built in order to obtain his nasty work would dry up if he got caught, but he didn't want to do it anymore anyway. He could find something far more lucrative to do, or just satisfy his need for mayhem in other ways. He knew he'd never stop completely, but he'd find a way to do it for himself. Maybe he'd go back to all those prior clients and blackmail every nasty one of them.

After a quick trip to the Greyhound Bus Station downtown, Cole returned to the room and created his letter. Sitting at his makeshift desk, he meticulously typed out a demand for a million dollars, an amount he thought Quinton could come up with quickly. The words were succinct, the threat clear, as he detailed the consequences of noncompliance. He asserted he had a file containing the evidence that Quinton was not who he said he was. He intimated that he knew Quinton's real name, although the Boss had never told him. All he actually had was the Boss's word for it, and how he'd discovered that Cole may never know.

The Boss didn't need the money, and blackmail was never part of the plan, but Quinton didn't know that, and if Cole was lucky, the Boss would not find out and he'd make his money coming and going.

With the message drafted, Cole put on gloves, opened a new ream of paper, inserted a few sheets into the printer, and printed the blackmail note. He folded it and inserted it into an envelope which he sealed with a touch of water on the glove from the bathroom sink. He smirked, reveling in the audacity of his plan. He placed the small envelope into a larger manila envelope, spread the metal clasp to seal it, then removed the gloves. He looked with satisfaction at the package, a ticking time bomb that could destroy Quinton's world.

As the minutes crawled by, Cole's anxiety heightened. Would Quinton pay up? Had he underestimated the consequences of betraying the Boss? After all, he was the one who controlled the strings. If Quinton didn't pay and the Boss found out, he'd be out of both incomes.

The anticipation gnawed at him, but deep down, a spark of liberation ignited within his soul. Tonight, he would break free from the shackles of his past and forge a new path, leaving behind the role of the obedient puppet for good.

Cole followed Quinton to the gym and made sure he was swimming laps before he drove over to Quinton's condo near the medical center. He pulled his hoodie up around his face, being careful to avoid the security cameras, which he'd scoped out on many other occasions when he'd followed Quinton. He waited for a young couple to use their pass-card to enter the building then piggybacked on their entry.

Cole took the stairs up to Quinton's floor and to his door, where he unzipped the hoodie and pulled the manila envelope from beneath. He opened the clasp at the end of the envelope, slid the smaller envelope containing the blackmail note onto the mat without touching it, and put the manila envelope back under his hoodie.

With the toe of his boot, he kicked the envelope closer to the door, and left it there for Quinton to find.

When Quinton arrived at his condo, he found the letter and took it inside. He was reluctant to open it and the can of worms he was concerned it possessed. He got a beer from the refrigerator, sat on the sofa, and opened the delivery with no small amount of trepidation. As he read the demand for money, a wave of nausea surged through him, nearly causing him to throw up. He quickly pulled a trashcan closer to his side, anticipating the worst.

The note contained a carefully worded message, outlining the dire consequences if Quinton failed to comply with the demands. The sender claimed to possess sensitive information that could ruin Quinton's life and reputation. Quinton felt a cold sweat forming on his forehead as he absorbed the gravity of the situation.

His hands trembled as he re-read the specifics of the blackmail. The note outlined a meticulous plan for the delivery of the money that Quinton was required to pay to prevent the exposure of the truth about his secret past. The note did not say what the secret was, but outlined terms that were stringent and left no room for negotiation.

The blackmailer instructed Quinton to place a bag containing one million cash in locker number 383 at the Greyhound Bus Station on Harrisburg Boulevard. Quinton knew it well from his arrival in town before he became Quinton. The instructions were explicit, detailing the exact location of the locker, the time of delivery, and the consequences of deviating from the plan. He was given a code to the locker and assumed that the blackmailer would later use the code to retrieve the cash.

As Quinton absorbed the details, a sense of helplessness washed over him. The demands were exorbitant, and the thought of parting with such a significant sum of money left him reeling. He weighed the potential fallout of refusing against the financial strain that complying would place on him and his ability to continue the case for Lily. What if he had to flee again regardless of paying off the blackmailer? He would have very little cash left to live on while on the run. If he called the cops, and they caught the blackmailer, he could reveal his secret to them. The blackmailer had obviously thought of that, and thought it a deterrent, as the asshole had to go back to the same locker to retrieve the cash.

Fighting back the rising panic, Quinton considered his options. The blackmailer had given him a tight deadline, adding to the pressure. He couldn't ignore the threat, and the consequences of exposure seemed too severe to risk. Should he cut his losses and leave now? How could he give up all he'd rebuilt as Quinton? He could ask Dart for help, but dare he let another in on his secret? What could Dart do to help him anyway? Broussard? He did owe him one, but not this much. He'd never keep the secret and might be the first to point the finger at him for Q's murder.

In a state of despair, Quinton began contemplating how he would secure the funds and execute the delivery without arousing suspicion. He had several days to pull the funds together and deliver them to the locker. His movements now became potential pitfalls in the intricate dance he was forced to perform to protect his secret. The ticking clock intensified the urgency, leaving Quinton with a sinking feeling that his life was no longer entirely under his control, if it ever was.

The pressure was weighing on Quinton, and he needed a game. He had been to The Dog Pound recently, but he broke his own rule of going only once a month and headed over anyway. He was now gambling almost once a week, and taking chances he shouldn't be taking.

The urge to gamble to blow off steam and relieve the pressures of work, Channing, the house was becoming stronger.

When he'd first returned to Houston, he frequently drove by his childhood home that he'd shared with his loving mother. He also drove by the house that he'd purchased for her when he became a successful trial lawyer. Now, he avoided both of those areas, ashamed of what she might think of him and his weaknesses.

Quinton hadn't had any traumatic episodes since the date in Judge Blaylock's courtroom, but he felt an ever-present pressure in the back of his mind, and often had headaches, which was unusual for him. He was glad to be in his new relationship with Channing, but never went a day without thinking of Joanne. He often thought of the exit from New York and the people who were killed or hurt in the process.

At first, he didn't notice the increased frequency of gambling, then ignored it, but it had eventually become obvious to him. Still, Quinton felt he could handle it.

Isn't that what every gambler says.

49

Hobbs started drinking early one afternoon when he'd grown tired of waiting outside Quinton's office. The lawyer worked late almost every night during the trial, and it was boring for Hobbs to sit in the parking garage and wait for Quinton to leave night after night.

Hobbs chose a bar nearby in case he decided to go back on Quinton watch, and because he was really needing the hair of the dog after his late night out the night before. The trial verdict was coming soon, and he feared it. He worried that he had been too hasty in refusing to settle, especially with STS still refusing to admit fault in overloading and improperly securing the haul. Now, he had second thoughts about the trial, and the alcohol caused paranoia he hadn't experienced in some years.

The bartender finally refused to serve Hobbs under the Texas Dram Shop Act when he saw him weaving back from the men's room, bumping a table full of drinks, and knocking over a barstool in the process.

"Sorry, buddy. No more alcohol tonight. It's the law. Let me call you a cab."

Hobbs was slurring his words. "Bullshit. Who you to becide if I need another dwink?"

The bouncer watched the exchange unfold, from across the room, and came over to assist. "Come on, buddy. Get some sleep and come back to drink another day."

Hobbs vomited in the back seat, and the cab driver pulled over and threw him out, about two blocks from the bar. He staggered back to his pickup in the bar's parking lot and vowed to make Quinton pay for all he was doing to him. He had been sober, had a business he owned, a life that had taken him time, money, and work to achieve, and Quinton had robbed him of it all, no matter how the trial turned out.

He drove back to the parking garage of Quinton's office building, backed in where he could see Quinton's new SUV, and passed out almost immediately. He was awakened a few minutes later by screeching tires as an office worker peeled out of the garage. Still drunk, but wanting more, Hobbs took a pop from the half-pint of Wild Turkey he kept in the glove box. Lucky for Hobbs, but unlucky for Quinton, the lawyer wrapped his day and exited the elevator a few minutes later.

Hobbs watched as he pulled on his driving gloves and took another swig of Wild Turkey. He waited for Quinton to clear the CCTV cameras that had been increased but were still inadequate to protect the garage from someone who knew what they were doing. When Quinton walked between a large concrete pylon and a car, Hobbs grabbed a baseball bat from the gun rack behind him, flew out of the truck, and ran full speed toward Quinton.

Hobbs took a swing aimed at Quinton's back, but not before Quinton felt his presence and deflected by twisting his body and allowing his shoulder and arm to take the brunt of the attack. Hobbs took another swing at the backs of Quinton's knees and put him down on the gritty concrete floor. Hobbs then hit him several times across the lower back and shoulders with the bat as Quinton defended himself as best he could. Quinton reached for the knife in his pocket, but Hobbs saw the weapon and hit Quinton's wrist with the bat, causing Quinton to drop the blade.

When Quinton stopped fighting back, Hobbs stood over Quinton and raised the bat high with both hands and just as he was about to sweep down for a fatal blow, Cole blasted his horn, probably to protect his investment in the blackmail more than to save Quinton, but nevertheless, caused a ruckus. Hobbs looked up and hesitated.

Quinton seized the moment of delay, pulled the last of his effort from the bottom of his will to live, and grasped the knife from the concrete floor. He swung it up as the bat came down, cutting a large gash in Hobbs's arm and causing him to drop the bat.

Cole, watching it all from his truck, turned on his headlights and flashed them. Hobbs realized he had an audience and ran to his truck, leaving the bat on the floor, and sped away from the garage.

50

———

Cole had already sent several email reports to his employer about Quinton's activities, and spiced them up with the antics of Hobbs, whom he identified as the defendant in one of Quinton's cases. But, when Hobbs sent Quinton to the hospital, Cole couldn't resist picking up the phone and calling the Boss in person. He activated the mini recorder as he'd done each time he'd called the Boss since hatching his blackmail scheme.

"Your boy just got the shit beat out of him and he's in an ambulance being unloaded at Hermann Memorial Hospital."

"What?"

"That's right, the drunk hillbilly finally snapped and sent Bell to the emergency room. I'm sitting in the parking lot right now watching Bell being wheeled into the ER at The Red Duke Trauma Institute. I followed the ambulance all the way over."

"Well, isn't that nice that we're getting some help torturing the guy."

"Yep. Didn't even have to get my hands dirty."

"Tell me everything."

Cole told the story blow by blow, not having to embellish much, and indicating his role as rescuer by honking and flashing his lights.

"You helped him out?"

"You said the hospital, not the morgue. I was following your orders even if I wasn't the one giving the beating. You said to make him suffer. Well, he's suffering, believe me."

The employer let out a hearty, evil laugh that turned into a cough that lasted several minutes. It caught Cole off guard. "You okay, Boss?"

"I couldn't be better."

Cole stood in the shadows in the corner of Quinton's hospital room and assessed the situation. Quinton was totally out, an IV snaking into his arm obviously delivering pain meds that would keep him under for a few days, if not longer.

Cole sighed, his shoulders slumping as he took in the sterile clinical surroundings. The rhythmic beeping of the heart monitor provided a dissonant backdrop to the disappointment that overwhelmed him. Being in the hospital only brought back painful memories of numerous visits with his wife as her health declined.

The promise of the money from the blackmail scheme now seemed a distant dream. Cole couldn't help but curse his luck, but he realized he had no control over the situation. Worse yet, what if Quinton died? That would leave him with no continuing money from the Boss and no blackmail either. The taste of bitterness lingered in his mouth.

A nurse entered, noticed Cole's presence, and said, "Visitors are not allowed this late. I'm sorry, you'll have to leave."

Dart and Anna sat by the side of Quinton's hospital bed waiting for him to awaken. When he finally came around, he could only see from one eye and could not move his neck or left arm which were both in traction.

Anna used a soothing voice. "Easy. It's Anna. Dart is here with me."

"Joanne?" Quinton muttered in a muddy voice.

"No, it's Anna and Dart. Do you remember what happened?"

Quinton mumbled. "A baseball bat."

Dart moved closer. "Broussard found the bat next to you in the garage. Someone called an ambulance but didn't hang around to help."

Quinton became more lucid. "Cops?"

"Broussard is looking into it. There are no fingerprints on the bat but there's blood where you cut him with that knife of yours. Good job."

"So, it came in handy after all."

Quinton succumbed to the pain meds and when he awoke again, both Anna and Dart were still there.

"Quinton?"

"Yes. I can see you, Anna. Go back to the office. I'm just going back to sleep now."

"There's something else we have to tell you."

Quinton answered but didn't open his eyes. "I'm listening."

"It's about Channing. Remember Van, the maintenance man at the office?"

Quinton mumbled. "Van the Man."

"I'm sorry to have to tell you this, but when Channing left the office the night that she delivered food, Van overheard a conversation she had on the phone with someone. He was in the hallway, but Channing didn't know it."

"What did she say?"

"She was reporting that you would not take the settlement. She said she had tried to convince you, but you weren't going for it and that the two of you had a spat about it."

"Who? Why? Hollingsworth? Hobbs?"

"Van didn't know."

Quinton closed his eyes and felt the pain of her betrayal outweigh the pain of his injuries. "I forwarded her the Hobbs alcoholism memo you prepared. I asked her for advice about sobriety rates. She knew I was going to spring it on Hobbs at trial."

Anna held back tears as Dart put his hand on Quinton's shoulder.

Dart was guarding Quinton in the hospital room when Channing dropped by for a visit.

"I can't let you in here."

"Why not? I just want to check on Quinton and see if I can help."

"Not today."

Quinton heard them talking and looked at Dart. He was out of traction, but still unable to sit up fully. He could see with both eyes, which looked like raccoon's.

"It's alright, Dart. Give us a minute."

"I'll be right outside the door."

"Thanks."

Channing placed her purse in a chair and moved over to the bedside with no small amount of trepidation. "What's going on? I came by the first night you were here, but you were out of it and I couldn't speak with you."

"You betrayed me. I know you've been feeding information to the other side." He wasn't completely sure about all she had done, but he was sure she was guilty of something and wanted to draw the information from her.

"What do you mean? What betrayal?"

"I know. You called them when you left my office."

Channing knew she was caught and gave in. Her eyes filled with remorse, but it was too late. "I'm so sorry, Quinton. I didn't know I was going to develop such feelings for you. I needed the money and..."

"How could you betray me like that after what happened with Joanne?"

"They chose me because I don't look like her. They didn't want me to remind you of her, just the opposite."

"Who chose you? Who are you reporting to? How did you get past Judge Garzon?"

"I'm sorry. I can't say any more." She grabbed her purse and turned to leave. "I'm so sorry."

Dart grudgingly let her pass.

51

Broussard entered Quinton's hospital room to find him out of traction and sleeping on pain meds, with Dart by his side.

"Hey, Broussard." Dart got up and the two men shook hands.

"How's Counselor Bell coming along?"

"He's still pretty much hamburger meat. Broken and bruised."

"You guarding him?"

"Yeah. Making sure they don't come back for another try."

"Has he been able to tell you what he thinks happened?"

"Not much. He went into the parking garage and somebody jumped him. Said it was a man with a baseball bat, but he didn't see his face."

"That's it? We found the bat but can't locate the ambulance caller. Burner phone."

"He said someone blew a car horn but didn't try to help him or stop the guy with the bat."

"Strange."

"Yeah. Unless he was warning the guy with the bat that someone was comin'. Nobody else showed up, though."

"I'll wait a bit for him to wake up. See if he remembers anything new. Want to take a break, maybe get some coffee?"

"I wouldn't mind going outside for a while. Hate this hospital smell."

"Me too. I'll be here until you get back."

"Thanks."

Broussard sat for about twenty minutes until Quinton started to stir. He looked at the detective, not sure if he was awake or dreaming.

"Welcome back to the living, Ami."

"Hmm." Quinton mumbled and pointed to a cup of water with a straw.

Broussard stood and handed him the cup. Quinton took a long sip and handed it back.

Broussard sat back down in the guest chair. "You look like Louisiana roadkill. Any idea who it was?"

"None. The cowardly bastard came at me from behind. Looked like he had a baseball bat or some type of long pole."

"Yeah. We have the bat with blood on it, but no DNA to match it to. It's not your blood. Whoever it was isn't in our system."

"Have you considered Sonny's buddies? They seem to like baseball bats."

"Yep. Ruled them out. Most of them have records, remember. No matches there."

Quinton considered without responding.

Broussard looked at Quinton. "What about the guy who vandalized your house? Nothing new there? Any more threats lately? Emails or mail from disgruntled clients? Love notes from haters?"

Quinton wanted to tell him, but he just couldn't trust

anyone with his secret. "Nothing new. All my clients are happy campers. I still don't know who vandalized the house."

Broussard's face turned serious. "You're a lying yellow dog."

Quinton was taken aback. "I've told you what I saw and I haven't had any new threats, or threats from clients at all."

"You've been holding out on me since I met you and you know more about this than you're saying. You think you have a poker face, but I read people for a living."

"Broussard, I'd love to help you find the bastard who did this so I could take him down myself, but I don't know who it was."

Dart came back in the room holding two cups of coffee with plastic lids. He offered one to Broussard. "They fresh outta chicory, but it's hot."

"No thanks. I'm finished here. Take care of our boy. He's going to need it."

52

All was lost. Quinton checked himself out and left the hospital, alone with the Uber driver, and went to his condo to brood. He had been betrayed by a woman he thought he could love and had blown his only theory for the case he was fighting. Worst of all, a blackmailer was threatening to take the last of his go money. No Channing, no strategy, no hope for Lily, and no backup plan.

To beat it all, he'd broken a cardinal rule and invested his own money in the case, further taxing his go money and ability to flee. How many times had his former partners in New York told him to never invest in a client's case? Always a retainer upfront, or at most, do it pro bono or for a percentage. Retainer or time only. Never cash.

He had been so sure he could win, and now he was about to lose not only his money, but the income for Lily. How would she survive? The little she had would be gone in under a year. He couldn't take it. The stress. The disappointment. The pain he was in that painkillers could only partially relieve, and not forever. He got himself into bed, took a double dose of the drugs, and slept for two days.

When the meds wore off, and the fatigue was relieved, he awoke with a start, his muted phone showing twenty-three text messages and over thirty emails. He ignored them and tried more medication to get ahead of the pain that had returned. His face had healed a lot, but his shoulder and arm were still sore. He could have managed at this stage with Advil or Tylenol, but he chose to stay with the heavy meds. His body was healing, but the pain was in his heart, and in his pride.

The full brunt of the last few weeks bore down on him, and he couldn't take it. He could not risk his secret anymore. Not for the case or for his law office, and not for his life as Quinton. He picked up the phone and made a plane reservation.

Run. Run.

Quinton boarded the plane at William P. Hobby Airport bound for Las Vegas. He asked the flight attendant for a shot of tequila, and used it to gulp down an additional painkiller. He was sore all over, but that was just an excuse. He was dodging the fact that he was losing in court and losing had never been an option for him. He didn't know how to lose. And worse, someone had the goods on him and he had no idea who it was. He didn't know how to combat the blackmailer, and he saw no way to bounce back. He only knew that he was afraid and that he hurt inside and out.

As he sank deeper into his window seat, the low hum of the engines reverberated through the cabin, the rhythmic sound provided escape as he drifted in and out on the pain meds and booze. He didn't want to question his impulsive decision or think about what he was doing. He just wanted to get away. He had to leave it all behind. He'd gambled and lost.

Quinton also wanted the feel of the cards in his hands, the flick of the deal, and the sounds and smells of the poker room. Mostly, he wanted something he could control. The bet was up to him, the cards were his to play, the power of the poker table called to him. He could control something in his life, even if it was just the turn of a card.

Quinton's last thought before he settled into a deep sleep was of Channing. The look on her face when he'd called her out. The stab he felt when he realized the truth of her betrayal. The loss of another woman that he'd cared for.

Mo Powers, as Quinton's second chair, skillfully navigated the courtroom, arguing for a continuance on Quinton's behalf. Judge Garzon, though displeased, yielded to Mo's assertion that Quinton was recovering in the hospital and unable to attend. Despite the judge's reservations, he reluctantly granted the continuance. He was not willing to risk having a higher court overturn his trial court decision. Besides, what else could he do? Mo could not try the case alone, and there was no one else to step in.

Mo served as the intermediary between the courtroom and the unspoken worries about Quinton's condition. Legal matters and medical updates became intertwined as Mo worked diligently to maintain a delicate balance. The continuance offered a brief respite, but the uncertainty surrounding Quinton's return lingered, leaving the fate of the case hanging in limbo. So far, she had continued to convince the court that he was in bed trying to heal.

When Mo had learned that Quinton left the hospital

without advising her or his office, she went to his condo to find him. She knocked on the door, and finally banged so hard a neighbor came out to check on the commotion.

"Have you seen Quinton Bell?"

The neighbor shook her head and closed her door, leaving Mo to worry and wonder where he was and what he was doing. *Could he be dead in there?*

The court would not wait forever, and it was becoming her responsibility to report Quinton's discharge from the hospital and absence from his office and home. Had the mugger found Quinton and finished the job this time? She called Anna at Quinton's office and asked her to report his absence to Detective Broussard and have him check to see if Quinton was okay.

Mo decided to give it the weekend. If Quinton did not resurface, she'd go to see Judge Garzon.

53

When Quinton arrived and navigated his way around Vegas, at first he felt relief. No one knew who he was and no one knew where he was. He purchased a few extra articles of clothing that he'd forgotten during his hasty packing in Houston, added a few disguises from the Goodwill Store on Sahara, and was ready for the poker rooms.

He made the rounds from one casino to the next, raking in a few thousand here and a few thousand there. He loved winning, and he loved the escape of it all. But, no matter how many card games he played, Vegas was not the cure he had hoped it would be. His wounds were healing, and he expertly covered the remaining bruises on his face with makeup techniques he'd learned from his days in Reno and from the plastic surgeon who'd reinvented him with Q's nose.

Today, he was playing at Binion's, formerly The Horseshoe. Quinton smoothed back the crown of his slicked-back blackened hair and adjusted his dark sunglasses, hiding his eyes. He wore a navy sport jacket that made him blend into the Las Vegas crowd. He'd taken a few precautions to avoid the watchful eyes of the Irish mob who might still be seeking retribution. Or, maybe it was just habit with him, to gamble incognito. Here he was again, hiding behind the facade of other people's personas.

He walked through the glittering entrance of the high-stakes poker room at the familiar casino and listened to the clinking of chips and hushed conversations. The smell of cigars and aged whiskey hung in the air as he approached the high-dollar poker table. That's when Quinton saw him. His hero, the legendary Texas Dolly himself, Doyle Brunson. The Dolly was sitting with his back to a wall in the far corner of the room, wearing his familiar cowboy hat casting a shadow over his aged, craggy face.

It was one of Quinton's lifelong dreams to play a round with The Dolly. Quinton went to the cage for a twenty-thousand-dollar tray of chips, then approached the table. The floor monitor took note of the large tray and allowed him through the velvet ropes. Quinton took a seat, exchanging a polite nod with the players already seated. The Dolly, reflective neon rainbows dancing around him, didn't look up.

The dealer shuffled the cards with an expert flourish and Quinton watched as the deck split and merged, the anticipation building with each flick of the dealer's wrist. The deal was smooth and polished as the dealer slid the cards across the velvet tabletop.

Quinton peeked at his hole cards, a pair of eights, heart and spade. It wasn't a stellar hand, but he had a lucky feeling, so he decided to ride it for a bet or two. The first three community cards were revealed on the flop: ten of hearts, eight of diamonds, and the four of spades. Quinton's heart raced as he now held three eights, a powerful hand. He maintained his poker face and watched the other players' reactions to their new cards. All experienced players, they revealed little.

Betting and checking went around the table, until the turn rested on Doyle Brunson, who raised the bet. Quinton considered, then called. The other players folded one by one, leaving just the two Texans in the hand, Quinton and The Dolly.

Quinton temporarily forgot his troubles, and instead remembered every word of the book by Brunson titled *Super Systems*. Quinton had read and earmarked it so many times, it was almost pulp when he'd abandoned it in Reno during his escape to Houston.

The turn was revealed, the four of hearts. Quinton now had a full house. He couldn't help but steal a quick glance at his opponent and idol, trying to decipher Doyle's expression through the shadow created by the hat. Doyle checked, and Quinton sensed an opportunity. With a confident, but hidden grin, Quinton pushed a large stack of chips forward, raising the bet. Doyle leaned back in his chair, studying Quinton's every move. As the tension rose, players began to gather around the outside of the velvet ropes dividing the high-stakes table from the rest of the room. After a tense moment, Doyle matched the bet, and the tension rose higher.

The river card was revealed, an ace of hearts. It did nothing for Quinton's hand, but what if the Dolly was holding trip aces? What if he now had four of a kind? What if? What if? Doyle checked once more, his eyes narrowing.

Quinton took a deep breath and pushed the rest of his chips into the center of the table. "All-in."

Doyle stared at the chips, his face unreadable. After a seemingly eternal pause, The Dolly matched the bet and said, "Call."

Quinton turned over his cards, revealing his full house. The Dolly slowly revealed his hand, three aces. Quinton's heart soared as he realized he'd won. He slammed against the chair back, so stunned he forgot to rake in the chips. The other players at the table and in the room applauded the thrilling moment, and Quinton felt a rush of excitement. He slipped a single one hundred dollar Binion chip into the pocket of his jacket, as a keepsake of an amazing experience.

In the next hand, the Dolly took back a large portion of Quinton's chips, as well as those of the players around him, but Quinton didn't care. He'd sat down at the table with the great man, arguably the greatest player of all time, and he'd won.

Quinton had left his troubles behind and didn't think about Houston or Lily Collins until the wee hours when he returned to his room and passed out on the bed with his clothes on.

Cole had watched Quinton as he made his way to the high-stakes table and taken a big pot off The Texas Dolly. Cole had been on Quinton's plane from Houston and had watched the pitiful display of self-indulgence and self-pity displayed by Quinton with the meds and booze. When Cole had reported it to the Boss, they'd both taken a special pleasure in Quinton's discomfort.

Now, his prey seemed to be in fine spirits. Sometimes, this Quinton guy was a lot of fun to follow and watch, buying new cars and gambling in Vegas. If all his jobs were like this, he'd never finish off the target, as he'd done so many times before. The Boss hadn't given the final word on this one, but he knew his employer was not going to fund the cat and mouse game forever. Cole had noticed a slight shift in interest the last time he'd reported in. Maybe the Boss had had enough, maybe Cole could stretch it out a bit longer.

Cole had planned to take Quinton out after the blackmail payment, regardless of the order from the Boss. It would just be safer if Quinton was out of the way when he left town. Of course, he had planned on collecting the blackmail before that happened. He had no real proof that Quinton was not who he said he was, but the Boss was sure about it and that was enough for him. He'd planned to ride it out until he collected the blackmail money from the locker, hopefully have the word from the Boss to take Quinton out, and either way, leave H-Town a happy man.

Now, he didn't know if he'd see the blackmail money at all. It wouldn't do much good to threaten Quinton in Vegas, he might hop on another plane and Cole might lose him. If he was on the run, the threat of blackmail wouldn't affect him anymore. Cole thought that maybe he'd turned up the heat a bit too high with the second blackmail note. Maybe Bell was more scared than he'd realized. *Too late now.*

Cole found his room, set an alarm, and passed out on the bed, four doors down from Quinton.

When Quinton awoke the next day around noon, he avoided the painkillers and ordered a pot of black coffee and toast from room service. He sat in his boxers in a chair in front of a big picture window overlooking the strip and had a "Come to Jesus" meeting with himself.

When he had presented his case in court, he had been confident that he would secure a fair and sizable verdict for his client, Lily Collins, and a return on his investment. Quinton had meticulously prepared for the hearing, poured his heart out to the jury, and invested his whole being in defending Lily and her dead mother, Charlotte Collins.

He knew something was amiss when, time after time, defense counsel, Hollingsworth, targeted his arguments as if he'd researched them in advance and predicted his every move.

Step by step, the case had slipped through his fingers like grains of sand, leaving him dumbfounded and humiliated. Even Mo was flabbergasted at the dance she was watching between Quinton and Hollingsworth. She'd been in court with Quinton many times, and she'd never seen him beaten.

When Quinton had finally discovered that Channing was his betrayer, it all made sense. Her disloyalty cut as deep as the courtroom failure. She'd finally admitted her complicity when he'd confronted her and seemed sorry for her behavior, but to what end? He'd never forgive her or trust her again. He'd debated whether to have her arrested, brought before the court, or heaven knows what. But he had no real proof, and there wasn't a remedy that would do him any good. The damage had been done.

He couldn't remember exactly when Channing could have gained access to his files and strategy, but there were several opportunities while he was recovering from their lovemaking. She might even have returned later if she'd stolen his keys and had copies made. Hell, he'd told her everything he was planning each time he saw her, thinking she was his ally and Lily's defender.

As far as he knew, Dart was still sorting it all out by researching CCTV footage. Anna was checking computer login records and comparing them to Quinton's calendar. Either way, Channing's betrayal was so cold and calculated that it had left him reeling and fleeing from the unbearable circumstance.

Now, he was sorry he had cut and run. Escape was becoming a habit that he didn't admire in himself. He'd run from Dannon in New York, and now from his stockpile of worries in Houston, including a blackmailer who was trying to bleed him like a stuck pig.

How could he abandon Lily like that? She had also been betrayed by Channing and he'd left the young girl to fight alone, with only the foster parents on her side, and they weren't trained to handle the legal side of things. What would his mother think of his behavior? She would not be proud. Sitting before the large-paned glass window, he felt as naked and vulnerable as he was, a small figure facing the mammoth Las Vegas strip and wondering what to do.

He beat himself up for a few more minutes, drank more coffee, and brooded further. He knew he couldn't wallow in self-pity forever. He needed to find a way to salvage the case, to turn the tide in Lily's favor. But how? How could he recover from such a devastating blow? And, how could he evade the blackmailer?

Nothing came to him, but he knew he had to go home to Houston. The trip had been a reckless escape from the mounting pressure. The pity party was over, and he had to go back. He'd had enough running. It was time to face the music.

54

Quinton's plane touched down at Houston Hobby airport and he felt deflated as he disembarked. The familiar Texas heat hit him like a wall as he exited the terminal, carrying his overnight bag and his ever-present go bag, and looked for his Uber.

The adrenaline of the casino floor had temporarily drowned out his worries, but that could not last. The truth was, he was not a quitter. The weight of his problems was heavy, but not as heavy as those of Lily Collins. How dare he compare his plight to hers, an injured child who needed him and was counting on him.

Cole trailed behind Quinton down the arriving flights area and through the airport. As he walked, Cole spoke into his mobile phone.

"He's back in Houston. We just landed at Hobby. Not sure what his plan might be."

The Boss clucked his tongue and considered. "Maybe it's time for an intervention."

Quinton had the Uber driver drop him directly at his SUV in the parking garage of his condo, and without going upstairs, he threw his bags in the hatch and headed to the beach house in Galveston.

Once there, he sat alone on the front steps of the Victorian home, listening to the waves crash in the turbulent waters of the Gulf of Mexico. Upon arrival, he had shed his clothes and put on a pair of beach shorts. Now he sat, barefoot and bare chested, still not knowing what to do.

He had come here to calm the turmoil in his mind and find solace in the sea's quiet rhythm, but it seemed that even nature conspired against him. A storm out at sea was causing dark clouds to hang overhead and huge waves to crash against the seawall. He took a long pull from a beer that still had sweat dripping from the bottle. Despite the sweet brew, the bitter taste of defeat and betrayal still lingered on his tongue.

He finished the beer, walked to the shoreline, and dove in. He swam so far out, he could barely see the seawall from the distance. He swam back, weak and shaky, walked the beach, plopped down on the sand, then waited and hoped his resolve would return. The lapping of the Gulf of Mexico against the shore became a mantra for him. "Fight, fight, fight."

The salty breeze ruffled his disheveled hair as the cloud cover began to shift. He waded in the waves to wash off the sand and knew that the answer was not here in Galveston, but back in his office in Houston. He had to summon the strength to fight back, to rebuild his case from the ground up, to pull a rabbit out of the proverbial hat. How? What could he do?

Don't forget your second wind.

He didn't have a plan, but he knew deep in his heart that justice could prevail. He had to try. He walked back to the house, showered and dressed, secured the premises, and headed to Houston.

55

Quinton parked his SUV in front of Kevin and Jess's house and felt a twinge of anxiety. Channing, as Lily's guardian, had been a pillar of support for her, and since she had disappeared from the case, he felt obligated to break the news to Lily and reassure her foster parents.

He sat in his car for a moment, gathering his thoughts. He had chosen a simple blue twill button-down shirt and a pair of jeans for the visit. He did not want to appear too stuffy in his usual coat and tie. He took a deep breath and made his way to the front door.

Kevin and Jess had been expecting Quinton's visit and welcomed him warmly as they had done every time he had visited Lily. They had promised to let him break the news to her, but she seemed to know something was up. She sat on the sofa in front of an animated film featuring a mermaid, but she was not looking at the screen. Her pink dress was pulled down over her knee, hiding the stump and revealing only one leg below the hem, wearing a pink sock and black patent shoe.

"Please, sit down. Would you like some iced tea?" Jess offered as she rounded the island into the kitchen.

"That would be great." Quinton took a seat in an overstuffed chair next to Lily who still hadn't acknowledged his presence. He used the most gentle voice he could muster. "Lily, I have something important to discuss with you."

"Is it about Channing? She's always with you when you visit. Did you have a fight?"

So, she was paying attention after all.

"The judge has transferred her to another case. He might appoint someone else, but if it's alright with you, I'd like to ask him to just let Kevin, Jess, and I make the decisions from here on out. I don't see a good reason to bring someone else in now, unless you want to."

"I don't want anyone new. I'd have to tell them the whole story all over again. Just you three look out for me, please." Trying to appear mature, her eyes welled up with tears and she looked down at her lap. "Did Channing not want to be my guardian anymore?"

Kevin and Jess exchanged worried glances, silently conveying their concern for the young girl. Channing had been a constant in her life since the accident, and her absence left a void and disrupted the carefully built bridge of trust between Lily and her adult caretakers.

Quinton reached out and placed a reassuring hand on Lily's shoulder. "I know this is tough, but sometimes things change. Lily, I want you to know that I'm here for you. I'm not going anywhere. I promise to do everything in my power to win your case and make sure you get the justice you deserve."

"Do you really mean that?" Her voice quivered and tears glistened in her eyes.

"Yes, Lily. You have my word. You can call me any time you

have doubts." He smiled at her to lighten the mood. "Do you still have my phone number?"

Lily pulled the drawing paper out of her pocket on which Quinton had written his phone number the first day they'd met. She showed it to him. He smiled again and patted her arm.

Lily managed a weak smile in return. "Thank you, Quinton. I believe you."

Now, just don't let her down.

56

Anna shooed Van out of the break room and put on a pot of coffee. She had been stuffing him full of cookies each afternoon in gratitude for his discovery of Channing's betrayal. Now, Anna told him to go back to work and ordered Chinese food to be delivered. It was going to be a long night.

Quinton had called from the Galveston house and put both Anna and Dart on notice that work was required. Neither had quizzed Quinton about his absence. Maybe they thought he was still healing from the beating. Maybe they, having delivered the news in the hospital about Channing, thought it was still too sore a subject. The small team gathered in the conference room, which had been converted to the war room for the case. Quinton pointed at the boxes and computers.

"Okay. We're going to go back through everything. There has to be something we can use in all these documents. No detail is too small. Start from the beginning. Try to read as if you've never seen the information before."

Each poured a cup of coffee, took a box of files, found a

chair, and started reading, sorting, and organizing the information from a fresh point of view. The team worked tirelessly for
hours, combing through the files and documents. Dart occasionally paced around the room, eating with a plastic fork from
a box of kung pao shrimp, his frustration showing with each
passing minute and bite.

Also exasperated, Anna said to Quinton, "We've been
through all of this multiple times. There's nothing new here."
Just as she was about to slump into her chair in defeat, Dart's
voice cut through the tension. "Hey, guys, I think I found
something."

Quinton looked up from a stack of papers. "What is it?"

Dart pulled his chair over and shared a document he was
reading. "It might be nothing, but I don't remember being given
a copy of an interview with this Jesse Peters, a motorcycle rider,
in the original discovery. You had me make a list of all the
witnesses and I checked them off one by one. This guy wasn't
on my list. I'd have remembered the bike."

"Check your spreadsheet of witnesses."

Dart opened his laptop and pulled up his list and scrolled
down to the P's. "Nope, not here."

Quinton leaned forward, his eyes narrowing in focus on the
newly discovered document. "This is just a memorandum, not
the full interview. Very cryptic. Maybe the defense tried to bury
this witness in the piles of discovery."

Anna read over Quinton's shoulder. "Is this the break we
need?"

Quinton's eyes gleamed with determination. "I don't know,
but at least it's something new. Dart, contact Mr. Peters first
thing in the morning. We need to get his full statement and find
out his account of what happened on the date of the accident."

Dart nodded. "Do you want to request the full document?"

"No. Let's let opposing counsel think we've missed it. Try to get the full story from Peters."

"I'm on it."

57

The next day, Dart drove through the gray, wet morning down I-10 toward Jesse Peters' home. He was out early because he wanted to catch the potential witness before he left for work. Dart hoped he was not a shift worker, and he'd come all this way just to miss him. The relentless rain hammered Houston's concrete jungle, transforming the city into a labyrinth of slick streets and gleaming reflections.

Dart nursed a cup of hot coffee, his eyes going back and forth from the rain-smeared window to the dashboard GPS, showing the way. Houston's dark and shadowy venue reflected the complexity of the case. Dart's journey to uncover the truth was paramount. He knew how much Quinton needed his help, and he was determined to give it.

As Dart turned onto Park Street in Jesse Peters' neighborhood, he began to count off the house numbers looking for the right house. The GPS showed a dot on the right side of the street, so he only looked there.

Upon arriving at the Peters' residence, Dart noticed a car in the driveway and parked his vehicle nearby on the street. He did not see evidence of a motorcycle, but it was probably safe from the rain and theft in the garage. He was hopeful as he approached the door and raised his hand to knock. Before he could make contact with his fist, the door was opened by a young man with a messenger bag over his arm, apparently headed to work. Peters stepped back at the sight of the hulking Dart and said feebly, "May I help you?"

"I hope so. Are you Jesse Peters?"

Peters relaxed a little, but not entirely. "That's me."

"I'm Dart Owens. I work for a lawyer in Houston named Quinton Bell. He's sent me out here to find you."

"What for?" Peters looked back inside the door where Viola had moved over and was listening behind him.

"Mr. Bell represents a party involved in the eighteen-wheeler accident that you witnessed. We just found out 'bout you yesterday."

Peters' initial surprise gave way to a look of apprehension. "I didn't witness the accident, but I was wondering why I never heard back from the police. I thought I'd hear from someone about my statement. They had sent out a plea over TV and seemed to be motivated to find the motorcycle driver. Then, crickets."

"Have you been followin' the case in the news?"

"We looked, my wife and I, but we didn't see much other than the fact that a class action was formed by a lawyer representing the drivers of the cars in the pileup. Is that your lawyer?"

"No, my boss only represents one plaintiff, a little eight-year-old girl whose mother was killed. I'm sorry no one got in touch with you, but we're here now and could really use yo' help."

"Well, like I told the authorities, I didn't see the accident. I didn't even know that it had occurred. I never put two and two together until I saw the plea for witnesses, and my bike, on the news."

"That's okay. We don't need you to testify to anything except what you did. I'd really like to have you come in and talk with Quinton Bell. He can explain all this much better than I can. I'm just glad I foun' you. It could lead to a crucial piece of evidence that might lead to justice being served for that little girl."

"How so?"

"We saw in your statement that you passed the white Camry. That's the car we're interested in. You may be able to help us. A little girl's future is at stake."

At this point, Viola pushed the door farther open and joined the conversation.

"What little girl?"

"Her name is Lily Collins, and her mother was driving the white Camry. Lily was in the back seat when her mother was killed in the pileup."

Viola gasped. "Oh my God. How awful."

Peters echoed her sentiments. "That's tragic."

"That's why I'm here. To get yo' help."

"What if they try to say that Jesse was somehow responsible for what happened?"

"That's not what we think, and I don't see how they could say that, but Mr. Bell can answer all those questions. Just a conversation. No obligation on yo' part. Please, both of you can come in together."

Peters looked at Viola. "I'm just not sure."

Dart played the sympathy card. "Lily lost one of her legs in the accident and is so traumatized, she needs help. Mr. Bell is the only one on her side. We really need you. Please."

Peters and Viola looked at each other again. "We'll have to talk it over."

58

Quinton sat at his desk flipping through stacks of discovery in the Lily Collins case. It was after-hours, and the sun was already set. Anna had left over an hour ago. He heard a knock on the door of the outer office and rose to see who might be calling so late. As he went through the reception area, he pulled on his coat and pushed up the knot on his tie. When he arrived at the main office entrance, he looked through the glass in the sidelight of the door.

There stood Channing Ward. Quinton shook his head at her. She looked at him with pleading eyes and yelled, "Just let me in for five minutes."

He opened the door and stepped aside for her to enter but blocked her going farther into the office. He did not invite her into the inner sanctum or offer beverages. *No way.*

Channing stood nervously in the entry, clutching a slender stack of files in her trembling hands. Her usually confident demeanor had been replaced by an air of unease and vulnerability. Her presence had once been magnetic to Quinton, but now he could taste the bitterness of her betrayal.

"Channing, what are you doing here?" His voice dripped with a cold detachment.

She hesitated for a moment, her resolve wavering. She knew the risk she was taking by revealing what she knew. Still, her heart ached and she had to try. "Quinton, I came here to tell you something important about the Collins case."

Quinton raised an eyebrow, curiosity momentarily overriding his resentment. "What could you possibly have to say that's worth my time?"

She took a deep breath, her fingers white-knuckled around the files. "It's about Judge Garzon. He's been working with the defense team on the case."

Quinton's eyes widened in surprise. "What? That's impossible. Garzon is a highly respected judge. He'd never compromise his integrity like that."

"I did."

"You're not a judge."

"I took an oath, just as he did. I thought the same, but I've seen the evidence, Quinton. He's been passing information to the defense, helping them to build their case, calling close ones in their favor, and undermining you."

Quinton was stunned. *Wasn't one betrayal enough?*

Channing took a step closer to Quinton, her desperation palpable. "I came to you with this information because I want to make things right between us. I can't undo what I did, but I can't bear to see you lose this case and your reputation because of what I did and what Judge Garzon is still doing."

Quinton's eyes locked onto Channing's tearful gaze. He felt a mixture of emotions, but love was not one of them. His voice was low and resolute. "Even if it's true, which I doubt, this doesn't change anything between us."

Channing's shoulders slumped. "I didn't come here for that."

"What proof do you have?"

"I brought these files. If you look at them carefully, you'll see how the meetings with Garzon always preceded your losses in court. I included notes with my best recollection of two ex parte communications between Judge Garzon, Hollingsworth, and me, along with the dates. I know I'm guilty too, and I'm sorry."

Quinton didn't respond and she turned and left, her footsteps heavy with her failed attempt at restoring friendship. As Quinton locked the door behind Channing, he knew he'd never see her again. Some betrayals ran deeper than broken hearts. She had deceived not only him, but Lily. It was unforgivable.

He stood there with the files in his hands, feeling the weight of the betrayals and the actions that the information required him to take.

Quinton arrived at the chambers of Judge Blaylock and was greeted by Bailiff Grant.

"Hey, George. How's it going?"

"Fine, thanks. Judge is expecting you." Then, he lowered his voice. "Any new episodes?"

"Nope. I didn't call the therapist you recommended because, at least so far, I've been able to handle things myself."

"Keep the number handy, just in case."

"Will do. Thanks." Quinton slipped through the door to the judge's inner chamber.

"Howdy, Judge. I come bearing gifts."

"Not wings and waffles, I hope. It took me two weeks to work off the last ones."

Quinton laughed. "Nope. Just a couple of Nitro Cold

Brews." He took the drinks out of a brown paper bag and placed one on Judge Blaylock's desk.

"That'll get me going." The judge pointed to one of the guest chairs and Quinton sat down.

"I hate to say you're going to need it."

"Uh-oh. What's up?" The judge sat back against his chair, took a long drink, then waited for the other shoe to drop.

Quinton nervously cleared his throat as he prepared to divulge the unsettling news. "I believe there's been some serious impropriety happening in the Lily Collins case. It involves Judge Garzon."

The judge raised an eyebrow. "Go on."

"I've received some information that Judge Garzon has been sharing privileged information in chambers with the defense counsel, Jacob Hollingsworth."

Judge Blaylock frowned. "That's a grave allegation, Quinton. Are you sure about this?"

In that moment it hit Quinton that he was breaking the law by just being there, acting as Quinton Bell and sitting on his high horse reporting a district judge. He had forgotten that he was just as guilty of crimes as anyone else who walked through the doors of the courthouse he was in. He could only nod and pass him a copy of the information Channing had given him.

Judge Blaylock flipped through the file. He stopped on the third page and read a passage slowly and carefully. "Is this correct? Channing Ward was removed from the case after she admitted to you that she was giving information to the defense team?"

"Yes, Judge. She removed herself. The rest of the file is about the additional ex parte meetings between Garzon and Hollingsworth. Of course, we can't know what was said, outside of the fact that Channing Ward was present for two of the meetings."

Judge Blaylock scratched his chin. "Any communication outside of your presence as plaintiff's counsel is unacceptable. I'll have to address this."

"Unfortunately, there's more. Judge Garzon approved sixty percent attorney's fees to push the settlement of the class action portion of the case."

"That's highway robbery."

"They hid the excess in the expenses and management fee. The judge and Hollingsworth offered me a similar deal. I refused, but I have no proof."

"I'll have to verify every bit of this. I can't accuse a sitting judge without a thorough investigation."

Quinton nodded. "It's very troubling. I'll leave it in your capable hands."

The next hearing on the Collins case was called by Judge Blaylock's bailiff, George Grant. The emailed notice instructed Quinton and all other counsel of record to meet in Judge Blaylock's court in lieu of Judge Garzon's.

Dart walked into Quinton's office to deliver the notice. "Does this mean they are going to disqualify him? What about Hollingsworth?"

Quinton had received a call from Judge Blaylock. He relayed that the investigation revealed a series of emails, text messages, and security camera footage that painted a damning picture of the misconduct. Still, there was no smoking gun to prove that Judge Garzon had been doing anything more than chatting about the weather, except for Channing's assertions, and she was in no place to testify about honesty and truthfulness. No one else had heard any of the ex parte communications. Quinton reported the gist of the conversation to Dart, leaving out the boring parts, then summed it up. "Garzon will just get a slap on the wrist, but at least he's removed from the case. Probably nothing for Hollingsworth."

"That's all?"

"Unless we can prove he was bending the case in Hollingsworth's favor, it's the best we're going to get."

Dart grunted. "Same as it ever was."

59

Jesse Peters realized the gravity of the situation and the injustice that would arise if he did not help in the Collins case. Along with support from his wife, Viola, this pivotal moment of moral reckoning led him to face his fears and testify.

In preparation for the trial, Quinton, with the help of Dart, and a video camera, recorded Peters' remembrance of the day of the accident and sent it on to their expert witness along with every other piece of evidence they had gathered concerning the crash itself. The expert performed the necessary tasks and returned to Quinton's office with a presentation for his team to consider.

Quinton, Dart, Anna, and Jesse and Viola Peters sat around the table in Quinton's conference room in preparation for Peters' testimony at trial. The reenactment expert, Jane Bering, stood before the team, very professional in a dark pantsuit, with a remote control in her hand.

Quinton signaled for her to begin. "Give it to us exactly the way you'd present it in court."

"Okay. First, I'd expect you to toss me a softball question about crashes in general."

"Got it. Ms. Bering, In your expert opinion, what are the primary differences between regular car crashes and accidents involving large trucks?"

"I'm glad you asked." It broke the ice as those around the table laughed.

"But seriously, there exists a chasm between the crashes involving regular cars and those with hulking semitrucks. Four distinct differences set these vehicular cataclysms apart, each one a pivotal factor in the ensuing chaos. First and foremost is the contrast in damage inflicted. When two cars meet in a head-on collision, the harm might be contained, a crumpled bumper or a dented hood. But introduce a semitruck into the equation and the scale of destruction multiplies exponentially. The sheer mass and force of these colossal machines can carve a path of devastation.

"Moreover, are the differences between the experience of the drivers. Regular car operators are equipped with standard-issue licenses, their skills honed through routine journeys and traffic regulations. However, truck operators are a breed apart, professionals wielding specialized licenses and comprehensive training. These road warriors navigate the asphalt with a practiced precision, their expertise forged through years of experience and an intimate knowledge of the rigs they drive. They are, in essence, masters of the road, their every maneuver calculated and deliberate.

"Another stark difference lays in the number of casualties incurred. A collision between standard-sized cars typically involves the drivers and, at most, a few passengers. The injuries are contained within the confines of the vehicles. However, the narrative drastically shifts when an eighteen-wheeler is involved. Their size and momentum endow them with a terrifying capacity to wreak havoc on a grand scale. They can lay waste to multiple cars, a bus, pedestrians, or even an entire road construction crew. The list of potential victims can grow long.

"Lastly, the size of the vehicles themselves plays a pivotal role in determining the outcome of a collision. The sheer magnitude of a semitruck dwarfs that of an average car. When these two entities collide, it is a battle of David and Goliath, where size overwhelmingly triumphs. The laws of physics favor the larger mass, leaving the smaller vehicle at an insurmountable disadvantage.

"Next, you should ask me a question about reenactments and how they are created and why."

"Consider it asked."

Jane began again. "Accident reconstruction is conducted by professionals who use cutting-edge tools and scientific accident reconstruction techniques to answer questions around why a collision occurred. Evidence such as the final resting position of the vehicles involved, damage to vehicles and property, footage of the incident, as well as tangible pieces of evidence are all considered. Using this method, reconstructions can help determine cause and liability.

"Now you want to tell me to play the video."

Quinton responded. "Ms. Bering, please play the video."

Jane clicked the button on the remote and the reenactment began on the screen, which looked like an animated cartoon. The video showed Peters' motorcycle avoid the eighteen-wheeler and continue on down the road. Then, the large truck began to sway and hit Allison Parker's car on the side of the highway. Next, it showed Hobbs lose control of the vehicle and jump from the cab as it jackknifed across the road. Lastly, it showed Charlotte Collins' white Camry slamming into the truck which was clearly in her lane. At that point, Jane hit pause and waited for questions or comments.

Quinton was impressed. "Excellent. How do we show the estimated speed of each vehicle?"

Jane restarted the video from the beginning. She used a pointer which showed a small number in the upper right-hand corner of the reenactment. The number changed as the truck moved, indicating the estimated speed of travel.

"This number shows the speed of the truck. All other vehicles are going more slowly, indicating that the truck was the fastest moving vehicle on the highway at the point of collision."

Everyone at the table had been holding their breath and there was a collective release as the video ended with the truck grinding down, then teetering on the overpass wall.

"Good job, Jane. Let's back it up just a little to show Mr. Peters passing Charlotte Collins' Camry before he becomes involved with Hobbs' truck. If you could show the motorcycle's speed at that stage, then, it's good to go. Thank you."

The team gave a round of applause as if they'd just seen a blockbuster movie.

Jesse Peters took the stand in Judge Blaylock's courtroom to a packed house. The case had drawn attention across the tort bar, as well as with those who'd been involved on so many levels in the original accident. Peters was sworn in and took the stand, looking dapper in his best church suit. Viola sat behind the plaintiff's attorneys in the gallery.

Lily Collins was absent from court today. Quinton, and Kevin and Jess Matherly, had decided it was in her best interest not to re-live the accident in open court. If she ever wanted to see the reenactment in the future, it would be there waiting for her.

Quinton froze the demonstration at the beginning of the demonstration on a screen which was set up for the jury and walked up to the witness stand.

"Good morning, Mr. Peters. Thank you for being here today to shed some light on what happened on that fateful day when Charlotte Collins was killed, and Lily Collins was injured."

Peters nodded at Quinton and waited for the questions that he knew were coming. Quinton took him through his age, occupation, place of work, and residence. Peters answered clearly and concisely as each question was asked.

Quinton then pointed to the frozen animation on the screen.

"Thank you. Now, is this animated depiction an accurate representation of you driving your motorcycle past Charlotte Collins' Camry on that day?" Quinton pointed at the vehicles. "You, in this lane, and her in that lane?"

"Yes, that's correct. We were both traveling west on I-10 and I passed her just after this shot. I do not recall how many other cars were in the various lanes; those shown are my best guess."

"I see. Now, when you passed the Camry, were you speeding?"

"No, I wasn't speeding before I passed her nor did I accelerate past the speed limit to pass her."

"Was Ms. Collins weaving or changing lanes or doing anything unusual or reckless that morning?"

"No, the car was moving in a normal way at a safe speed of travel for traffic at that time of day."

"Okay, now if you were not speeding, and you passed Ms. Collins here, could she have been speeding?"

"No, I don't know her rate of speed, but it was slower than mine and I was not speeding."

"Okay, now you weren't actually involved in the accident, were you?"

"No. In fact, I didn't even know there had been an accident until much later when the police posted a photo of my motorcycle and asked that the rider come forward."

Quinton pushed the button on the remote and allowed the reenactment to run a few frames forward.

"Okay, Mr. Peters. Tell the jury, do you have any monetary stake in this case?"

"No."

"You're not being paid for your testimony, and you're not part of any settlement negotiations or lawsuits related to the accident?"

"No."

"Okay. Thank you. Now, did you provide the information necessary to show this portion of the reenactment where you encountered the eighteen-wheeler driven by Mr. Hobbs?"

"Yes. That's why I remember the Camry and the day so well. The eighteen-wheeler, which was speeding, attempted to change lanes without regard for my presence, and caught me between the truck and an SUV beside me. I accelerated and shot out of the bind. At that point, I was speeding and glad for it."

"Did you see the crash occur behind you?"

"No, I just took off, not realizing that anything else had occurred."

"Did you do anything else? Honk? Yell? Pull off the road?"

Peters looked at Viola in the gallery and hesitated. "Do I have to say?"

Judge Blaylock looked at Peters. "The witness will answer."

"Yes, sir. As I drove off, I flipped him the finger."

A small ripple of laughter passed through the gallery.

"Thank you, Mr. Peters. No further questions."

After the break, it was Hollingsworth's turn on cross-examination to question Peters. No matter how many ways he asked his questions, he could not get the witness to deviate from his testimony. Finally, he asked one last question.

"Mr. Peters, do you expect this jury to believe that you passed a Toyota on the highway all that time ago and you remember it, the color, and the speed it was traveling? How could you possibly remember something that happened before you ever encountered the eighteen-wheeler?"

"I remember because when I passed the white car, a little girl in the back seat held up a pink stuffed teddy bear and caused it to wave at me. My wife and I had been hoping for a child for some time, and it was both charming and poignant. I remember asking God to bring me a darling child of my own."

Hollingsworth stopped and looked at Peters, sincerity dripping off of him. "No further questions."

After the break, it was Jane Bering's turn on the witness stand. Quinton went through her pedigree, the length of time she'd been creating reenactments, and the assertion that she had created one for this trial. Next, he began the dog and pony show that they had rehearsed in his office with her testimony about who wins a battle between a car and a truck, how reenactments are created, and the use they have in trial. Finally, he picked up the remote and pointed it at the screen.

"Ms. Bering, is this the reenactment that you created?"

"Yes, in my expert opinion, it represents what happened on the date of the collision involving the parties in this case."

Quinton hit the button and the entire animation played out

for the jury to see. It was just as impressive as it was in his office, and there was no question in his mind that the jury believed every single frame.

60

Just when Quinton thought things were looking up for Lily and her case, Charlotte Collins' alleged common law husband, Philip Lyme, turned up again. He had a new lawyer, a young hotshot named Cassidy West, who was trying to get a practice started and would take just about any business that walked in her door. They set a meeting for later that week, and Quinton put Dart on notice.

"This guy, Lyme, stinks. He's a liar and a cheat. I know there's something back there we can use on him."

Dart nodded. "On it."

Dart called Broussard. "Remember that favor you owe Quinton for the help with Sonny's case? Well, it's time to pay up."

"Oh yeah? We paid his bill, what makes you think I owe him a favor?"

"'Cause you said you did."

"Oh, right. Me and my big alligator mouth. What do you want, Dart?"

"You hear about Quinton's big case for the little girl?"

"Of course. It's all over the news."

"Well, some lowlife name Lyme shows up saying he the girl's step-daddy. Has some affidavits that the first judge let into court to let him inherit from the mama. I need to find those folks. They just up and disappeared."

"Email the names and what addresses you have over to me and I'll take a look. No promises."

"Thanks."

Anna showed Lyme and his attorney, Cassidy West, into Quinton's office, offered coffee, and disappeared back to her desk. The three stood near the small conference table at the end of Quinton's office, as the large conference room was still set up as the war room for the Collins case.

Cassidy West offered her hand, which Quinton shook, but did not in turn offer his hand to Lyme.

"Ms. West, please have a seat."

The three settled around the table. "You can call me Cassidy or Cass."

Man, she was green. Short and petite, face like a high schooler, no stage presence whatsoever, not a threatening bone in her body. Quinton almost felt sorry for her. He remembered when he'd hung around Judge Blaylock's courtroom, hoping the judge would throw him a case or two. It's tough to start a law firm from scratch with no clients and no reputation to trade on.

"Okay, Cass. I understand you're preparing a lawsuit on behalf of your client?"

"That's right. Here is the draft." She slid a document across the table to him. "We want to see if we can work something out with you before we file it."

Quinton assumed that Lyme didn't want to put his name on anything, much less testify in open court. If he was lying, jail wouldn't be far behind. He read through the pleading which stated that since Judge Garzon had deemed the common law marriage valid, Lyme was entitled to a portion of any settlement or jury verdict won by Charlotte Collins' estate.

Quinton looked at Cass, then at Lyme. "I see. What did you have in mind?"

"Well, in Texas, as I'm sure you know, a spouse is entitled to one half of all accrued assets during the term of the marriage and half of the estate. Since Mr. Lyme and Charlotte Collins were estranged, but not legally divorced, it could be argued that Mr. Lyme is entitled to half of any income from the civil case. Of course, Lily Collins is entitled to all of her award or settlement and the other half of Charlotte Collins' award or settlement. If there was a house, car or other assets in the Collins' estate, Mr. Lyme would receive one-half of those as well."

Quinton listened respectfully to her recitation of the Texas Probate Code that any law school graduate would know. She did not seem to be wise to Lyme's character or any deceit he might be perpetrating. She just seemed to be trying to act as a good lawyer.

Cass continued. "We did some research and did not find any real estate in the name of Charlotte Collins in Harris County, so we assume she did not own a home at the time of her death. Mr. Lyme is not interested in any personal property that might have been in her rental."

That's big of him, Quinton thought. He pushed a button on the office intercom. "Dart, would you join us, please?"

Lyme squirmed a bit in his seat. Cass just looked curious.

Dart joined them at the table with six file folders, each containing several documents.

"This is my associate and investigator, Dart Owens. He's done some research into the alleged marriage between Mr. Lyme and Charlotte Collins."

Dart handed Cass three of the file folders and kept three duplicates, opening the first one. "If you'll open the file marked Robert Ewers, you'll see that Mr. Ewers has recanted his sworn affidavit. If you'll go to the second page, you'll see that he's executed a new sworn affidavit stating that not only did Mr. Lyme and Charlotte Collins not hold themselves out as man and wife, but Mr. Lyme swore that he was a 'rolling stone' who could never settle down, and that he left Charlotte Collins and Lily after about a year together."

Cass looked bewildered. "Why would he sign this?"

Dart responded. "Not in the documentation, but in confidence, Mr. Ewers advised that Mr. Lyme and his attorneys paid him one thousand dollars to sign the first affidavit."

Quinton added, "We did not pay him to sign the second affidavit but did threaten to report him to the new judge if he didn't tell the truth. The other two folders contain similar affidavits by the other two affiants that were filed in court."

Cass looked shocked. "I didn't know any of this. I would never participate in such a fraud on the court." She looked at Lyme with disgust.

Quinton said in a kind voice, "Maybe you should have done a little more homework before taking on the case."

Cass blushed pink from her blonde hair down to the top of her blouse. "I see that now. I thought since Judge Garzon ruled in Mr. Lyme's favor, it was safe to assume the affidavits were accurate."

Quinton looked at the young lawyer. "I can see why you'd think that. I tell you what, just so Mr. Lyme doesn't keep popping up and ruining my day, why don't we put this to bed once and for all?"

Cass recovered a bit. "How can we do that?"

"Well, I'll be presenting the new affidavits to Judge Blaylock, and you could come into court and argue that Mr. Lyme and Charlotte Collins are still married." There was an alternative hanging in the tone of Quinton's voice.

Cass picked up on the hint. "Or?"

Lyme slumped in his chair.

"You can join us in our information to the judge, and we can settle all claims against the estate right here and now."

Lyme piped up. "Do I get to keep my part of the class-action suit for my own pain and suffering that I got from The Hammer?"

Cass looked disgusted at her own client.

"As long as no one else comes after you. We won't be bothering."

Lyme took over his own case. "How would this work so I don't get in trouble?"

Quinton addressed Cass. "If we can settle on an amount, I can wire the money to your escrow account today. Mr. Lyme can leave town before Judge Blaylock hears about this. The rest is up to him."

Lyme looked as if he was liking the sound of it. "How much are you offering?"

Quinton scoffed and turned to Lyme. "You deserve nothing, but we'll add ten thousand dollars to what you already got from The Hammer. I assume your attorney will keep a third. You can be on the highway by tomorrow morning."

Cass nodded then looked at Lyme. "I think you're lucky it's not jail. I advise you to take it."

Lyme spat. "Well, I bet you do. You'll get a third for doing almost nothing."

"Take it or not. I won't be representing you further."

Lyme snarled at Quinton, "Fine. You have a deal."

Dart went to Anna's desk and instructed her on the documentation Quinton needed. In short order, the paperwork was prepared, printed, and executed by Lyme and Cassidy West, and notarized by Anna. The money was wired, and Phillip Lyme slithered out of town the same way he'd slithered in.

61

Q uinton sat with his client, Lily Collins, in the courtroom of Judge Blaylock. The air hummed with anticipation as the soft echo of footsteps on marble floors and the distant murmur of conversations were the only sounds that filled the noble room.

Quinton did not feel threatened by the environment today, as he had come full circle and what he could not do for Joanne, he could now do for Lily. And, if he was honest, for himself. He had overcome his fears, found some help in Dart, Broussard, and Anna, and although he was still hiding in plain sight, he was not alone.

Quinton also had a new talisman that he called The Dolly Chip. It was the one hundred dollar poker chip he'd slipped in his pocket, at Binion's in Vegas, on the day he'd won the round with The Texas Dolly. Today, he touched it in his pocket, for luck. They were going to need it.

Quinton patted the hand of young Lily, as her eyes darted around the room, taking in the unfamiliar surroundings. Judge Blaylock addressed the gathering. "We're here today to consider the motion of plaintiff's counsel, Quinton Bell, that his client, Lily Collins, be allowed to testify in open court. Mr. Bell, you set the hearing, please present your argument."

Quinton stood, shot his cuffs, and cleared his throat to address the court. "Your Honor, as you're well aware, the law regarding admissibility of a minor's testimony in open court must be weighed against the probative nature of her testimony. As there is no specific age requirement for a child to testify, it's within your discretion to allow Lily to speak in open court. The criterion for determining a child's competency to testify is their ability to understand and answer questions truthfully. We assert that Lily is very capable of doing that, and if necessary, we will be happy to have her capacity proven up before the questioning begins."

Opposite Quinton, Jacob Hollingsworth sat with a cold and calculating expression. He had no intention of allowing Lily to testify, a point he was about to argue vociferously. Her baby face and missing leg would end any chances his client might have in front of a jury, and he was not about to lose because of a baby-faced girl. Hollingsworth stood.

"Your Honor, may I be heard?"

"Go ahead."

"As the court is aware, Texas Family Code Section 104.003 is analogous to the current issue at hand. This section provides for a parent to be present if a child testifies. It is suggested in the Family Code that if a child is to testify, they do so by video-taped prerecording."

"Mr. Bell?"

"Your Honor, it would be unconscionable to deprive my client from testifying because her mother is not alive to be in court due to the very negligence of the defendants."

Hollingsworth, still standing, jumped in. "Your Honor, children's testimony has long been suspect and discouraged by the courts, especially in cases where a great deal of emotion is involved. We do not doubt Miss Collins' veracity, but she can be coached, and she can be mistaken, which often happens in cases involving child testimony. In addition, the most relevant testimony is the use of expert witnesses when an accident is involved at trial. The testimony of a child sitting in the back seat of a car cannot possibly add anything to the cause or outcome of the accident."

Quinton refuted the argument. "Lily's account of the accident is not only relevant, but also holds probative value in determining the truth behind this tragic accident. She was a direct witness to the accident, and her perspective is invaluable to what actually transpired in the car as her mother died and she lay wounded. We are down to the question of damages, and pain and suffering on the part of my client is the majority of those damages. She is capable of asserting her emotions and feelings around what happened and should be allowed to do so. For these reasons, Your Honor, we respectfully request that Lily be allowed to testify in open court."

Quinton paused, looked at Lily, then wrapped up his argument. "Most importantly, Your Honor, I believe in the power of Lily's words to bring justice for her mother and herself. She wants to tell her story, and I believe she has the right to do so."

With a nod from Judge Blaylock, Hollingsworth spoke. "Your Honor, we understand the emotional strain that this young girl has gone through, but the law is open to interpretation on minors testifying in court, and there are many reasons that Lily Collins should not testify in this case."

Lily looked at Quinton with questioning eyes as if to say: Will this man keep me from testifying? They both looked back at Hollingsworth.

"All right, I've heard enough, and read your briefs." Judge Blaylock furrowed his brow and considered the arguments before him. "Mr. Hollingsworth, while the law does limit the testimony of minors in open court, there are exceptions when their testimony is necessary for the interests of justice. I am reluctant to deny a grieving child her right to be heard. That said, the stress of being on the witness stand before a jury, a room full of reporters, and the pressure of cross-examination are weighing heavily in my decision."

Hollingsworth's face looked hopeful. Quinton, concerned that the opportunity might be slipping away, interjected. "Your Honor, may I propose a compromise?"

"Go ahead."

"We're willing to have Lily testify in your chambers, ensuring that her voice is heard while avoiding undue distress. You may ask the questions yourself so that they remain friendly and fair. Then, if you believe the testimony has probative value, we can play the testimony before the jury."

Judge Blaylock considered.

Hollingsworth was on his feet. "Your Honor, I object to the compromise. It still allows the testimony of a young girl to come before a jury without my client exercising his right to cross-examination. It's blatantly unfair and unduly prejudicial."

Judge Blaylock gave Hollingsworth the stink eye, as only he could. "Mr. Hollingsworth, do you doubt my ability to properly question this witness and evaluate whether any parts of her testimony should be shared with a jury?"

Hollingsworth was flummoxed. "Of course not, Your Honor, I only meant..."

"I know what you meant. Everyone be seated."

Quinton sat, patted Lily's hand, and held his breath. This could be the turning point. His pat on her hand was a prayer for justice and resolution. The whole ordeal had gone on long enough. It was time to put the matter to rest.

Judge Blaylock made his decision. "I will allow Lily to

testify before me in chambers. We'll set a date for the proceeding, and I will ensure the presence of a court reporter for a full record. That will preserve your appeal, Mr. Hollingsworth, if things don't go your way."

With the matter settled, Judge Blaylock banged his gavel and concluded the hearing.

Quinton leaned over and whispered to Lily, "We won this round. Fingers crossed for the rest."

Hollingsworth asked that the afternoon recess start early so that he and his team could prepare a response to the reenactment and Jesse Peters' testimony. The truth of it was there was not much they could ask or say other than to call Peters a liar or challenge his memory from the day of the accident. This tactic could backfire and make the defense team look petty at best, and stupid at worst. It was determined in a closed strategy session, led by Hollingsworth, that the test for contributory negligence could not be met the defense team.

In addition, with Judge Blaylock having granted the order for Lily's testimony in chambers, the defense counsel folded. Fearing the verdict, Hollingsworth phoned Quinton with a request for a settlement meeting. This time, Quinton had all the leverage he needed. He knew he could win at trial, so he was a bit cocky in his response.

"You know, Hollingsworth, I'm all 'meetinged out' and keeping company with cheaters like you has never appealed to me. Why don't you just send me an email with a number and we'll let you know if it's good enough. I don't intend to waste any more time going back and forth. You know the national average verdict on these cases, and we expect something in that ballpark."

Quinton was actually confident enough not to settle at all and take the big verdict he thought he could get from the jury, but nothing in court is ever guaranteed, and he wasn't that cocky. His largest remaining concern was that the companies would string things out with appeals and even a possible bankruptcy threat, and Lily needed money now. He wanted the trial to end so that she and he could get on with their lives, and the defendants probably preferred that it be over as well.

It was a glorious moment with the theme from *Chariots of Fire* playing in Quinton's head. He smiled all the way to the gym for a swim; this one for fun.

———

Quinton walked into Judge Blaylock's chambers juggling a bag of something that smelled delicious and a cardboard tray holding two coffee cups with lids.

Judge Blaylock looked up from the thick book he was studying. "Oh, I see you brought gifts. You must really need something this time."

Quinton laughed, put the coffee and food on the desk, sat in one of the guest chairs, and said, "You caught me."

"What's in the bag?"

"I see you have your priorities straight. Food first." Quinton removed a to-go carton. "Wings and waffles again from the Breakfast Klub."

"Are you trying to kill me?" Judge Blaylock laughed. "I'll have to workout double this week."

"You don't have to eat it." Quinton laughed and lifted a second carton from the bag. "I'll be swimming extra laps, but I'm going in."

Both men popped the folding lids from the clam shell

containers and the aroma made them throw their heads back and smile.

Quinton bit the end off of the wrap on a plastic fork and extracted the utensil. He tucked a napkin into his collar over his tie and dug in. Judge Blaylock followed suit, pouring a to-go syrup over his waffle, and both men chomped wings and waffles without speaking for a full five minutes.

Judge Blaylock took the top off his coffee, drank a long hot sip, and let out a sigh of satisfaction and said, "Okay, spill it. What do you want?"

Quinton wiped his greasy hands, from the wings, on a napkin and leaned into the chair back. "I think we're about to settle the Collins case."

"Thought you might."

"You didn't throw it my way, did you?"

"Nope. I did the right thing; it just happened to be what you needed."

"Well, thank you. Now I have this dilemma with my client, Lily. She has been waiting to tell the story of her mother and her loss for so long, and if we settle, she will not have her opportunity to speak. Her foster parents think it would be in her best interest to participate in her fate in some way if at all possible."

"So she's not victimized any more than she already has been?"

Quinton nodded. "Exactly."

"What do you propose?"

"I can't make it a condition of settlement that she testify. Once the settlement is concluded, there's no reason for her to give her statement."

"I know, but wonder if you might allow her to answer your questions in chambers, as we had originally planned at the hearing. She could come in, we could have a court reporter and video the Q and A. I could give you a list of questions that would do her the most good, then you could wing it with the rest. What do you think?"

"You didn't have to bring in Breakfast Klub, I'll be happy to hear her testimony."

"The wings and waffles didn't hurt."

"No, they didn't hurt."

Both men sipped their coffee and shared a satisfied smile of doing the right thing.

62

Broussard had been working Quinton's case ever since the arson of the Afton Oaks house and the hospitalization from the beating in the parking garage. Unbeknownst to Broussard, he was dealing with two perpetrators, not one. He assumed that the same man who'd vandalized the SUV and house, and set the fire, was the same man who'd assaulted Quinton. Since there was no clear CCTV footage capturing the image of the assailant, he was left with forensics and Quinton's report from his hospital bed during the initial interview. He also had a bat, and some blood; he just needed to find someone to match it with.

Quinton was not aware that Broussard was working the case so diligently, so he was spared the added stress of the detective possibly finding out his secret. Part of Broussard's diligence was the shadow of something hanging around everything that happened involving Quinton Bell. He knew something was going on and his dogged detective mind just wouldn't let it go.

Broussard walked through the garage at Quinton's office building, assessing the scene of the assault once again and hoping for lightning to strike in terms of a clue or intuition about how to find the perpetrator. He looked up at the useless security cameras and lamented how much people relied on them for a sense of security that really wasn't there. He passed the elevator to the lobby and continued on to a door at the end of the wall marked *Maintenance*. He pushed it open and found a cluttered space filled with mops, brooms, and a variety of cleaning supplies. In the midst of it all, hunched over a mop bucket was Van, who jumped when he saw Broussard.

"Sorry, man, didn't mean to scare you. I'm Detective Clive Broussard." He took his badge out of his pocket and showed it to Van who settled from the surprise, then guffawed his funny laugh and wiped his hands on a rag. "No problem. What can I do for HPD?"

"I saw in the police report that you were here the day they found Quinton Bell after he was assaulted. I wonder if you saw anything."

"Like I told the cop that day. I didn't see anything. I was working upstairs, fixing a plumbing leak on the fifth floor. By the time I got down here, it was all over and he was in the ambulance."

"Maybe you've remembered something since then? Sometimes people do."

"I'd tell you to look at the security footage, but I'm sure you already did that. It's for shit down here. Hardly covers anything in the garage."

"Yeah, it's hardly worth having except to record the license plates of those who come in and out. We're still going through the plates, but so far nothing of note."

"I've seen lots of people sit in their cars and work on their phones or set up a map before they take off. Nobody that's been here for long. 'Course, I don't hang out here much, just in and out of this room." Van wrinkled his nose at the smell. "Not the nicest place to be."

Broussard nodded and handed him a business card. "Right. Well, if you think of anything, please give me a call."

"Will do, HPD." Van guffawed at his attempt at TV humor.

Broussard left the maintenance room and headed to his car.

Van popped out the door and called after him, "I remember something."

Broussard turned back. "What?"

"There were these broken bottles of Wild Turkey. You know the small kind like drunks get at the liquor store? Funny thing about it, they were broken by the same parking spot three or four times over about a two-week period. Very strange. I had to clean it up over and over. I wondered if there was a squatter down here, but there's no place for them to hide for long, and I know they haven't gotten into the main building."

"Could you show me where the glass from the bottle was left?"

Van walked Broussard over to the spot where Hobbs had sat and drank three times a week, watching Quinton come and go.

"Right there." Van pointed to the line designating the parking spot.

"Here, on the edge of the spot. So, if someone was drinking in the car, they could drop the bottle beside it and drive off without rolling their tires over the glass."

"I guess so."

"Hmm. Maybe something. If it happens again, could you put some cones around the glass and call me?"

"Sure. Would you like to have the glass that I cleaned up?"

"You have it?"

"Yep. It's in there." The men walked back into the maintenance room. "I don't put broken glass in a trash bag. It rips. I put it in a box and when it's full, I close it up and take it out to the dumpster." Van pointed to a medium-size cardboard box with Amazon printed on the outside. It was folded over at the top with the four sides alternating and the last fold tucked under to hold it closed. Van popped it open.

Broussard squatted by the box and looked inside. There was a mix of broken glass, some lightbulbs, pieces of mirrors, and several labels that said Wild Turkey. Shards of glass were clinging to the sticky side of the labels. Broussard used a pen from his breast pocket to gently move the glass around.

"May I take this?"

"Sure. Save me some trouble." Van guffawed as if it was the most hilarious thing he'd ever said.

Broussard looked at him and smiled.

Broussard dropped by the law office and asked Lacey if he could have a few minutes with Quinton. Anna came over and offered to help, which disappointed Broussard because he didn't get to watch Lacey walk across the room.

"Yes, please. I just need a minute or two. I have some news on his assault case."

Anna pointed to a guest chair. "Please wait here and I'll check. I'm sure he'll be pleased to hear it."

Broussard sat for a while and watched a couple of lowlifes leave Quinton's inner office. Anna took him in and offered coffee and a seat.

"You work for the likes of those guys walking out of here?"

"Yes, Broussard. Those 'likes' are most of my clients. You know, criminals."

"Just when I thought I might actually like you, Cher."

"Well, it's good to see you too. What brings you by?"

"It was Hobbs."

"What was Hobbs?"

"The guy who assaulted you in the garage. We assume he set the fire and vandalized your car and house, too."

Quinton was astonished. "Hobbs the truck driver?"

"How many Hobbs do you know?"

"Well, I just find it hard to believe."

"It's him. Thanks to your maintenance man, we found his fingerprints on some glass debris left in the garage, and we matched it to his truck driver's license when we ran the prints through our database. He didn't wear gloves like he did with the bat. Left his prints all over the broken glass and labels. His blood is a match for the DNA where you cut him. We also found a notebook in his glove box. He's been following you and keeping a diary of when and where."

Quinton fell against his chair back. "Well. I never would have guessed. Are you sure he was at the house, too?"

"No way to know for sure, but how many people are out to get you these days?" Broussard laughed.

"Yeah, right." Quinton laughed too. "Did he say what he hoped to accomplish?"

"He didn't say much. Said you took his job and his life. Lawyered up after that."

"It's no excuse for the beating I took, but if someone took away my livelihood, I might be desperate too." Quinton stopped himself before he said too much.

He can't be the blackmailer, and the guy in my back yard wasn't Hobbs. Totally different build and height. Who else is after me?

63

Quinton was working in his condo when a knock at the door caused him to go into high alert and peek through the peep hole, but he saw no one. He cracked the door with the chain on and saw a small envelop on the floor. He removed the chain, picked up the envelop, slammed, and relocked the door. Using a kitchen knife, because his diving knife had been taken as evidence, he cut open the envelope and slid out the note from the blackmailer.

It said: Welcome Back. How was Vegas? Nice to see you at the bonfire. Want more? You have twenty-four hours. Same locker, same code, same time.

Quinton paced his condo, trying to think of a way around the blackmailer. If he didn't pay, would the follower actually out him? Would he do something far worse, like try to kill him or wipe out his home or office with another fire? He had never used his real name. Did he actually know who he was, or just know that he was not Quinton Bell?

From the message in the latest demand note, Quinton was now sure that the blackmailer was the perpetrator of both the vandalism and arson at the Afton Oaks home. He'd let Broussard think that Hobbs was the solo actor, but he wasn't sure that would hold him for long. Broussard was the least of his worries right now. The blackmailer required an immediate response. If money was all he wanted, maybe that would get rid of him for good.

He could pull together a million dollars in twenty-four hours, thanks to his fees in the Collins case, but he was terrified to go to the bus station alone. What if it was a trap? What if it was a ploy to get the money and take him out?

Seamus Devlin's evil mind could concoct such a scenario. What if he was running low on travel money? What if he wasn't working for Dannon anymore and needed cash? But there was no indication that Devlin was back or even alive, and how would he know that Quinton was really Byron? Hadn't that all been put to rest in the first chapters of this ongoing life story? It could be Tua Dannon, but Dannon would not bother with a measly million dollars. He would have wiped Quinton out the minute he knew he was really Byron.

The list of possible people who could know his secret was so small. He wracked his brain. Why couldn't he figure out who it was? Even if he paid, what about the next time? A million dollars only lasts so long if you're on the run, or if greed takes hold. The secret would be out there, and the blackmailer could come back at any time for more. What could he do?

Quinton decided to take it one step at a time. He'd put together the million in cash and have it handy. He'd be ready if he had to go through with it. In the meantime, he needed to trust someone. Quinton decided that someone was Dart.

Quinton met with Dart in the office after-hours so they could be alone, and Anna could not eavesdrop. After Anna's help bringing Channing's actions to light, Quinton trusted her, but he didn't want to have to explain himself to her, for her benefit as well as his. He had grown fond of her and wanted to keep her safe from any harm around his secret life.

Dart ambled in with a Big Gulp in his beefy hand. "Wassup?"

"Hey, Dart. Have a seat."

The big man tucked himself into a guest chair in front of Quinton's desk and Quinton came around and sat in the other chair. He turned to face Dart. "I need your help."

"Sho'."

"I mean, I need it for personal reasons. Not work. I've got a problem."

Quinton hated to deceive Dart, but he felt he had to. He had prepared a story in advance and launched into it now.

"Shoot."

"When I was back in my Q days, I did some things I'm not very proud of."

"We all did."

"Right. But now, one of those things has come back to haunt me. I'm being blackmailed and I've decided to pay. I want you to go with me and watch my back when I deliver the money."

"Will guns be involved?"

"No, I don't think so. I just need to drop the money off at a locker and I want to make sure that the blackmailer isn't really there to get me after he gets the money. I don't think so, but I don't want to go in there with no backup."

"You sho' you want to pay this bastard? You thought it through?"

"I have."

"How much we talkin'?"

"One million dollars."

"Whoa. No shit? For a million dollars, I'd jus' take him out."

"You're kidding, right?"

"Yeah, but it's tempting. What the hell did you do?"

"I don't want to tell you about it because I don't want you to get pulled into the past. This way, you can deny knowing anything."

"And, you don' want me to know what you capable of?"

Quinton paused. "True. Regardless, I've thought it through, and I think I should pay."

"Okay, but I'm bringin' a gun. Jus' in case."

"That's probably not a bad idea."

"When and where?"

64

When the Boss decided he'd had enough of the cat and mouse with Quinton through his proxy, Cole, he jumped on a plane and headed to Houston. He had not decided how he would take credit for the torture he had caused Quinton and wasn't sure what his endgame would be. One option was to have Cole take him out and leave town, never having Quinton understand who was behind it. But that was not something the Boss was able to do. He had a burning need to punish Quinton and let him know exactly who was responsible for his distress.

He let Cole know that he was in Houston and that it was time to end the whole Quinton Bell fiasco. The Boss knocked on the motel room door and Cole answered, stood aside, and let him in. No greetings, no handshake. These men were not friends and would never run in the same circles.

The Boss looked around at the cheap bedspread and carpet and frowned. He handed Cole an envelope. "It's all there, as agreed, plus a little extra. Cash. No paper trail."

"Thanks."

"You've done a good job on this, but it's time to end it. You're free to go. I'll take it from here."

"Okay."

"I want you to delete all of our emails and destroy anything else that ties us together."

"I understand." Of course, Cole had no intention of hiding the paper trail and had been carefully preserving it for weeks, along with the recordings of their phone calls.

The Boss felt a little uneasy as he gauged his employee one last time. "I guess that's it. I'll leave you to pack."

The Boss left and Cole looked in the envelope. All there. He put the money in the room safe, looked at his watch, and headed to the bus station for his second payday. Just one more step and he and his lovely wife would spend her last days together. After that, he'd decide what was next. If things were progressing as they had been last time he'd gone home for a visit, they would not have long.

Outside, and out of sight, the Boss sat in his vehicle, a dark Lincoln Navigator that he kept at his second home in Houston, and waited. He didn't trust Cole as far as he could throw him and wanted to see how long he took to pack and vacate the city.

Shortly, Cole came out of the motel room, no luggage in hand. He entered a Ram pickup truck parked near the door and took off. The Boss followed, keeping a safe distance until Cole wove his way downtown and into a surface parking lot near the Greyhound Bus Station.

Dart entered the bus station half an hour ahead of the scheduled drop off time. As he passed through the sliding glass doors into the cold concrete ambiance, he saw a sign that said: PURSUANT TO SECTION 30.05 PENAL CODE (CRIMINAL

TRESPASS), A PERSON MAY NOT ENTER THIS PROPERTY WITH A FIREARM.

There was no metal detector at the entrance, and the single guard with a wand was way too busy to check even a small fraction of the passengers who waited for their departures. Dart knew this, as he'd done a dry run the night before, right after his meeting with Quinton.

Per Quinton's instructions, Dart relocated the correct locker number and found a lookout point near the baggage area where he could see anything that went on in the aisle. He thumbed through a Michael Connelly novel as he waited, trying to look like a typical traveler.

Quinton entered the bus station with a small tan satchel in his hand, that weighed about thirty pounds, and a note with the locker number and code on it in his pocket. He planned to drop the money, signal Dart, and run like hell. It would all be over in a matter of minutes. *Hopefully.*

After the code was entered, the money placed inside, and the locker re-secured, Quinton went over to the area where Dart was waiting and watching.

"Let's go."

Dart didn't move. "Not yet. Let's see who this bastard is."

"No, if he sees me here it will make things worse. The instructions were to deposit the money by five o'clock and leave. What if he's watching now?"

Dart was stubborn. "Just a few minutes. If he doesn't show, we'll cut out."

Quinton sat beside him and grabbed an abandoned magazine in an empty seat. He used the magazine to partially hide his face as Dart continued to pretend to read *The Concrete*

Blonde. They didn't have to wait for long. A fit man of medium height and age, in a dark hoodie, approached the end of the appointed aisle, looked around the room, walked toward the locker, and applied the code to the keypad. Quinton recognized him from the gym and maybe somewhere else, too, but he couldn't quite place him.

"I know that guy. I've seen him a couple of times. Once for sure, he was working out at my gym. Maybe Vegas? I can't be sure, but he might have been the guy in my back yard."

"Do you know who he is?"

"I have no clue, but he's been following me. I see that now."

Cole took the tan bag out of the locker and slipped it inside a black garbage bag that he took from his pocket and shook open. He tied the top, looked around again, and started out of the locker area.

Dart started to stand. "Let's get him. He's alone and there are two of us."

Quinton hesitated, then pushed past his fear, and ran toward the guy with his money. Dart used his shoulder to push Cole into the locker and Quinton got in his face.

"Who are you?"

The Boss had parked his car at the other end of the surface lot and watched Cole go into the bus station. He waited a beat, then followed him inside, staying clear of the main departure area and hugging a side wall. The Boss saw Cole round a corner and duck into a row of lockers.

After a moment, two men approached Cole and tackled him against the locker wall.

The Boss, recognizing Quinton and reading the situation,

was enraged. He ran up to Cole and yelled, "What do you think you're doing?"

Quinton took a step back. "Alcott, what are you doing here?"

"I'll get to you. Right now, I have some business with this traitor."

Dart recognized Alcott Wyatt as Joanne Wyatt's brother who'd paid him to do research during her murder trial. He was so surprised he let go of Cole who clutched the garbage bag and ran toward the exit. Wyatt ran across the waiting area after him and Dart ran after the money. Quinton brought up the rear, running after everyone.

Wyatt chased outside after Cole, yelling for him to stop. Cole crossed the parking lanes where several buses were loading and unloading passengers as Wyatt followed. Cole continued across the grassy curbed area surrounding the facility and was stopped by heavy traffic going one way on Harrisburg Boulevard. All he had to do was get to his pickup truck in the surface lot and he'd be free.

Wyatt was closing the gap between them. Cole saw an opening coming in the traffic and stepped off the curb, ready to dive behind a Greyhound bus that was his only barrier to escape. He waited, waited, then felt something from behind as Wyatt pushed him directly into the oncoming bus. Cole flew into the air as Dart and Quinton caught up to Wyatt.

The garbage bag containing the satchel bounced off the bumper of the bus and landed at Quinton's feet. He grabbed it and watched Alcott run off as Dart checked Cole's pulse to see if an ambulance would do any good. He looked up at Quinton and shook his head. Security from the bus station came running along with several looky-loos, one of whom began to record the scene on his mobile phone, panning over to Quinton. Before the onlooker could record him, Quinton knocked the phone from the hand of the observer, who yelled and fell on his butt. Dart pushed passed the guy, and he and Quinton followed Wyatt to the end of the block where he crossed the street at the light and ran over to a surface lot. Quinton and Dart ran after him until they saw him jump into a Lincoln Navigator and peeled out of the parking area, tires squealing.

Both men bent over with hands on knees to catch their breath.

Dart stood up. "Pretty good move knocking that phone down."

"You weren't so bad yourself tackling that guy into the locker."

"I see you still got your million bucks."

Quinton looked down at his right hand that had a choke hold on the top of the black garbage bag. "I guess I do."

Dart laughed.

Quinton thought for a moment. "We have to go back. The cameras in there will identify us and if we leave, it will look like we did something wrong. Best to go back now and tell the cops something."

"You draggin' that bag back over there?"

"No way. I was hoping you'd secure it for me in your car, then come back and corroborate my story."

"Thought so. I'll try to resist stealing it." Dart laughed. "Just kidding. I'll be right there."

Quinton returned to the bus station, gave his statement, and indicated that he had no idea who had run into the path of the bus. He said he didn't know either of them and could not give a very good description of the one who ran away. If he pushed the dead guy, Quinton said he didn't see it.

Dart joined them and gave a similar statement, indicating that they were in the bus station to pick up a new client for Quinton's firm who never showed.

Quinton went directly back to his office and dialed Alcott Wyatt's mobile number. He picked up on the first ring, as if he were waiting for the call.

Quinton yelled. "In my office. Now. I'm sure you know where it is. If you're not here in under an hour, I'm calling the cops."

"You won't call the cops, but I'll be there. I have a few things to say to you."

When Wyatt arrived at Quinton's office, there was no warmth between them. Dart searched Wyatt, then stood just outside of Quinton's office, and allowed them some privacy, while making sure Wyatt didn't try to do to Quinton what he'd done to the blackmailer.

"For now, the police think that guy ran into the bus. We'll see how long it takes me to modify my statement, depending on your answers to my questions. Who was he and how do you know him?"

"His name is Dalton Cole. I hired him to follow you." Wyatt seemed happy to take responsibility for Quinton's anguish.

"Why? What purpose could that possibly serve? Did you tell him to vandalize and burn down my house?"

"I told him to get creative. How he did that was up to him."

"Why? What have I ever done but try to be your friend? I gave you every cent that Joanne left me in her will."

"You, my friend? You think this is about money? You killed my sister. If you'd never come into her life, she'd still be alive today."

"How did you find out my secret? Did she tell you?"

"Of course, she did. Do you think Joanne would have kept it from me? She was my only sibling. We shared everything. I was all she had until you came along and blew up her life."

"If it's not about money, why were you trying to blackmail me?"

"That was Cole. I'd already paid him and sent him on his way. I was coming to see you for this very conversation. He was a traitor and got what he deserved."

"You lay down with dogs…"

"It was worth it to see you squirm. I got video of each painful moment you experienced, and I enjoyed every bit of it. Running off to Vegas and crying in your cups. What a coward you are."

"Maybe I am, but you're no better. You could have come to me."

"For what? A friendly chat? Fuck that. You deserved every second of pain I dished out to you, and more."

Quinton realized there was no reasoning with Wyatt. His bitterness was too deep, and his vengeance too important to him. He also didn't want Wyatt to blurt out his real name in case Dart could hear them.

"Well, I hope you're satisfied with your pound of flesh. Regardless, Dart and I both saw you push this Dalton Cole character into the bus. If I ever hear from you again, you'll be arrested for murder. If you reveal my secret, I'll reveal yours, and don't think you can let it slip out without my knowing. You're the only one it could be."

Wyatt was in no position to ever bother him again. If he did, he'd be in worse trouble than Quinton. They were at detente like two superpowers with atomic bombs at their disposal. Neither could make a move without harming himself equally and blowing up their own life.

"Don't worry. I'm finished with you. I never want to see your face again."

65

Clive Broussard walked into Quinton's office and didn't bother to knock. Quinton looked up from his desk and raised an eyebrow.

"Come on in, Detective."

"This isn't a social call. I've got a bone to pick with you. Death and destruction seem to follow you around, Bell."

"So, now it's Bell again. What happened to being friends?"

"I've stumbled around you since the first day we met. It's getting old, and I'm getting tired of walking in here."

"Well, I represent criminals, so there's going to be disorder from time to time," Quinton quipped.

"I read your statement to the cops at the bus station. Do you really expect me to believe that you just happened to be in the same place as Dalton Cole when he gets hit by a bus and you saw nothing?"

"Who is Dalton Cole?" Quinton pretended not to know.

"He's the one whose fingerprints were at your burned down house. The guy whose fingerprints are in the database. He's wanted in several jurisdictions. What's his beef with you?"

"I really can't say, Broussard. The only thing I can guess is that he followed me to the bus station. Dart and I went to pick up a new client. Simple as that."

"Oh, really. And, you expect me to believe that. You think I'm couyon?"

"No, I don't think you're crazy. I think you hate coincidence and loose ends. It's part of your detective nature."

"We have a saying in Louisiana, it's 'de'pouille.' It means a mess. That's you, Bell. You, and everything around you, is a mess." Frustration was evident in his tone.

Quinton replied with a shrug. "I represent what you call the bad guys, Broussard. Chaos is part of the package. It gets a little untidy."

"I owe you one, but this is it. My patience is worn thin. Next time a red flag hits my desk about you, I won't stop until I know the truth. Clear?"

Quinton softened. "I know what this must look like from your side. It is a mess, but that's my life, for now. I'm trying to live it as best I can without getting anyone hurt."

"Like Joanne?"

"Yes, like Joanne. I hear you. I'll do my best to stay out of your lane and keep my mess off your desk."

Broussard softened too, but not entirely, and wanted the last word. "You do that."

66

Judge Blaylock sat behind his mahogany desk, the weight of his responsibility sitting heavy on his shoulders, as Quinton escorted young Lily Collins into the room. She wore her favorite pink dress and used a crutch on one side, to balance out her missing leg. Kevin and Jess followed slowly behind and took a seat in the corner of the room. They trusted Quinton, as Lily's attorney, to get her through the ordeal she was about to endure.

Quinton sat beside Lily on one side and the court reporter sat on the other side. A videographer manipulated a camera, behind and to the left of the judge, pointing across his desk and straight at Lily.

Judge Blaylock began the proceedings. "Thank you for coming today, Lily. It's very important to me and to the court to have your testimony memorialized. Did Mr. Bell, Quinton, tell you what would happen today?"

Lily nodded.

"I'll ask you some questions. Mr. Landon will video your

statement, and Ms. Rossi will take it down on this machine called a stenograph. Is that all okay with you?"

Lily nodded.

Quinton looked at her. "Lily, you must answer verbally so that the stenographer can write down what you say. Okay?"

"Okay. I understand." She looked at Ms. Rossi. "Sorry." The stenographer smiled sweetly at her.

Judge Blaylock began with his first question. "Please state your name, age, and grade in school for the court."

"Lily Marie Collins, age nine. I would be in third grade, but I'm homeschooled."

"Now, Lily, would you please tell the court what occurred on the day you and your mother were going to Austin and the accident happened?"

"Yes, sir, Your Honor." She began, her voice barely above a whisper. "We were driving on the freeway, and I was reading a book in the back seat. I heard a noise and I looked up. All of a sudden, a truck swerved and then it was blocking all the lanes." As she described the accident, her voice quivered with the traumatic memory that haunted her. "My mother tried to stop, but it was too late. It all happened so fast."

The judge listened intently, his heart aching with every word that spilled from her lips.

"My next question, Lily, might be hard to answer. If you don't want to respond, you don't have to. Understand?"

Lily nodded, then corrected herself. "Yes, sir."

"After the car crash, when you were in the back seat and waiting for the police and ambulances to arrive, what happened to your mother?"

Tears began to stream down Lily's cheeks. "I could hear her crying and groaning. She said my name over and over. She was hurt and I couldn't get out of my seatbelt to help her. I tried; I really did."

Tears welled up in Quinton's eyes as he watched the girl's anguish unfold before him.

Judge Blaylock used a soothing voice. "That was not your fault, Lily. You could not help her, no matter what you did."

She looked over at her foster parents. "That's what Jess says." Jess smiled reassuringly at the girl who was still crying.

"Well, Jess is right. Would you like to try one last question?"

"Yes, sir." Lily took a swipe at her runny nose and Quinton handed her a tissue. She used it to do a little better job of cleaning herself up.

"What happened when you were removed from the car?"

"I could see the policemen trying to pull the door open, but they couldn't. Then, it got so loud. I couldn't hear my mother anymore. A big machine came at me, cutting through the roof of the car. I didn't know if it would stop or if it would cut me in two. It was like a big mouth full of teeth."

"That must have been like a nightmare."

"It was. It was exactly like a nightmare. I still see it in my dreams, and it makes me scream and wake up."

"I understand, and I'm sorry that happened to you. I hope you know that your testimony here today will go a long way toward making things right. It will take a long time, but I hope this will help you heal, knowing that you helped so much. Thank you."

Lily nodded. "Thank you, Judge Blaylock." The judge signaled to Quinton that they were finished.

Quinton patted Lily's hand. "You did a really good job. I'm so proud of you."

Lily smiled at him through her drying tears. "Thanks, Quinton. You did a really good job as my lawyer."

67

Quinton met his new contractor, Buddy Barnes, at the Afton Oaks house to give him a walk-through and show him what he wanted in the new build. Quinton was using some of his attorney's fees from the Collins case to get the home construction going again. He felt a sense of purpose and hope. It was his chance to start anew.

Quinton felt safe and secure, as Lily was healing, Hobbs was in jail, Cole was dead, and Alcott Wyatt was in no position to ever bother him again. Lily occasionally texted him a legal question and had told him during his last visit that she wanted to become a lawyer when she grew up. She was being fitted for a prosthetic leg in the coming month, and Jess had found her a new therapist. Broussard was still a thorn in his side, but Quinton hoped he had him at bay, at least for now.

Quinton escorted Barnes into the kitchen area. A few metal pipes stuck up through the concrete where an island belonged. The debris had been cleared from the slab throughout, leaving a footprint on which to build the new home. "This room is probably where the fire was started."

Barnes nodded, took notes, and asked questions when appropriate. They proceeded through all of what was formerly the bedrooms and baths and out into the pool area in the back yard. By the time they were finished, Quinton felt he was in capable hands.

The two men stood by the empty pool and Barnes said. "The architectural drawings should be completed later this week and I'll have them sent over to you."

"Sounds great. If you've seen all you need to for now, I'll walk you out."

The two men proceeded back across the slab through what was formerly the living room. A soot-covered stacked stone fireplace was all that remained of the long wall at the far end. Quinton froze as he looked over at the hearth. A souvenir model of the Staten Island Ferry was sitting on the stone, untouched by char or smoke. It had obviously been placed there after the fire.

Quinton walked over and picked it up. *Please, no. Not again!*

He turned it over in his hand and felt sick to his stomach. On the bottom was written: HELLO BYRON.

THE END

Can Quinton continue to hide in plain sight? **COMING SOON:** Alive By Proxy, the next page-turner in the Proxy Legal Thriller Series !

Sign up for Manning Wolfe's FREE newsletter and get a FREE book. Claim your copy:
www.manningwolfe.com/giveaway

PLEASE LEAVE A REVIEW!

Thank you for reading **Hunted By Proxy**. Help future readers
find their way to this series.
Click here, or go to Amazon and Goodreads. Thank you.

ALSO BY MANNING WOLFE

Merit Bridges Legal Thrillers

Proxy Legal Thriller Series

Bullet Books Speed Reads

MANNING WOLFE, an award-winning author and attorney, writes cinematic-style, smart, fast-paced thrillers and crime fiction. Manning was recently featured on Oxygen TV's: Accident, Suicide, or Murder, and has spoken at major book festivals around the world.

* Manning's Merit Bridges Legal Thrillers features Austin attorney Merit Bridges, including Dollar Signs, Music Notes, Green Fees, and Chinese Wall.
* Manning's new Proxy Legal Thrillers Series features Houston attorney Quinton Bell, including Dead By Proxy, Hunted By Proxy, and Alive By Proxy.
* Manning is co-author of Killer Set: Drop the Mic, and twelve additional Bullet Books Speed Reads.

As a graduate of Rice University and the University of Texas School of Law, Manning's experience has given her a voyeur's peek into some shady characters' lives and a front-row seat to watch the good people who stand against them.

www.manningwolfe.com

Visit Manning Wolfe's website:
www.manningwolfe.com

Follow Manning Wolfe on Social Media:
www.facebook.com/manning.wolfe
www.twitter.com/ManningWolfe
www.instagram.com/manningwolfe/
www.tiktok.com/@manningwolfe

Sign up for Manning Wolfe's FREE newsletter and get a FREE book.
www.manningwolfe.com/giveaway